W9-BMI-983

the good daughters

ALSO BY JOYCE MAYNARD

Fiction

*Baby Love*

*To Die For*

*Where Love Goes*

*The Usual Rules*

*The Cloud Chamber*

*Labor Day*

Nonfiction

*Looking Back*

*Domestic Affairs*

*At Home in the World*

*Internal Combustion*

# the good daughters

JOYCE MAYNARD

wm

WILLIAM MORROW

*An Imprint of* HarperCollins*Publishers*

This book is a work of fiction. The characters, incidents, and dialogue are drawn from the author's imagination and are not to be construed as real. Any resemblance to actual events or persons, living or dead, is entirely coincidental.



HarperCollins books may be purchased for educational, business, or sales promotional use. For information please write: Special Markets Department, HarperCollins Publishers, 10 East 53rd Street, New York, NY 10022.

FIRST EDITION

*Designed by Lisa Stokes*

Library of Congress Cataloging-in-Publication Data has been applied for.

ISBN 978-0-06-199431-9 (hardcover)
ISBN 978-0-06-201516-7 (international edition)

10 11 12 13 14 OV/RRD 10 9 8 7 6 5 4 3 2 1

*For Laurie Clark Buchar, Rebecca Tuttle Schultze,*

*Shirley Hazzard Marcello, and for Lida Stinchfield—*

*all, like myself, daughters of New Hampshire (two native born, two transplanted).*

*Each a sister, not by blood but by choice.*

the good daughters

PROLOGUE

# Hurricane Season

*October 1949*

IT BEGINS WITH a humid wind, blowing across the fields from the northeast, and strangely warm for this time of year. Even before the wind reaches the house, Edwin Plank sees it coming, rippling over the dry grass, the last rows of cornstalks still standing in the lower field below the barn, the one place the tractor hasn't got to yet.

In the space of time it takes a man to pour his coffee and call the dog in (though Sadie knows to come; the wind has sent her running toward the house), the sky grows dark. Crows circle the barn, and starlings, looking for the rafters. It's not yet four o'clock, and daylight savings will be ending soon, but with the sun no longer visible behind the low, flat wall of cloud cover rolling in, it could be sunset, and maybe that's why the cattle are making their long, low sounds of discontent. Things are not as they should be on the farm, and animals always know.

Standing on the porch with his coffee, Edwin calls to his wife, Connie. She's still out in the yard with a basket, taking down the laundry she'd hung out to dry this morning. Four girls make a lot of laundry. Cotton dresses, Carter's tops and bottoms, all pink, diapers, naturally—and her own sensible white cotton undergarments, but the less said about those the better, in Connie's book.

Gathering up the last of the clothing not yet dry—rescued from the line before the wind gets to it—Connie is already thinking that if the lights go out due to the storm, as very likely they will, and he can't listen to the ball game on the radio, her husband may bother her in bed tonight. She had been hoping the World Series would keep him occupied a while. His Red Sox won't be playing; the team folded in September as usual. Still, Edwin never misses the series.

They knew the hurricane was coming. Bonnie, they're calling this one. (In their eight years of marriage, has Edwin ever failed to catch the weather report?) He has already taken care of things in the barn, put away his tools, made sure the hay is covered and the barn doors secured. The cows are in their stalls, naturally. But on the roof, the weather vane—the same one that has stood there for a hundred and forty years now, through a half-dozen generations of Planks—spins like a top.

Now comes the rain. A few drops first, then sheets of it, pounding down so hard Edwin can no longer see his tractor, the old red Massey Ferguson that sits out in the field, in whatever spot he finished up his work that day. The rain's so loud, he has to raise his voice now as he calls in his two elder daughters—Naomi and Sarah. "Go check your sisters, girls." The little ones—Esther and Edwina—should be waking from their nap any time now, if the sound of the rain hasn't wakened them already.

In the yard, Connie is struggling with the laundry basket—wind in her face, and rain. He sets his coffee down and runs to meet her and take the load. Already soaked, her dress clings to her short, utilitarian body. Nothing about her resembles the women he sometimes thinks about, afternoons on the tractor, or during the long hours he spends in the barn, milking—Marilyn Monroe, of course, Ava Gardner, Peggy Lee. But at that moment, with wet fabric accentuating her breasts, he is thinking how nice it will be, when the children are in bed tonight—knowing the game will be canceled due to the weather—to lie under the covers with his wife, hearing the rain on the roof. A good night for making love, if she lets him.

Connie hands her husband the basket. He puts his free arm around her shoulders to help her up the hill—the wind is that strong pushing against their bodies. He has to raise his voice over the roar of the downpour.

"She's a doozy, this one," he says. "Looks like we may lose power."

"I'd better get the girls," she says, brushing his hand away. "The baby will be frightened." She means Edwina, the one named after him. He might have thought he'd have been disappointed, not to get a boy that last time, and perhaps he was, but he loves his girls. There's something about walking into church with the line of them—every one built like their mother, from the looks of things so far—that fills his heart with tender pride.

This is when the phone rings. Surprising that it even works in all this wind, and in another few minutes it won't. But for now the dispatcher has managed to get through, to say a tree is down on the old County Road, and would Edwin get his truck out there, and a chain saw, so people can get through—not that anyone's likely to try, until the storm dies down. Edwin is the captain of the volunteer firemen in town, and on call at moments like these when a job needs doing.

He has his work boots on already. Now comes the yellow slicker and a check to make sure that the batteries in his flashlight are working. A final shot of coffee in case the task takes longer than he hopes. A kiss for his wife, who turns her cheek to receive it with her usual brisk efficiency. She is already lighting the stove to put the beans on for the children.

Less than five minutes have passed since the phone rang, but the sky has gone black, and the wind is wailing. Edwin climbs into the cab of his truck and starts the motor. Even with the wipers on, the only way he makes it down the road is because he knows it so well—he could drive this stretch blindfolded.

The radio is playing. Peggy Lee, oddly enough, the woman he had just been thinking about not one hour ago, bringing the cattle into the barn. There's a woman for you. Imagine making love to a gal like that.

They interrupt the broadcast. Hurricane warnings upgraded to full-scale storm emergency status. Power lines coming down all over the county. No drivers on the road, except for rescue workers. He is one of those.

It will be a long night, Edwin knows. Before it's over, he will be soaked through to his long johns. There's danger for a man out in a storm like this one, too. Falling trees, loose power lines on the road. Floodwaters.

He thinks about a movie he saw once—one of the few times he ever went to the pictures, in fact—*The Wizard of Oz*. And how, when the storm hit (a twister, if memory serves), the farmhouse lifted right up off the ground and landed in this whole other place nobody ever knew about before.

That was a made-up story, of course, but wild weather can come upon a person in the state of New Hampshire, too. Right around the time he saw the Judy Garland movie, in fact, they had the biggest storm in a hundred years, the hurricane of '38. That one took the oak tree in front of the house where his tire swing used to hang. And a few hundred others. A few thousand, more like it. Even now, all these years later, people around here still talk about that storm, measure time even, by "before '38" or "after."

From the looks of it, this hurricane could do some serious damage. He does an inventory of the places on the farm where they might run into trouble. No danger of losing crops this time of year (with only the pumpkins left in the field, and not many of those), but there's the barn roof, and the shed, and a stand of hickory he loves, up along the strawberry fields. Always the first to go in a storm, hickory. He'd hate to see those trees snapped off, and it could happen tonight.

Then there's the house, built by his great-grandfather, and still standing firm, with those four little girls and his good wife inside. He doesn't like leaving them alone in a storm.

Still, making his way along the darkened road, with the rain coming down in sheets and the body of his old Dodge trembling from the wind, Edwin Plank registers an oddly pleasant sense of anticipation. One thing about a hurricane: it turns everything upside down. You never know how things will be once the wind dies down. All you know for sure: the world will look different tomorrow. And perhaps it is a sign of some restlessness in his nature, or more than that even, a hunger for something he has not yet found, that Edwin Plank heads out into the wild night with his heart beating fast. Life on this patch of earth could be totally different come morning.

# PART I

# RUTH

## Beanpole

MY FATHER TOLD me I was a hurricane baby. This didn't mean I was born in the middle of one. July 4, 1950, the day of my birth, fell well before hurricane season.

He meant I was conceived during a hurricane. Or in its aftermath.

"Stop that, Edwin," my mother would say, if she overheard him saying this. To my mother, Connie, anything to do with sex, or its consequences (namely, my birth, or at least the idea of linking my birth to the sex act), was not a topic for discussion.

But if she wasn't around, he'd tell me about the storm, and how he'd been called out to clear a fallen tree off the road, and how fierce the rain had been that night, how wild the wind. "I didn't get to France in the war like my brothers," he said, "but it felt like I was doing battle, fighting those hundred-mile-an-hour gusts," he told me. "And here's the funny thing about it. Those times a person feels most afraid for their life? Those are the times you know you're alive."

He told me how, in the cab of his truck, the water poured down so hard he couldn't see, and how fast his heart was pounding, plunging into the darkness, and how it was, after—outside in the downpour, cutting the tree and moving the heavy branches to the side of the road, his boots sinking into the mud and drenched from rain, his arms shaking.

"The wind had a human sound to it," he said, "like the moaning of a woman."

Later, thinking back on the way my father recounted the story, it occurred to me that much of the language he used to describe the storm might have been applied to the act of a couple making love. He made the sound of the wind for me, then, and I pressed myself against his chest so he could wrap his big arms around me. I shivered, just to think of how it must have been that night.

For some reason, my father liked to tell this story, though I—not my sisters, not our mother—was his only audience. Well, that made sense perhaps. I was his hurricane girl, he said. If there hadn't been that storm, he liked to say, I wouldn't be here now.

It was nine months later almost to the day that I arrived, in the delivery room of Bellersville Hospital, high noon on our nation's birthday, right after the end of the first haying season, and just when the strawberries had reached their peak.

And here was the other part of the story, well known to me from a hundred tellings: small as our town was—not even so much as a town, really; more like a handful of farms with a school and a general store and a post office to keep things ticking along—I was not the only baby born at Bellersville Hospital that day. Not two hours after me, another baby girl came into the world. This would be Dana Dickerson, and here my mother, if she was in earshot, joined in with her own remarks.

"Your birthday sister," she liked to say. "You two girls started out in the world together. It only stands to reason we'd feel a connection."

In fact, our families could hardly have been more different—the Dickersons and the Planks. Starting with where we made our home, and how we got there.

The farm where we lived had been in my father's family since the sixteen hundreds, thanks to a twenty-acre land parcel acquired in a card game by an ancestor—an early settler come from England on one of the first boats—with so many greats in front of his name I lost count, Reginald Plank. Since Reginald, ten generations of Plank men had farmed that soil, each one augmenting the original tract with the purchase of neighboring farms, as—one by one—more fainthearted men gave up on the hard life of farming, while my forebears endured.

My father was the oldest son of an oldest son. That's how the land had been passed down for all the generations. The farm now consisted of two hundred and twenty acres, forty of them cultivated, mostly in corn and what my father called kitchen crops that we sold, summers, at our farm stand, Plank's Barn. Those and his pride and joy, our strawberries.

Ours was never a family with money, but we had mortgage-free land, which we all understood to be the most precious thing a farmer could possess, the only thing that mattered other than (and here came my mother's voice) the church. (And we had standing in the town that came from having history in a place where not just our father's parents and grandparents, but their great-grandparents and great-great-grandparents before them, all lay buried in New Hampshire soil.) More than any other family in town that was what made us who we were—history and roots.

The Dickersons had drifted into town (my mother's phrase once more) a few years back from someplace else. Out of state was all we knew, and though they owned a place—a run-down ranch house out by the highway—it was clear they were not country people. Besides Dana, they had an older boy, Ray—lanky and blue-eyed—who played the harmonica on the school bus and once, famously, arranged himself on the tar of the playground at recess, motionless and staring blankly in the direction of the sky, as if he'd jumped out a window. The teacher on duty had already called the principal to summon an ambulance when he hopped up, dancing like Gumby, all rubber legged and grinning. He was a joker and a troublemaker, though everybody loved him, particularly the girls. His badness thrilled and amazed me.

Supposedly, Mr. Dickerson was a writer, and he was working on a novel, but until that sold he had a job that took him on the road a lot—selling different kinds of brushes out of a suitcase, my mother thought—and Valerie Dickerson called herself some kind of artist—a notion that didn't sit well with my mother, who believed the only art a woman with children had any business pursuing was the domestic variety.

Still, my mother insisted on paying visits to the Dickersons whenever we were in town. She'd stop by with baked goods or, depending on the season, corn, or a bowl of our fresh-picked strawberries, with biscuits hot out of the oven for shortcake. ("Knowing Valerie Dickerson," she said, "I wouldn't put it past that woman to use whipped cream in a can." The idea that Val Dickerson might serve her shortcake with no cream at all—real or fake—seemed more than she could envision.)

Then the women might visit—my mother in her sensible farm dress, and the same blue sweater that stayed on her for my entire childhood, and Val, who wore jeans before any other woman I'd met, and served only instant coffee, if that. She never seemed particularly happy to see us, but fixed my mother a cup anyway, and a glass of milk for me or, because the Dickersons were health food nuts, some kind of juice made out of different vegetables all whirled up together in a machine Mr. Dickerson said was going to be the next big thing after the electric fry pan. I hadn't known the electric fry pan was such a big idea, either, but never mind.

Then they moved away, and you would have imagined that was the end of our family's association with the Dickersons. Only it wasn't. Of all the people who'd come in and out of our lives over the years—helpers on the farm, customers at Plank's, even my mother's relatives in Wisconsin—it was only the Dickersons with whom she made a point of not losing touch. It was as if the fact that Dana and I were born on the same day conferred some sort of rare magic on the relationship.

"I wonder if that Valerie Dickerson ever feeds Dana anything besides nuts and berries," my mother said one time. The family had moved to Pennsylvania by now, but they'd been passing through—and because it was strawberry season, and our birthdays, they'd stopped by the farm stand. Dana and I must have been nine or ten, and Ray was probably thirteen, and tall as my father. I was bringing in a load of peas I'd spent the morning picking when he spotted me. It was always an odd thing—how, even when I was young, and the difference between our ages seemed so vast, he always paid attention to me.

"You still making pictures?" he said. His voice had turned deep but his eyes were the way I remembered, and looking at me hard, like I was a real person and not just a little girl.

"I was reading this in the car," he said, handing me a rolled-up magazine. "I thought you'd like it." *Mad* magazine. Forbidden in our family, but my favorite.

It was on this visit—the first of what became a nearly annual tradition of strawberry runs—where the word had come out that Valerie was now a vegetarian. This was back in the days when it was almost unheard of for a person not to eat meat. This fact shocked my mother, as so much about the Dickersons did.

"Some say the American consumer eats too much beef," my father said—a surprising view for a farmer to set forward, even if his main crop was vegetables. My father liked his steak, but he possessed an open mind, whereas anything different from how we did things appeared suspect to my mother.

"Dana seems like a particularly intelligent girl, didn't you think, Edwin?" she said, after they pulled away, in that amazing car of Valerie's, a Chevrolet Bel Air with fins that seemed to me like something you'd expect to be driven by a movie star, or her chauffeur. Then, to me, she mentioned that my birthday sister had won their school spelling bee that year, and was also enrolled in the 4-H Club, working on a project involving chickens.

"Maybe it's about time you thought about 4-H," she said to me.

This kind of remark—and there were many such—no doubt formed the basis for my early resentment of Dana Dickerson. As the two of us moved through childhood and then adolescence, the girl seemed to provide the standard against which my own development and achievements should be measured. And when this happened, I could pretty much rely on falling short, in anything but the height category.

Most of the time, of course—given the irregularity of the reports—we didn't know where things stood with Dana Dickerson. Then my mother made do with speculating. When I learned to ride a bike, my mother had commented, "I wonder if Dana can do that yet," and when I got my period—early, just after turning twelve—she considered what might be going on for Dana now. One time, on my birthday—mine and Dana Dickerson's—my mother gave me a box of stationery with lilacs going up the side. "You can use this to write letters to Dana Dickerson," she said. "You two should be pen pals."

I didn't write. If there was one girl in the world I didn't want to correspond with, that girl would be Dana Dickerson. Our families had nothing in common and neither did we.

The one Dickerson who interested me was Dana's older brother, Ray, four years older than us. He was a tall, impossibly long-limbed person, like his mother, Valerie, and though he wasn't handsome in the regular way of high school boys you saw on TV (Wally Cleaver and the older brothers on *My Three Sons*, or Ricky Nelson), there was something about his face that made my skin hot if I looked at him. He had blue eyes that always gave you the sense he was about to burst out laughing, or cry—by which I mean, I suppose, that there was always so much feeling evident—and eyelashes so long they shaded his face.

Ray had this way of coming into a room that took your breath away. Partly it was the look of him, but more so it was his crazy energy, and all the funny and amazing ideas he thought up. He did things other boys didn't, like building a raft out of old kerosene drums and taking it down Beard's Creek, where it got stuck in the mud, and performing magic tricks wearing a cape he'd evidently sewed himself. He had taught himself ventriloquism, so one time, at Plank's, he made this pair of summer squashes talk to each other without moving his lips. Years before, when I was five or six, he pulled a silver dollar out of my ear, so for the next few days I was forever checking to see what else might be in there, but nothing ever was.

One spring Ray Dickerson built a homemade unicycle using a few old bike parts he'd found at the dump. That was Ray for you. When other boys were out on the ball field, he rode that contraption around town playing his harmonica.

At one point, he'd tried to teach his sister how to ride the unicycle, and Dana had taken a fall bad enough that her arm ended up in a sling. You'd think Mrs. Dickerson would have confiscated the thing after that—or that she'd be upset at least, but it didn't seem to bother her, though my mother had a fit.

Not much bothered Val Dickerson, or appeared to. She was an artist, and generally absorbed in that more than whatever might be going on with her children, was my impression. Where my mother kept close tabs on every single thing my sisters and I did, Val Dickerson would disappear into a room she called her studio for hours at a time, leaving Dana and Ray with an enormous bowl of dry Cheerios and some odd assignment like "go put on a play" or "see if you can find a squirrel and teach him to do tricks." The strange thing was, they might. When Ray talked to animals, they seemed to listen.

My father couldn't ever take time off in summer, because of all the jobs that needed doing at our farm, but my mother established a tradition of making a road trip every year during February vacation, when there wasn't so much that needed doing on the farm, and what there was he could, reluctantly, trust to his helper, a small, wiry boy by the name of Victor Patucci who'd first shown up at our door when he was only fourteen or so, looking for work. Victor was about as unlikely a person as you could have chosen to be a farmer—a smoker, who wore so much Brylcreem his hair reflected light, who followed race car driving and turned up his transistor radio whenever they played an Elvis Presley song, and never seemed to go to school. His father worked in the shoe factory, and my father said he wasn't a good man—words that stood out for me because my father so seldom spoke ill of anyone.

"The boy could use a helping hand," my father said when he'd signed Victor up—and though initially my mother protested the thirty-dollar-a-week expense, it was Victor's presence on our farm that made our annual Dickerson visit possible, and for that she was thankful.

So every March we set out to see the Dickersons. Before embarking on our road trip, my mother filled a cooler with sandwiches and jars of peanut butter and things like beef jerky that didn't go bad. Then my sisters and I would pile into the backseat of our old Country Squire station wagon with the fake wood paneling and a stack of coloring books and Mad Libs to keep us busy. We'd play I Spy or look for license plates from unusual states and now and then we'd stop at battlefields and historic monuments, and sometimes a museum, but our ultimate destination was whatever run-down house or trailer (and one time, a converted Quonset hut) the Dickersons were living in that year.

The point of this, as always, was what my mother imagined to be my attachment to Dana Dickerson, but for me, the one significant attraction of the trip was knowing I'd get to see Ray Dickerson.

Young as I was, I understood he was handsome, and the knowledge of that made me shy, though I was drawn to him too. The odd thing was that even when I was very young—eight or nine, and he twelve or thirteen—he seemed to take an interest in me over my sisters. On one of our visits, he had spotted a drawing I'd made in the car, of a camel I'd copied off an empty cigarette pack I'd found—only I added a man dressed like Lawrence of Arabia riding on it, and a girl tied up, like a prisoner, on the camel's other hump.

"Cool picture," he said. "I'll give you a Lifesaver for it."

I would've given Ray Dickerson my picture for nothing, but I couldn't speak.

After that, whenever we made trips to the Dickersons, I had lots of pictures ready. Things boys might like: spacemen and cowboys, and a portrait of my father's favorite player on the Red Sox, Ted Williams.

"Just a few more hours, girls," my mother would say when we complained about the length of the journey, the discomfort of all those hours in the car. But the most uncomfortable part was what happened when we arrived, and Mrs. Dickerson greeted us with that bemused and irritated expression (even as a child, I could see that), offering us lemonade, but never a meal.

The first year after they moved we drove to Pennsylvania to see them, and though that time we fit in a visit to the Liberty Bell, to round out the trip, most of the later trips we made—to Vermont, Connecticut, Vermont again—were made for the sole purpose of catching up with the Dickersons. My mother told Mrs. Dickerson that we were passing through. (Passing through? To where?) The visit might last an hour. Never more than two.

Dana and I shared nothing (she was a tomboy; I was interested in art), but her mother would always suggest we go upstairs to play, at which point I would ask Dana to show me her Barbies—Barbie being a kind of doll my mother didn't believe in, due to her physique and the provocative clothes the Mattel Company made for her, not that we would have spent the money anyway.

Dana never seemed interested in dolls herself, but Valerie kept giving her new ones, along with an incredible collection of official Barbie outfits, unlike the kind most girls I knew back home had—home sewn by their mothers and grandmothers, often crocheted and picked up at church fairs.

The real Barbie ensembles all had names that I knew from studying the Barbie catalog. My favorite was called "Solo in the Spotlight"—a strapless evening dress with sparkles on the hem that came with a tiny plastic microphone, for nights Barbie performed in nightclubs.

Once, when Dana was in the bathroom, I had stuffed the Barbie gown into my pocket. Dana had so little interest in this kind of thing she hadn't noticed, but as we were leaving their house, Ray had put an arm around my shoulder and whispered, "You forgot something." He handed me an odd-shaped package, wrapped in many layers of toilet paper and sealed with tape, and later, when we were on the highway, I opened it. The microphone.

I thought about him all that year. How had he known, for starters—though, of course, it was already proven he was magic. But more important: what did it mean, that Ray Dickerson, so much older than me, and so handsome, had chosen to present me with the treasured item?

The next spring, when we made our pilgrimage to see the Dickersons, I brought him a present of my own—a harmonica I'd bought with money I earned from weeding the strawberries, with mother-of-pearl on the case. But Ray—the main attraction of the trip—was off on his unicycle, so I never got to see him that time. Meanwhile, downstairs, my parents and Valerie Dickerson chatted about people back home, barely known to Valerie, and my mother inquired after Dana's religious education, such as it was. She'd brought a Junior Bible as a gift.

"That was so thoughtful, Connie," Mrs. Dickerson told her. "I wish I could invite you to stay for dinner, but I'm taking an art class."

"Art lessons, a woman her age," my mother commented to my father as we made our way home along that same long stretch of road, after the lemonade—my father's back straight at the wheel, his eyes on the road and no place else. "What is Valerie Dickerson thinking?"

"I guess she's got talent," he said. Then, after a minute's silence in the car, or even longer, he added, "Maybe Ruth should take art lessons. She's got that gift too."

Sitting in the backseat—the way-back, actually, this being the days before seat belt regulations—I felt a small, hopeful surge of promise, like a faint, thin shaft of light coming through the door, or the hint of breeze on a sweltering day. I loved to draw, a fact my mother hadn't seemed to notice.

My mother said nothing. Why would she want to pursue any activity that linked me closer to Val Dickerson? Even as my mother sought the woman out, she seemed so filled with judgment and reproach.

"There's a Howard Johnson's up ahead, girls," she said. "We'll get you each a cone. Just not chocolate. It stains."

Afterward, standing in the parking lot, licking my ice cream—the one person in our family who chose coffee, when everybody else favored strawberry or vanilla—I thought about a picture I'd seen on the wall at the Dickersons.

It was a print by an artist who was popular at the time, an image of a thin girl with straggly hair and big eyes that filled up half her face. She was holding a flower. The feeling it gave you, looking at this picture, was that the girl the artist had painted was the only person in the world (and very likely this was the only flower). Nobody could be more alone than that girl. And the funny thing was that though I lived in a big family—with my four sisters, crammed into three bedrooms—this was how I felt, too, growing up in that house.

Not that she ever did anything so different, but I had a sense that in some odd way I could not understand, but registered in my heart, my mother never took to me as she did to my sisters. I would feel it when I saw her with one of the others—Naomi, whose hair she liked to braid, or Esther, for whom she had found the nickname "Tootsie," or Sarah, known as "Honeybun."

"What's my nickname?" I asked her one time. She had looked at me with a blank expression then, as if the thought of coming up with yet another endearment was beyond her capacity.

"Ruth," she said. "That's a fine name."

This was when my father stepped in. "I think I'll call you Beanpole," he said.

I was different from my sisters. Different from my mother most of all. They didn't know this about me, but I made up odd stories, and sometimes, as I did, I drew pictures of the things I dreamed up, and sometimes these pictures were so strange, and possibly even shocking, I hid them in my sock drawer. Though there was one person I showed them to, when I had a chance. Ray Dickerson.

The second time we visited them in Vermont, I brought Ray a picture of the two of us—Ray and me—on a spaceship, both of us in spacesuits but still clearly recognizable, with an image of Saturn out the window. At school we'd just done a unit on astronauts and they'd told us about Ham, the chimpanzee they sent into space—an idea that had haunted me, because my teacher never mentioned any plans for bringing the chimp home, only launching him—meaning he was destined to orbit the earth forever, I guessed, until the food ran out and all that was left was a chimp skeleton. In my picture, I was half girl, half chimpanzee. Ray looked like a chimpanzee too.

"Sometimes, I feel like that chimp they launched into space," he said, when I showed him my picture.

"Only it wouldn't be so lonely if you had company," I said, thinking of how in the picture there had been two of us.

He just looked at me then. Maybe he was thinking, *What am I doing talking to a little kid?* He looked like he might say something—an expression he often had, actually—but he didn't speak. He just grabbed his unicycle and took off down the driveway, though not before stuffing my picture in his jeans pocket. This was another thing about Ray: he disappeared abruptly. One minute you were having the best conversation. Then he was gone.

Driving home that afternoon, we passed him on the road—his long, angular form cruising on his unicycle. He didn't see me, but for that one flash of time, I had taken in his face. Long enough to decide I loved this boy.

# *Dana*

# Where Trouble Lay

TO MY BROTHER and me, our parents went by their first names, Valerie and George. In all the years we lived with them, I don't think we ever called them Mom or Dad. It said a lot, our not using those names for them. I'm not sure I ever felt I had parents. Not parents as you normally think of them, anyway.

It's an odd feeling, growing up in a family where it seems like the adults are the ones who need to grow up. Even when I was very young, I felt that way. They just seemed so unreliable to me. They were so wrapped up in themselves they sometimes seemed to forget they had children.

I was five or six when George quit his job selling ad space at the newspaper in Concord, to write a novel about life on another galaxy where the people wore no clothes. This was the only thing I remember about George's book. Even when I was little, this fact shocked me. George's goal was to become a world-renowned writer, which was why we left New Hampshire, the place I was born.

Valerie's father had just died, and her mother was dead already, and since there were no brothers or sisters, she inherited what he had. This wasn't much, considering her dad had been a steelworker all his life, but it was enough for George to decide to quit his job and sell the house and live off that money until his ship came in as an author. His goal was not to be simply a writer but "an author." I never understood what the difference was.

Meanwhile, we'd live in Valerie's father's old place, just outside of Pittsburgh. Even then I remember thinking, what if this ship doesn't come in? I had heard George telling the story for this novel of his—it was something he liked to do on long car rides when we were going somewhere, as was often the case, but every time he did, my mind would wander, which didn't seem like a good sign. My brother, Ray, also a lover of fantasy, had read me a couple of J. R. R. Tolkien books by now, and C. S. Lewis, and though they were never really my style, either, I could tell a good fantasy from one that made no sense, meaning the kind George was writing.

As for me, as soon as I could read I gravitated to nonfiction, biographies mostly, of people like Annie Oakley and George Washington Carver. Also true stories about animals and nature. My all-time favorite was *Ring of Bright Water*, about a pair of otters. I loved it that the illustrations were photographs.

I worried that while we were waiting for that ship of his, George would spend all the money. If he didn't sell his book, then where would we be? I was in the third grade at this point, but as it turned out I was right. Where we would be, and were, was in a trailer park in Pennsylvania, and after that, a house in Vermont without indoor plumbing. It's unclear to me now how George and Valerie decided on these places for us to settle down, for a while anyway. We never stayed for long.

We were living in the Vermont house when George announced that he was going to become a country-and-western songwriter. He had an idea for a romantic ballad that would be perfect for Les Paul and Mary Ford—though by the time he got it together to record his demo, they were getting divorced. But even without the problem of the singers' relationship, there seemed to be some pretty big obstacles to this plan.

"Don't you have to know how to play the guitar or something if you want to write songs for people?" I said. He thought this was a good idea, and bought one, along with a book on how to learn to play guitar in fourteen days. I did not find this reassuring.

Back in the days of reel-to-reel tapes, he created a recording studio to work on his demos, in what had been the garage of the house we rented, this time in Connecticut. I wasn't sure the owner of the house would appreciate it that my father cut a hole in the garage door to let in more light, never mind what he was going to do in wintertime, when it would get pretty chilly in that uninsulated garage.

By winter the checks would have started rolling in, George told me. Then he could get himself a real place to work on his music, and things like an electric organ. We might even move to Nashville, he said. That's where the action was in country music.

Even then, I knew this wasn't happening, as did Val and my brother probably, though I was the one in the family with the firmest grasp on reality. Even as a kid, I always had the ability to see down the line to where trouble lay, or truth. George used to complain that I expected the worst out of life, but it wasn't that. I simply recognized that just because the sun was shining one day didn't mean it would the next. Frost would come, and so would snow. The fact of rain did not rule out the possibility of drought. You could call it pessimism. I based my attitudes on what I saw in the world around me. Not what I dreamed up.

"Dana has her feet firmly grounded on earth," one of my teachers wrote about me on a report card. I remembered this because to me it seemed like the nicest kind of compliment, but I could see that for my mother, this was a disappointment.

"Don't you ever want to use your imagination?" she said, but I was more the type who based her thinking on what was real—the things I could touch and see.

I was not one to believe, the way my father did, that things would always turn out the way you wanted them to, or—like my mother—that we should surround ourselves only with what was beautiful. Life wasn't like that. Even as a child, I knew and accepted this.

I think I always had an understanding of the seasons and recognized that all of them—winter as much as summer, fall as much as spring—were necessary to sustain the cycle of life. I might be the youngest, but I kept track of the bills. Where the others whistled in the dark, I considered how we might get by in the event of a worst-case scenario. From what I'd seen of the world, those were far more likely to take place than the paydays George kept expecting.

I loved my brother, Ray. He was the only one in our family who showed me a certain interest, for a while there anyway. But I understood that I was the only truly reasonable person living under whatever roof happened to be sheltering us that season.

Except for one uncle, we saw no relatives. No cousins. There was one grandparent that I met one time and one time only. All I knew of my heritage was George's story: that his father had performed in silent movies, where he met my grandmother—the woman, he told us, who had posed for that image we saw at the beginning of every movie made by Columbia Pictures to this day. He called her a legendary beauty of Hollywood. He said she could stop traffic with her amazing body, well into her sixties.

Traffic? What traffic? My grandparents had lived in Vermont. Due to some kind of falling-out that had something to do with my mother, though we never got the details, I met my grandma only once, when I was five or six, but in distant memory she was an ordinary-looking person who served us meat loaf and called my father Georgie.

George was a fair-weather type. He wanted every day to be sunny, and never believed, as long as it was, that the sky would ever darken again, as it always did over the broad green horizons he imagined for us all. He liked the idea of having children and being a father, but only long enough to cook up some project for us, which he'd forget about shortly after.

A picture from our Vermont days: One time at the feed store, where he was buying materials to build a pen for the baby chicks he'd gotten my brother and me for Easter—with no idea what we were going to do with them when they got big—George spotted a wildflower seed mix for sale. He came up with this idea of digging up our lawn and planting the whole thing with wildflower seed instead.

Back at our rented house, he gave my brother and me paper cups filled with seeds and instructed us to toss them in the ground wherever we wanted, to make the flowers grow in a more natural-looking pattern. He had abandoned the idea of rototilling up the lawn at this point. George preferred to let the seed find its own way into the soil, he said, filling in the patches where the grass was thin.

I knew, even then, no seedlings would take root that way. Even as he was telling Val how we'd set up a flower stand in summer, selling bouquets, I knew we wouldn't.

After his first round of the country-and-western phase, George had a fling with photography. He took up puppeteering. He had this idea he could make a living taking educational puppet shows to schools, teaching children about the importance of good nutrition.

They were ahead of their time, Val and George, as health food types, vegetarians. George's plan to make a killing selling vegetable juicers, and juicer franchises, came sometime after that. Then there was the yogurt culture he bought from a guy he met at a truck stop in Virginia, that we would use to set up a yogurt-making business, with pure Vermont honey (we were back up north by this point) for sweetener. After that failed (and despite the fact that neither of them touched seafood) came the clam shack in Maine. In between these projects there were inventions and—this never changed—country songs.

The years we lived in New Hampshire—where I was born in July of 1950—represented the only time I can remember in which my father held down regular employment. I was eight when we moved, my brother, Ray, twelve. But for years after that, my mother reminisced about the house we lived in there—a place way out on a dirt road that we'd actually bought with a five-thousand-dollar down payment given to my parents by my mother's uncle Ted, who had made some money from part ownership in a bubble-gum company, of all things.

Maybe it was the knowledge that a person could get rich from something like bubble gum (or if not rich, that he could end up with an extra five thousand dollars in his pocket, anyway) that inspired George's own dreams of overnight fame and fortune. Though, quick as he'd earned the bubble gum money, my mother's uncle had lost the majority of the cash, reinvesting the proceeds, as my mother told me, in a scheme for edible crayons or something like that.

Perhaps it was a similarity to this uncle of ours that first attracted Val to George. Though what kept them together was harder to figure. And whatever it was, it didn't keep them together much. The clearest picture I have of George is the sight of him with that briefcase of his, walking out the door headed to some greener pasture, or the twinkling lights of some city where someone had an amazing deal for him, or some grand harbor where, just over the horizon, our ship was coming in.

# RUTH

## Just Fine

THERE WERE FIVE girls in our family: Naomi, Sarah, Esther, Edwina, and me, the youngest, Ruth. Edwina was the only one who bypassed the biblical name, perhaps because by then my mother had begun to realize there might not be a son to carry on her husband's name, and this would have to do. Once her fifth daughter came along, she had accepted daughters as her destiny and returned to the Old Testament for inspiration.

My mother did not actually come from New Hampshire, where we lived, but from the Midwest, Wisconsin. Cheese country, she said, and it was cheese that brought her to the farm. The Planks raised cows, and wanted to learn cheese making.

Her father had come east to deliver some kind of cheese-making equipment. He'd brought his daughter on the trip, to mark her high school graduation and show her the world. As it would turn out, this was as much of it as she would get to see beyond prayer groups in Maine, now and then, and those road trips to check in with the Dickersons.

She was eighteen when she met my father, nineteen when she married him, though he was seven years older. There were hardly any men around in those days, with the war going on, but my father had been granted an exemption from military service, to stay back home and run the family farm. As the oldest of the three Plank brothers, the rest of whom had enlisted in the armed services to fight in Europe, my father was needed at home, and even the government agreed.

All his life, the fact that he had not fought in the war was a source of shame and guilt to my father, but the absence of competition in the form of other available suitors had no doubt also made it possible to persuade my mother to marry him, even if, as she told us regularly, the role of farmer's wife had never been her ambition.

Once she was installed on Plank Farm, though, she did not question it, or him. For all the years of my growing up, and plenty after that, my mother put in fourteen-hour days, in the kitchen mostly—baking bread and tending the baked beans and feeding our laundry through the wringer washer, hanging my father's overalls on the line every morning, canning vegetables in the pressure cooker to get us through the winters and, of course, running our farm stand.

Ours wasn't the kind of family she'd grown up in—the cheese business having been more lucrative, evidently, than farming was for us—but she displayed not an ounce of nostalgia for the life she'd left back in Wisconsin, and anyway, that was over. Once she made her bed, she liked to say, she'd lie in it.

For my father, there was never a day in his life he didn't know who he was or where he was headed: to the barn first, to milk our cows, then out to the fields, to start up the Massey Ferguson. Except for winters, that's how his days went, and he waited out the winters with a controlled impatience, preparing to start the cycle all over again in the new year, beginning with the arrival, every January second, of the new catalog from Ernie's A-1 Seeds.

My father's family were lackluster Presbyterians, but my mother brought a stronger dose of God into the mix, coming as she did from midwestern Lutheran stock. And though, in most departments, my father's word dictated how we lived our lives, when it came to religion, my mother steered our course.

Back then she was a rare midwestern transplant in New England. Her two sisters and her parents remained out in Wisconsin. Money being in short supply, and with a family our size, we didn't go there. That was the reason our mother gave us at the time, anyway, for why we never visited. I never questioned this, or wondered why, among the framed photographs of Plank ancestors that covered our mantel and every wall on our old farmhouse, no image of her own family was part of the display. I questioned little in those days.

I think now my mother must have led a lonely life on the farm—my father not much of a talker, the women of the church having all come from around those parts and, even after twenty years, after thirty, viewing my mother as something of an outsider. She attended women's Bible study and Rainbow Girls gatherings during which recipes and household hints were exchanged, and remedies for childhood ailments, and where, once a year, the women got together to perform skits based on lessons from the New Testament.

When the annual holiday bazaar rolled round, she made her pot holders to raise money for starving children in Africa, but my parents didn't socialize with anyone outside church. My father didn't go out anyplace but the feed store and to meetings of the volunteer firemen. Evenings, our mother read Agatha Christie novels, or the Bible, though once we got our television, she developed a deep and surprising affection for Dinah Shore—a woman of the Jewish persuasion, she said. But with a voice like an angel.

"If that Dinah Shore lived here in town, I know we'd be friends," she told me once. Later, when Dinah took up with a younger man, Burt Reynolds, I found a copy of the *National Enquirer* at the bottom of my mother's sewing basket, with a photograph of Burt and Dinah on the front. Whatever my mother made of that one, she never said.

My mother's only real-life friend (not counting Val Dickerson, and Val Dickerson could not be counted) was Nancy Edmunds, wife of our insurance agent, who lived down the road. The two of them got together for coffee—not often, because my mother was always busy with the chores, but every now and then. Nancy liked to do hair, and though my mother would never have paid money to visit a beauty parlor, she let Nancy give her a permanent wave once, and another time (this was long after, when they both must have been nearing fifty) Nancy dyed my mother's hair. It came out jet black, and if the objective had been to make her look younger—to cover the gray—the experiment failed.

"You were just fine the way you were, Connie," my father said, when he saw the results. The closest to a compliment I ever heard out of him, perhaps, though you might say it was just the opposite, and said less about how good she'd looked before the hair dye than how odd she had looked after.

A few years before this, around the time the oldest of the Edmunds kids and I were entering high school, it was discovered that Nancy's husband, Ralph—our agent with Granite State for as long as my father had run the farm—had been embezzling money from the company. Next thing you knew, Ralph Edmunds disappeared.

A week later it turned out he'd taken a train to Las Vegas, in the hopes that he might win back everything he'd lost, but that wasn't what happened. They found him at some motel next to a casino, hanging from the shower rod, with a note on the bed addressed to Nancy, apologizing for ruining her life.

Most people in our town stopped having much to do with Nancy and her kids after that, but my mother stuck by her friend, even after they lost their house and their car and Nancy Edmunds had to take a job at Perry's Meat Market. My mother found some Bible verse that applied to the situation, she said, but really, I think, it was more the upbeat Dinah Shore philosophy than the scriptures that guided her. A person didn't abandon her friend in hard times. That's when they needed you most.

# *Dana*

## Roots

AFTER THE NEW Hampshire house was sold, we became renters, and we were always renters after that. This may explain why one of my earliest resolutions for my own life was that I would own a piece of land some day. What kind of structure might stand on it barely mattered, but soil did, and a deed of ownership. Roots.

Val and George never cared about those things that much—though Val wanted one thing, which was a place to do her art. All those years, there was always paint under her fingernails and some picture in the works, though more often than not, when we moved, she'd have to leave her canvases behind. When she died, there was almost nothing to show of all those years she'd spent making those strange, sad pictures. They were of faces, mostly, and people she dreamed up, places that didn't exist.

As a young girl growing up in Pennsylvania, my mother had wanted to be an artist, but there was never any money for art school, and anyway, she told me once, her parents—her father worked at a steel mill; her mother kept house—didn't think "artist" was a real job.

She was working as a waitress in Pittsburgh when a man had given her his card. "With that long, thin figure of yours, you could be a model," he told her—an old story, but not one she'd ever heard. "Call me if you come to New York City and I'll set you up."

She didn't care about modeling. But New York sounded good, and getting away from her parents sounded better. Uncle Ted fronted her a hundred dollars, and five days later she was on a bus to the big city.

It turned out the modeling job involved walking around a Times Square bar in four-inch heels carrying a tray of cigarettes and candy and wearing an outfit that was basically underwear decorated with bits of fluff and a few sparkles. "A Peachy Puff Girl," she was called. Thursday nights she went to look at the art at the Metropolitan Museum and sometimes brought a sketch pad to copy some painting she liked.

But art school wasn't happening. Simply coming up with rent money was enough of a challenge, particularly for a girl like Valerie, who was never good with finances, and who—every time she had a few extra dollars—did something crazy with it like buying a deluxe set of pastels or a gold leather purse she saw in the window of Macy's, even though she had no place to take it.

It was on her rounds as a Peachy Puff girl that she met George, who was having a drink at the bar where she worked. He told her he was a writer. He had come to the city to meet with an editor who wanted to publish his novel. They were working out a few last details of the deal. (Later, it turned out the details included a five-hundred-dollar down payment, *from* George *to* his publisher, for getting *Vanquished Desire* into print. But that night, at least, George was one step away from becoming the next Erle Stanley Gardner.)

After all the traveling salesmen she'd met (though soon enough, she'd be married to one) the idea of knowing a writer struck Valerie as exciting. She told him she wanted to be an artist.

"Hey, we should go someplace like Vermont or New Hampshire and live off the land," he said. "I'd write best-selling novels and you'd make beautiful paintings."

In two weeks they were on their way north.

Years later, when Val and George were well into their forties and living in a funky apartment near Cocoa Beach, Florida—the last place they shared before George took off for good—George went to an art auction he read about in the paper. He came back having spent most of their savings—eight thousand dollars, if memory serves me—on a bunch of artwork he told my mother they could resell for three times what he paid, or more. A few days later he arranged for an appraiser to come over and take a look at his collection.

Among his purchases that day was a painting alleged to have been made by Salvador Dalí, and another that was by Fernand Léger, and a Frederic Remington statue of a cowboy, and a drawing the auctioneer attributed to a student of Leonardo da Vinci, with a letter taped on the back supposedly confirming this.

It took the appraiser less than five minutes to examine the collection. They were all fakes. George had fallen for one of the oldest tricks in the book.

The appraiser was just getting up to go when he spotted a portrait over our couch, of a woman in a red hat, smoking a cigarette. "Who did this one?" he said, with a tone of renewed interest. "You've actually got something here."

The painting was Val's. We had a storage room full of more of her work. There was no market for them, however—then or ever. Eventually, in her later years, after George was long gone, she made a little money doing greeting cards and pastel portraits of people's children. Fifty dollars a portrait, seventy-five if there were two heads in the frame rather than one.

All in all, we were about as unlikely a family as you could imagine to have befriended people like the Planks. We didn't exactly befriend them, of course. In fact, over the many years we kept receiving cards and letters from Plank Farm—forwarded from some previous address more often than not—Val often commented to us on the strangeness of Connie's stubborn insistence that the two families remain in touch.

One night Val read a letter out loud to us over our dinner of lentils and celery and beet juice, imitating Connie's voice as she might have spoken the words, and laughing in a way that struck me even then as unfair.

"Tell Dana for us that our Ruth has now entered the beautiful and special phase of womanhood," Connie had written. "I know she'd enjoy hearing from Dana about her own experiences in that regard."

My brother, Ray, had practically spit up his juice, hearing this. "The special phase of womanhood!" he said, gagging.

"Like I'd really write a letter to some girl I hardly know," I said. About menstruation, of all things.

We made fun of the Plank family, if we thought of them at all, which wasn't that often, though there was always the Christmas card, and oddly enough, Val always sent them a Christmas letter—which was a linoleum print she made, sometimes accompanied by the photograph George took of us each year, using a timer on the camera so he could be in it too. We even paid a visit to the farm stand most summers, usually around the time of Ruth's and my birthday, which was strawberry season.

I think it actually mattered to Val more than she liked to admit, to know what this family was doing, and what they thought of us. Connie Plank was like that kind of hungry and determined cat that shows up at your door with such persistence—not all the time, but often enough—that you finally decide you might as well start feeding it.

"I feel sorry for Edwin," Val said one time. "He goes along with that woman, but you know she drives him crazy. He should never have married someone like her."

But here was the oddest thing: somewhere along the line, on one of those Christmases when the letter from the Planks arrived as it always did, with the same reports (how many calves were born that spring, the girls' education, church events and the annual bazaar, followed by the yearly thanks to God for all his many blessings), it occurred to me that if the day ever came when Connie ceased to write, I would miss the presence of the Planks in our life. I had come to enjoy, in particular, our summer visits to the farm stand. I liked the dependability of the farm, for one thing—the fact that there was one place in my life—one place only, perhaps—that was always going to be there, where nothing much was ever going to change.

And I loved learning about the farm—those times on our strawberry season visits when (busy as he was, and he was always busy) Edwin Plank would drop what he was doing and show me some new development. He explained to me the reason he kept two kinds of cows—Guernseys for cream, Holsteins for milk. He was trying out a certain kind of Chinese bean with seeds brought to him by his one Chinese customer. ("Chinaman" was the term he used. This was the early sixties. That was what you said in those days.)

Another time he had reached into his pocket and pulled out for me a potato he said he'd noticed while digging up one of the hills.

"What do you make of this?" he said. "Darned thing's the spitting image of Lyndon Johnson."

Looking back, it was surprising how he seemed to recognize, early on, that I was a person who'd be interested in such things. I remember one year he was excited (as excited as a person like Edwin ever appears) over a new variety of butter-and-sugar corn that blended the best of both worlds: the flavor of yellow corn with the sweetness and crunchiness of white corn. Another time he told me the story of the Big Boy tomato, the first real commercial hybrid variety, developed by the son of a Ukrainian farmer, that was brought out by the Burpee company the year before my birth and Ruth's—1949.

"Imagine thinking up a whole new vegetable," he told me, as he handed me a sample.

"Now that would be a legacy to leave your grandchildren," he said.

Though I was still young when we had these conversations—once a year at most, walking the rows, while back at the house Connie served Val coffee from the percolator, not instant—I liked our visits. I appreciated Edwin Plank's sober reflection on the pride and comfort he found, early mornings in the barn, milking the cows, and most of all, running his old Massey Ferguson across his fields, knowing the furrows he was carving out were the very same ones his own father and grandfather before him had turned over in decades past.

"They're long dead now, of course," he said. "The only things that carry on for sure are the seasons and the crops."

Young as I was, hearing him say this moved me. Some part of me admired the Plank family's steadiness and constancy, the order with which their lives unfolded, particularly measured against the untidiness of our own. I loved the idea that a handful of corn seeds, properly planted and tended, would lead to tall, straight stalks, and food. Girls weren't supposed to care about these things—particularly in those days—but I was never a girl who cared about Barbie dolls or dresses. Even though Val, who loved those things, kept giving them to me.

I liked to put my hands in the dirt, felt drawn to it. I wished I could drive a tractor. Upstairs, alone in my room, I tried on my brother's jeans and rolled up the cuffs. I used to say, when people asked me, that I wanted to be a nurse when I grew up. That or a mother, because that was what girls said in those days, even a girl like me, with a mother like mine.

I told no one this, but the truth was, I dreamed of being a farmer like Edwin Plank.

# RUTH

## A Long Line

FOR ALL THE generations of the family I grew up in—ten of them, by the time I came along—it was having a son to carry on the farm that mattered most, and so, for a Plank, the birth of nothing but daughters, one after the other, had to have been a cruel disappointment on at least one level. But my father never treated the fact of our gender as anything besides a marvel. He spoke of us as "my girls," and it always seemed, when he did, that he took a particular pride in the fact of having fathered such a brood. If he ever allowed himself to imagine the son he didn't have, he never let us know.

But there remained a question nobody spoke of, though we all knew it was there: what would happen to the farm when he was no longer able to tend the land? Who would carry on, after?

I was never so young that I didn't know what it meant to be a Plank—that we were marching at the end of a long line dating back a few hundred years with the responsibility to tend our land well and turn it over to the next generation. The people would come and go. It was the farm that endured, and in our family and the world at large, it was believed this was a man's job.

Nobody ever doubted that my father loved us all, but it had not been a natural idea for him to share his work with a girl child. With my older sisters, there seemed no interest on their part to know our father's world of the barn and the fields, but I longed to be with him. Not so much for love of farming, perhaps, as for the love of him. And perhaps because by the time I came along, he'd given up on fathering a son, he acquiesced to my joining him for his morning chores.

I had to wake before dawn if I wanted to accompany him out to the barn, his workday began so early. Those mornings I'd jump out of bed and pull on my pants and shirt, step into my Keds without even lacing them, and scurry down the stairs just as he set his coffee mug down and headed out the door with our dog, Sadie, close behind. He might greet me, might not. My father inhabited another world when he had milking and crops on his mind.

I usually trudged a few steps behind him. I had a hard time keeping up, his stride was so long, but it was important to get to the barn when he did, so I could slip in with him. The door, on its heavy iron hinges, was way too heavy for me to open by myself, but he held it open for me, as long as I didn't lollygag.

Entering the barn, I'd be hit with the aroma of the manure and the fragrant hay up in the loft, where my father had put up a swing for my sisters and me. Hanging on the wall were the worn leather harnesses and collars our old workhorses used to wear. They'd been retired back when I was very little, but my father always said they deserved to live out their days in the home they started out in and the pastures they knew.

First off we headed to the feed supplies. This would be when my father might at last look up at me and nod. "You want to lend a hand here, Ruthie?" he said.

One by one then, we fed the animals—my father up ahead, and me, his eager helper following behind. Wordlessly, my father forked the silage into a wheelbarrow, then worked his way down the rows, making sure every cow got her share. I followed along, trying to whistle the way he did. I'd use my hoe to gather up the manure and then scrape it into the gutter, which ran the length of the barn, where we collected it.

As I worked I loved to think about how connected everything was on our farm—that the hay and silage our cows were munching had been grown here on our land, and that the manure the cows would create, from eating it, would ripen and be returned to that same land come spring, to fertilize the soil and start the process all over again.

While the cows were eating my father did the milking. My job: filling a bucket with a mix of water and disinfectant for wiping down the udders of each of our four cows—two Guernseys, two Holsteins—to keep them healthy. And sometimes, if I finished before my father, I climbed up into the prized Model T Ford he kept in the barn, and sat behind the steering wheel, pretending to drive.

My father said we didn't need a fancy milking setup. The old-fashioned way was good enough. He'd lower his long frame onto a three-legged stool, with his forehead leaned against the cow's flank and his fingers rhythmically working the teats, with a bucket below to catch the warm stream of milk and our old barn cat, Susan, waiting expectantly for her share. Her reward, my father said, for keeping the mouse population in check.

After we finished in the barn, we headed out to the truck and began our rounds of the farm. From his silence, you would have thought he didn't even know I was there, except he'd never start the ignition until I'd climbed up beside him and Sadie, on the seat of his old Dodge truck. On the dashboard he kept his farm log, in which he recorded every day's observations of rainfall and weather conditions and planting data—with comments like "Poor resistance to bottom rot. Plant in drier ground next time" or "Too much leaf, not enough yield. Don't use again."

We made our stops like milkmen—checking in on the cabbages in one field, the carrots next, to see what rows needed weeding or thinning that day, and what crops were ready for harvest. My father always kept a bucket of clippers and knives on the floor for cutting broccoli or cabbage or lettuce when they were ready. Sometimes I'd munch on a carrot he pulled for me as we worked.

We hardly ever talked on those mornings, or if we did, it was just a few words. Mostly he worked in silence, or whistled. But I loved those times with my father, when I had him all to myself. I waited for the end of his long workday to come, when we'd head to the irrigation pond and take a swim—my father in his shorts, me in my underwear, our two pairs of shoes (his heavy boots and my Keds) lined up along the shore, side by side.

My sisters never liked the water, but I was a fish, he said. So he taught me how to hold my breath underwater, and do the crawl, and then, the summer I turned seven or eight, how to dive off the big granite boulder at the far end of the pond. He said I had the build of a diver, meaning the same build as him.

After, we'd head up to the house for dinner with the family. My mother must have noticed our wet hair, but she never made a comment, though I sensed a certain edge of disapproval. She was afraid of the water and kept her distance from the pond, same as my sisters did. Swimming belonged to my father and me alone. The irrigation pond was our spot and ours only.

## *Dana*

# Windowsill Garden

WALKING HOME FROM school, sometimes, I'd study other kids with their dads and wonder what it would be like to have a father like that. Mine, when he was home, seemed more like a lodger than a member of our family. He'd turn up in between what he referred to as his business trips, wearing some fancy shirt and, if his latest project had taken him to some warmer climate, a tan. For my brother, George's greeting was a slap on the back of the kind businessmen or fraternity brothers might give one another. Though even as a kid, Ray was never the backslapping type.

For me there was a kiss on the cheek, or he'd pat my head as if I were a puppy. He brought me hotel soaps and shower caps, and once, a shirt with rhinestones on the front that said I LEFT IT IN LAS VEGAS. I often wondered, did he know me at all? How could he, and think I'd wear that shirt?

With Val, George seemed to adopt a kind of sharp and bitter humor lacking anything that passed for affection. They'd disappear into the bedroom shortly after his return from one or another of those trips, but I never saw them kiss, and when he spoke of her, it was usually to make fun of something—her poor housekeeping skills, her hopeless cooking, how much money she spent on paint.

I was too young to understand, but there was always an edge in his voice that left me anxious. "Your mom find any new boyfriends while I was away?" he'd ask. Or once, to my brother, he said, "Take a piece of advice from me, buddy. You're better off with an ugly woman. Those are the ones you can count on to stay out of trouble."

Val never said anything when he made these comments. None of us did. At times like this my brother could be counted on to head off on his unicycle, or pull his harmonica out of his pocket and start blowing on it. Val disappeared into whatever space she'd set up for herself to do her artwork. My father usually headed out for a beer. He no longer gave any indication of working on his novel.

As for me, I went to the library and checked out a new biography of some inspirational figure—Nellie Bly, reporter; Clara Barton, founder of the American Red Cross; Harriet Tubman, conductor on the Underground Railroad. I tended my windowsill avocado plants and concocted interesting combinations of organic materials—coffee grounds, crumbled-up eggshells, and old vegetable peels put through our juicer—to use as fertilizer. I conducted experiments with bean sprouts and bread mold. I dreamed I was living in the country somewhere, raising chickens and living off the land, with no people around to mess things up.

# RUTH

## Staying Within the Lines

THINGS WERE NEVER easy with my mother, but I adored my dad. My father alone, of all the people in our family, seemed to appreciate me, even if he didn't always understand what was going on in my head. Where my mother remained distant and dismissive, my father offered nothing but love. Stern as he could be if I'd neglected my chores in the barn, or there was mold on the blueberry bushes I was supposed to be looking after, he seemed only delighted by all the ways in which I revealed myself as different from the others.

"My beanpole," he called me. "After all these years of tending corn, someone up there must've thought I should have a daughter with hair the color of corn silk."

"I didn't get a son," he said. "But I got an artist."

All those years growing up, I had felt my mother's coolness toward me. She was never an easily affectionate person. But where her quiet, contained expressions of affection for the other girls came naturally—if not in abundance—with me, she always seemed to have been following directions, going through the motions of brushing my hair or kissing my cheek, in the same diligent manner with which she would go through the steps for canning tomatoes correctly in the pressure cooker or making pickles. There was always, in her behavior toward me, a sense that she was having to remind herself "Don't leave Ruth out." Her touch had a mechanical quality. Her words of encouragement, a script.

She'd compliment Esther or Naomi on a paper they brought home from school, or tape up a drawing they'd made—then, as if following a checklist, add, "What about you, Ruth? Show me what you did today." Worst of all was when she hugged me. Her lips on my cheek felt dry and frozen. I imagined that she must be counting the seconds before dropping her arms from that stiff embrace. One one thousand, two one thousand. Then, abruptly, release. A relief to us both.

I'd show her my drawings, of course, that being what I did best. I loved art class, and hungered for access to oil pastels and paints, and things like glue and glitter, markers and construction paper and silver foil, that we never had around. At our house, the same box of Crayolas had remained on the shelf for as long as I could remember. Jumbo, but so old now that all the best colors—like purple and orange, pink, bright yellow, crimson—were used up or worn down to the nub.

I asked my mother once if we could get a new box. "They wouldn't get used up so quickly if you didn't press down so hard," she said. "And anyway, there's plenty left." Meaning brown, gray, beige. In my mother's book, colors were interchangeable.

And oddly, though I was always the one who loved to draw, my mother demonstrated a strong preference for the pictures my sisters brought to her. Winnie's specialty was coloring books, where she, better than any of the rest of us, had mastered the ability to stay within the lines. Naomi had become particularly skillful at copying *Peanuts* characters.

"We should send this in to the newspaper," she said one time when Naomi brought her a likeness of Charlie Brown standing in front of the doghouse, with Snoopy on top.

"It's a copy," I said, but only to myself. Why would the newspaper want to publish my sister's drawing, when they already had the real cartoons?

My own pictures were full of made-up images that I worked on out in our barn, in the hayloft—fantasy figures, beautiful girls in dresses fancier, even, than the outfits of Dana Dickerson's Barbie. It was one of the many things I liked about drawing, the way—on paper—you could dream up anything you wanted, your only limitations those of your imagination, which in my case meant no limits at all.

It was viewed as a problem in our family—this fantasy life of mine, and my capacity to think up stories and scenarios. To my mother, this kind of activity suggested a deceitful character, and a susceptibility to the temptations of impure thought. All the stories we needed were right there in the Bible. Why go further?

But in my bed I did. I lay there sometimes, with my sister Esther asleep across from me and Winnie on the bunk above—and thought up characters and situations they'd find themselves in.

Sometimes I acted them out, but only in my head. I imagined an orphan girl who works on a farm, weeding strawberries until one day a woman pulls up and sees her there. First she buys all the strawberries. Then, as the girl is carrying the flats of ripe berries out to her limousine, the woman asks, "Where do you live?"

"Over there," says the orphan girl, pointing to the barn, where she sleeps next to the cows on a hard pallet her cruel employer has given her, with only a scratchy horsehair blanket for cold nights.

"I'm taking you away with me," the woman says.

"What about my clothes?" the girl asks, meaning a few rags and a pillowcase with holes for her head and arms that the cruel farmer's wife has given her.

"Never mind those," the woman says, stroking the girl's head and pressing her tight against the soft white fur of her cloak. "We'll buy you everything you need when you come to live with me in Hollywood."

Of course the woman turns out to be a movie star. The two of them make a movie together, in which the orphan girl, whose name is Rose, plays the star's beloved daughter. She's famous now. Off-screen, Rose is adopted by the beautiful movie star.

One day the cruel farmers go to the movies.

"That pretty little girl up on the screen looks familiar," the farmer's wife says to the farmer.

"Oh my God, it's Rose," he tells her. "If only we'd treated her better. Now it's too late."

Later I'd tell myself a different kind of story. I did this at night still—or times at the farm, when I'd be driving the tractor or hoeing the tomatoes. Around age twelve—at about the age my mother sent the Dickersons that mortifying announcement of my recent entry into womanhood, with little in the way of additional explanation for me concerning this development besides the information that I'd better be careful now, and my sisters would answer my questions if I had any—I started including a new set of characters in my stories.

These were boys around the age of the ones my father tended to hire to help out in the summer, but handsomer. Not Victor Patucci, though he was always around. Victor had acne—from all that hair cream I figured—and instead of calling our cows by their real names, he referred to them by the names of *Playboy* centerfolds, whose pictures I found when I was up in the loft one day, in a secret stash he'd evidently tucked behind some hay bales. The kind of boys I liked were more along the lines of Bob Dylan, whose album—with a soulful picture of him walking down a street in New York City with his beautiful long-haired girlfriend—I played on Sarah and Naomi's record player as much as my sisters allowed me. I kept this to myself, but the harmonica parts always made me think of Ray Dickerson.

Sometimes I dreamed of Bob Dylan. Sometimes Ray. Where my old stories featured shopping trips for dresses and rooms with four-poster beds, the pictures that filled my head now showed these boys taking my clothes off, though I never could picture how it would be if they'd taken off their own. In one, Bob Dylan was brushing my hair. Then he was kissing me. Then his hands were touching my breasts, and I was touching them, too, as I thought about this. Then lower. The place my mother did not ever talk about, except to say that babies came from there.

Not just babies.

WHEN I WAS LITTLE, MY father had brought home a book called *Harold and the Purple Crayon*. My mother never had much use for children's stories, but my dad used to take me to the town library—rainy days, when there was no way to work in the fields and nothing much was going on in our greenhouse that couldn't wait till tomorrow.

In this book, the boy named Harold gets a magic crayon and starts drawing things with it, and as he does, the lines he makes come to life, so when he draws an apple, he can actually eat it, and when he draws a rocket ship, he rides on it to space.

The message was clear to me: a person who can draw can do anything, go anywhere. This was the kind of person I wanted to be, and the fact that my father recognized that well enough to pick out that book for me was what I loved about him. One of the things.

I also believed my father—my father, alone—recognized and felt pride in my artistic talent. When we needed a sign for the farm stand (FIRST PEAS! SPRING ONIONS! PLEASE DON'T PEEL THE CORN! WE PROMISE THERE'S NO WORMS!), I was the one given the job of making it. When our dog, Sadie, died, he asked me to paint a picture to remember her by.

My father hardly ever took a day off work, besides those car trips every February to wherever the Dickersons lived at the time, and every now and then down to where the state agricultural school was, if some pest was giving him trouble and he needed advice, or soil testing. These were rare times my father set aside his Dickies overalls and put on his brown pants and regular shoes. He'd make an appointment to visit the lab, and when we walked in, carrying our soil samples, or a Tupperware container with a pinch of leaf mold or a fungus that was worrying him, or a new strain of potato bug, one of the professors would analyze the situation.

My sisters never came along on those trips, and I loved it that I got him all to myself then—sitting next to him on the bench seat of our old Dodge truck listening to the radio, or just the sound of him whistling, or talking about things in a way that never happened when my mother was around. Stories from the old days, when he was growing up on the farm. The time he spent a whole summer cultivating a pumpkin with the hope of winning first prize in a 4-H competition at the fall harvest fair, and then the night before the competition, a hailstorm had destroyed it. A trip he made to New York City—home of Greenwich Village, home of Dylan!—with his grandfather to the 1939 World's Fair.

The war, and my father's obligation to run the family farm, had ended my father's plans for a college education. He wanted that for me.

Meanwhile, he loved visiting the agriculture professors, and talking with them about issues on the farm. They had the book learning, he had the field experience. "If we could just get together on this stuff," he said, "there's no telling what us farmers could grow."

I loved those days, just my father and me, traipsing over the university campus, carrying our soil specimens and plant samples. After we were done talking with some professor there, my father took me over to the experimental barns where they bred the cattle. They had this one bull there, a new breed they'd been developing, though still in the experimental phase. I asked my father what he meant by that.

"This is a prize bull," my father told me. "Back home we breed cows the old-fashioned way, but here at the university the students extract the semen from him and inject it into cows they've selected for the purpose of improving the breed. Eventually, they hope they'll come up with a whole new breed, created right here in the state of New Hampshire."

We were standing outside this bull's pen at the time. The sign on the front of his stall said his name was Rocky. He was the biggest bull I'd ever seen, though the fact that he'd been confined within such a small space, and he looked so angry about that, no doubt contributed to the sense you got looking at him that this bull was enormous. I got the feeling he might at any moment break right through the bars and stomp on us, but I felt safe, because I was holding my father's hand, and I always felt safe when he was there.

I asked him how they got the semen. If I'd known better what it was, I might have felt embarrassed but I didn't. He would never have talked about these things if my mother was around, but when it was just the two of us, as it often was, my father loosened up considerably.

"One of the things I love about being a farmer," he said, "is having the opportunity to put together totally different genetic strains and come up with a whole new breed of living thing. Could be a cow. Could be a watermelon. That's how it is when a man and a woman get together too. You mix up the bloodlines and come up with the best of both, if you're lucky. Like I did with you."

Later that night, the bull entered my dreams. He was stomping his huge hoof in the sawdust of his pen, and his eyes were red, and there was drool coming out his flaring nostrils. He was scary, but something about him was exciting too.

When I came down to breakfast the next morning, my mother was at the stove, as usual, making the oatmeal. My sisters were already at their places.

"Did you and your father have a nice time at the university?" she said.

"Yup," I said. "Very educational."

## *Dana*

# The Idea of Love

THE FIRST THING people noticed about Val was usually her height, which was closing in on six feet. She stood a little taller than George, in fact. But that wasn't the only striking aspect to her appearance. She had this long blond hair, and blue eyes, and she moved like a dancer. Her fingers, though they were always covered with paint, were the kind you'd see in a magazine advertisement for hand lotion or diamond rings, not that she had one. She wasn't beautiful in the way movie stars and fashion models might be, but she had this very long, thin face, with a surprisingly wide space between her nose and her upper lip, which gave her a faintly animal appearance. She was the type of person other people looked at when she came into a room, without her making any effort to produce that result.

Unlike myself. I was short, with hair of a shade people tend to call dirty brown, and where my mother's legs stretched long and thin, with elegant narrow ankles and high arches like a ballerina's, I had thick calf muscles and wide, broad feet. Even in girlhood—long before menopause sealed the deal—I had a short, thick waist that inspired my mother to comment that I had the kind of body high-waisted dresses were invented for.

But the truth was, I didn't like any kind of dresses. I have always felt most comfortable in jeans or overalls or, if the situation calls for it, wide, cuffed men's trousers with a tucked-in shirt, never mind if it makes me look boyish and thick. Why pretend? I am.

The way Val kept presenting me with frilly clothes and things to put in my hair, even after I'd cut most of it off, always seemed bizarre to me. Every year on my birthday I got a new Barbie doll that I might never have taken out of the box if it hadn't been for those times Ruth Plank and her sisters came to visit. I would have given them the whole lot, but I knew my mother wouldn't want me to. She was the one who really loved those dolls.

Who she wanted for a daughter was someone she could have done things with, like try on clothes, or play with hairstyles, or do craft projects and make dollhouses. Val loved making things with fabric and bright colors and glued-on sequins—beaded necklaces, hand-painted shawls, ruffled outfits. Dirty as her fingernails were most of the time from painting, she would probably have loved going to one of those nail salons to get a manicure.

I never got the impression that there was love between Val and George, but Val had a big-time romantic streak. She used to do things like turn out all the lights and put candles all over the house, if George had been away for a while on one of his trips, and she'd have music going, like maybe Peggy Lee or Dean Martin, and then she'd meet him at the door in some amazing outfit she'd cooked up, with scarves and lace and possibly not that much else, which freaked out my brother in particular. He learned to make himself scarce on those nights.

I got the feeling she always ended up disappointed though. Val was a woman who loved the idea of love—more, possibly, than the reality of loving someone. She liked the trappings and the drama.

Her real love—more than George, and more than my brother and me when you got down to it, though I believe she loved us in her way—was going into whatever odd, cramped little space she'd made for herself in whatever place we'd touched down, and making artwork.

She painted faces mostly, generally women. Sometimes she cut pictures out of magazines to use for inspiration. She painted herself often, though always in made-up circumstances—riding a horse, on a trapeze, dressed in an evening gown at some imaginary ball. I used to wish she'd make a painting of me, but if she had, she would have had to study my face for a long time, and I had the oddest feeling that she didn't like to look at me. Not that she didn't love me. She just preferred not to consider my face too closely, having surely recognized long before that it contained not even the faintest sign of what she loved best, which was beauty.

I KNEW, VERY YOUNG, THAT I liked a certain kind of woman, a strong one. A woman nothing like my mother, though I could be drawn to beauty too.

The first woman I remember having a crush on was the actress who played Perry Mason's secretary on TV, Della Street. Perry might win the cases, and his big tall buddy, Paul Drake, stepped in when a little muscle was needed, but Della had this cool, calm, organized manner, like nothing ever flustered her, and underneath her gentle exterior there was a firmness and command I liked. Unlike the woman I lived with—my mother—this one had a handle on things.

I imagined how it would be if Della came to our house. How she'd get rid of all those variously dated and mostly out-of-date yogurt cultures on the windowsill, the frozen orange juice cans with paintbrushes lying around, my father's tapes spooling off the reels, my brother's *Mad* magazines, my mother's sequins and hair ornaments littering the floor, and all those unopened bills from the phone company and some recording studio where George made a demo one time, forwarded from whatever town we'd lived in before.

I watched *The Patty Duke Show,* about two identical cousins—one of whom grew up in London, the other in a place near New York City called Brooklyn. The proper, refined London girl, Cathy, comes to live with the family of the Brooklyn girl, Patty, who is a fun, wild, American teenager type. But I always liked Cathy best. She was sensible and cautious, where Patty was boy-crazy and immature. Patty got on my nerves.

In fact, I watched television a lot in those days, searching for women to model myself on. I liked Julia Child's big, confident voice and how she handled a roasting chicken, and the runner, Wilma Rudolph, who won three medals at the 1960 Olympics even though she'd been born with polio. I liked Donna Reed, not only because she was beautiful, but because she seemed kind, and steady, in a way I longed for my own parents to be. I loved *The Beverly Hillbillies,* but not because the ridiculous antics of the Clampett family amused me. The one I related to was the no-nonsense secretary Miss Jane Hathaway, the one sane character in the bunch. Something about her long thin frame and her plainness, even homeliness—particularly set off by the frilly excesses of Elly May—stirred my heart.

I was thirteen when I realized that how I felt about these women differed from how my brother viewed certain male celebrities and hero types.

For me, the women whose images covered the walls in my room were not simply people I admired, or ones whose music or performances appealed to me. I didn't just *like* these women. I thought about kissing them, and for the first time that I remember—having been all my life a person seemingly lacking in imagination—I imagined what I'd like to do with them.

I pictured the women wrapping their arms around me, and their legs, and pressing their hands into my flesh, running their fingers through my hair and down my neck.

I didn't know the word for who I was or how I felt, when I first started getting these feelings. I only knew I wasn't like other girls, who screamed when they saw the Beatles on television, or hung pictures of Elvis Presley and Ricky Nelson on their bedroom walls.

I didn't want a boy, I wanted girls—real girls, girls at my school—to feel about me as they did about some boy. To show that kind of interest, but in me this time. How could it be, I wondered, that they could fall all over themselves for some pimply loser with a bulging Adam's apple who snapped their bra strap, when I would kiss them tenderly and love them?

The first time I ever acted on my feelings for a girl was in seventh grade, shortly after we moved to Vermont. Her name was Jenny Samuels, and we had math together, and gym. Our lockers were next to each other, which meant we'd change side by side. This was wonderful and terrible, having her naked, or almost naked, up that close to me, and wanting so badly to look at her, and afraid if I did she'd know.

Most of the girls were modest about getting naked at that stage. A few even changed in the toilet cubicles, rather than let anyone see them without their underwear on. Or they'd come out of the shower with their towel around their chest, and shimmy into their underpants with the towel still on. Then turn around and hook their bra with their back to you, so the most you'd see was a flash of their nipples as they slipped their breasts into the cups. Not much to see in most cases, this being seventh grade.

My own breasts were so small I didn't really need a bra, and didn't want one, but Val said if I didn't have one on it would look funny, and there might be these two dark dots showing under my shirt if I wore something light-colored.

"I'll wear an undershirt," I said, but she said no, that's not what girls do.

This particular day, I had my bra and panties on already. I had made sure to get out of the shower quick, to be ahead of Jenny, so I'd have more time to position myself. I had this plan to be fiddling with my locker combination at the moment that she dropped the towel, and to drop the lock at the exact same moment, so I'd have an excuse to get down on the floor and then look up, which would be the moment I'd catch a glimpse of her.

Jenny had amazingly large breasts for a seventh grader. The boys had all commented widely on this. She must have been accustomed to having her breasts be a topic of interest at our school, but not in the girls' locker room, generally.

As it turned out, we were the only ones in our part of the room that day, because all the other girls had stayed in the gymnasium a few extra minutes to get the lowdown on cheerleading tryouts and see a demonstration of the cartwheel and the jumps they'd be asked to execute. The cheering coach herself had shown up, to offer pointers for those who wanted a little one-on-one work, which turned out to be everyone but two.

I had no interest in being a cheerleader, not that they ever would have picked me. Somewhat to my surprise, given her body, neither did Jenny.

Now she was coming over to our spot with her towel on. Now she was wiggling into her panties under the towel, on schedule. Now I was fiddling with the locker, dropping the lock, just as the towel fell on the floor beside me.

I looked up.

Jenny Samuels loomed over me, naked from the waist up, those two enormous breasts of hers sticking out so far I couldn't even see her face at first. Surprisingly, she was making no effort to put on her brassiere. The two bare pink breasts of Jenny Samuels that I'd longed to catch sight of all that fall were right there—even bigger and fuller than I had imagined.

She was just sitting on the bench that way, with her round pink nipples and her white freckled skin and her pink flower panties with lace around the edges cutting into her full pink thighs, and her breasts were hanging down even more dramatically than they might have if she were upright, because she was bent over now, with her hands over her eyes. She was crying.

I was almost too stunned to speak but I managed. "What's the matter?" I said. And then, because of my guilt, "What did I do?"

"You didn't do anything," she said. "It's all those boys that are always hanging around watching me. A bunch of them were waiting on the bleachers for the cheering tryout. I could tell they were figuring they'd get to see me jumping. That's the kind of thing they do. I get so sick of it."

It took me a second to get what she meant.

"These," she said, touching the gigantic, perfect breasts I had dreamed about touching. And more. "They like to watch them jiggle."

I put my arm around her. Not the way I'd pictured, when I imagined the two of us in a field someplace together, naked, mud wrestling. Or scrubbing each other in the shower and, afterward, putting our tongues in each other's mouths, and Jenny bending over me then, when we lay down side by side, and lowering her gorgeous breasts over my face, guiding her perfect pink nipples into my mouth.

The way I put my arm around her then was strictly for comfort, the way my brother put his arm around me sometimes, when I was feeling bad about something that happened at school.

For that moment, anyway, I was more like a sister, a friend. "They shouldn't make you feel that way," I said. "They're idiots."

"I wish I was flat like you," she said. "No offense."

"I think you're beautiful," I whispered. I couldn't help myself then. "I love them." Her breasts, I meant. I couldn't say the word, and the word *boobs,* that all the other girls used, seemed ridiculous and inadequate. Like what they had on top was some kind of a joke, instead of something wonderful and beautiful.

I kissed her. On the mouth.

She let out a noise, not like a scream exactly. More like my mother when she opened one of the yogurt containers and found a bunch of mold on top.

"You're a freak," she said, grabbing the towel. "I'm telling Miss Kavenaugh."

When I was older, looking back on this moment, the realization would come to me that if anyone in our school was likely to understand how I had felt at that moment, it might have been Miss Kavenaugh, our gym teacher. But at the time, all I knew was I had ruined everything.

By three o'clock our whole school would know, Dana Dickerson was a lesbo. This part was true. The only saving grace was that our family moved a few months later. For once I was glad we had never stayed anyplace that long.

# RUTH

## Outside the Rules

BESIDES OUR VISITS to the laboratories and barns of the University of New Hampshire College of Agriculture, I can remember only one other occasion, ever, when I went someplace besides the feed store or the dump with my father.

It happened over Christmas vacation the year I was in seventh grade, right after my mother left for Wisconsin to attend the funeral of her father—an event that had not seemed to fill her with much grief, I noted. She took my sisters, but when I told her I'd just as soon stay home, she didn't argue.

The five of them planned to take a Greyhound bus over that stretch of days between Christmas and New Year's, when nothing much was happening at the farm. Every year, as dependable as sunrise, my father would receive his new Burpee's catalog and the one from Ernie's A-1 Seeds, on January 2, and get to work with the ordering, but until then even he had time on his hands.

Two days after Christmas—a year in which my father had given my mother a new hay rake for the tractor as her gift, the same thing she'd given him—we drove my mother and sisters to the bus station in Boston, my sisters in their church clothes for the trip, my mother in a suit. I figured we'd head home right after, or maybe, if I was lucky, stop at Schrafft's for an ice cream. I knew about that place from the one other time I'd been to Boston, when our mother took us there to hear Bishop Fulton J. Sheen preach. Not a Lutheran, but she'd made an exception in his case.

As we pulled onto the road leading out toward the Charles River, my father handed me a Coke from the cooler in the back. "What do you say we take in an art museum, since we're in the neighborhood?" he said.

He might as well have said, "What do you say we go to a bar and get drunk?" or "Let's go bet on horses." The suggestion was that bizarre. But wonderful.

The place he had chosen to visit, oddly enough, was not the Museum of Fine Arts. That one I'd discover on my own years later, when I went to school not far from there. But that day we visited the Isabella Stewart Gardner Museum. You had to wonder how he'd heard about it.

"When I was a boy, my father took me once to Fenway Park, to watch Lefty Grove pitch," he said. "Seems like the kind of thing a dad should do at least once in his child's life, take her someplace out of the ordinary."

The fact that it was only me he was doing this with, and that he had chosen an art museum—rather than the Old North Church, or the Museum of Science, or the ballpark—filled me with pride. I had worried, when we walked in the doors and saw the admission price—four dollars—that he might decide the museum was too expensive, but he didn't hesitate. He opened his wallet and took out the bills, counted them one by one, and handed me my ticket so I could give it to the woman at the entry spot myself.

"You might want to hold on to the stub," he said. "Memento and all."

We were walking up the staircase to the first room of exhibits—running ahead, I was so excited to be at a place like this, a mansion—when my father called out to me.

"What do you know, Ruthie," he said. "Look who's over there."

The Isabella Stewart Gardner Museum definitely didn't seem like the kind of place my father and I would have run into anyone we knew, so for a moment all I could think was that he'd spotted a celebrity—the newscaster we watched on the local Boston station maybe, or some player on the Red Sox, though it didn't seem too likely they'd be in this place either.

But it was Val Dickerson, coming up the steps with her ticket stub. No Dana or Ray with her. Just Val.

Other times I'd seen her over the years, she was usually dressed in her painting clothes, some old pair of jeans and a man's shirt—George's no doubt—rolled up around her elbows, with her long blond hair pulled back in a ponytail. This time, she was wearing a dress and high-heeled shoes, which made her even taller than usual, of course, and she had lipstick on. I hadn't realized before how beautiful she was.

"What a surprise," she said, standing back as if to assess me. Maybe she was doing the same thing my mother always seemed to do, comparing me with Dana. Suddenly I felt awkward, gangly, stupid-looking. My pants legs were too short, and I had a pimple on my chin.

But Val Dickerson wasn't looking at me in the way I had come to expect from my mother—finding fault. Her eyes were locked so intently on my face that I had to look away. She stroked my cheek then, and when I looked at her again, I saw there were tears in her eyes.

I didn't know what to make of that. In all my twelve years, I'd never seen my mother cry, not even hearing the words she'd recently received from Wisconsin. But it wasn't news to me that Val Dickerson was nothing like my mother. Who could say what went on in her head? I was thinking that maybe being around all this great art touched her off. With Val you never could tell.

I didn't know what to do, so I studied my museum brochure, with a map in it of where to find the different artworks.

"She's beautiful, Eddie," Val said. This was the only time I'd ever heard anyone call my father Eddie. To my mother, he was Edwin. To his brothers, Ed.

"She's lucky she didn't inherit her old pop's mug," he said. "Dodged a bullet there, I'd say."

"How amazing that you two would have shown up here the same day as me," she said. Though this didn't begin to say it, actually. The amazing thing was that we were here at all. That my father, a man who'd never visited an art museum in his life, would have brought me to this one, on the very day Val Dickerson, who lived somewhere in Maine at the time, if I remembered right, would also have dropped in on this, of all museums, and on this same marble staircase, at the very moment he and I were mounting the steps together.

"What do you say we get a cup of coffee, Val?" my father said. "Catch up."

Something about the tone of his voice seemed odd to me, unfamiliar. My father was always quiet, and shy, but he had an agitated sound as he spoke, and his voice seemed to have gone up a half octave. Maybe he registered this, too, because he cleared his throat.

"We just got here," I said. "I want to see the paintings."

"Of course she does," said Val. She seemed to have gotten ahold of herself a little by this point, though her eyes were still moist, as if she was a minute from tears even though she probably wasn't really.

"Ruth here's a real art lover," he told her. "You should see the pictures she brings home from school. That's something you two have in common."

"I'd love to see your work someday," Val said. Nobody else had ever referred to the drawings I made as my "work." To my mother, they were pictures.

"I guess it's been a while since you've seen my girl here," my father said. "She's shot up since the last time. Must be all the good vegetables."

Val was studying my father's face now too. She had stepped back a little, the way a person would if she touched an electric fence. "You took me by surprise here, Edwin," she said. (Edwin now, not Eddie.) "I don't know what to say."

"Maybe we could take this place in together," my father said. "You could probably tell us about the artists, Valerie. I'm not much for knowing this stuff myself."

For a moment, then, the two of them had just stood there. My father was looking at Val Dickerson, it seemed to me, in a way I had never seen him look at my mother, a way I'd never known my father might look. The thought came to me that he must be in love with her. As for Val, the person she was looking at again was me. Then it seemed as if the two of them collected themselves—or Val did, anyway, and she turned back to my father.

"Isabella Stewart Gardner was a wild woman," she said. "She lived outside the rules, ahead of her time. This place used to be her home, you know."

I had run ahead now, impatient to get to a room I saw down the wide corridor, with golden furniture inside and a velvet couch, and paintings of angels on the ceiling. Though maybe part of it was not wanting to see what I guessed I might if I'd stayed standing in that spot. Whatever the two of them said to each other after that, I didn't want to know. I was looking at a portrait of a woman in an old-fashioned dress by an artist named John Singer Sargent. This was safer, and also interesting.

A minute later, my father joined me.

"What happened to Mrs. Dickerson?" I said.

"Something came up," he told me, his voice back to normal, more or less. "She had to go. I guess we won't be having that coffee after all. But when we're done, I'll buy you a hot chocolate at the refreshment stand."

That was how much my dad knew about art museums. He thought they had refreshment stands.

We didn't stay at the museum that long. My father seemed to think that what you did at a place like this was stroll through the rooms, reading the brass plaques posted next to every artwork, stopping just long enough to take in the name of the artist and when he was born and died—or she, in the case of the one I liked best, a painter named Mary Cassatt.

The unfamiliar agitation I'd observed in him when we ran into Val Dickerson stayed with him. He seemed anxious and distracted, so I did not protest when he finally said, "What do you say we call it a day? There's a barnful of cows waiting for me who don't know it's Christmas vacation."

He said almost nothing, driving home, but somewhere around Peabody he commented, "It might be best if your mother didn't know we ran into Val Dickerson. You know how she is about those Dickersons."

I did know and I didn't. Our relationship with the Dickersons had always baffled me, and now there was one more event involving a Dickerson that made no sense. Or—this was worse—an event that seemed comprehensible, but in a way that frightened me. Suppose my father and Mrs. Dickerson were in love? Suppose they ran away together, and left me alone with my mother and my sisters? And then Dana Dickerson would get my dad. And what then of my secret love for Ray Dickerson?

Only I knew my father would never leave Plank Farm. Whatever it was he felt about Val Dickerson—and seeing her, I thought, how could he not?—my father would never abandon us, or his crops and animals, or our farm.

Still, I struggled to make sense of the afternoon. How was it, for instance, that Mrs. Dickerson—who must have just paid the four-dollar admission when we ran into her—would leave without seeing a single room in the museum? Why was she so dressed up? When did she start calling my father Eddie?

"She had a long drive back to Maine," my father said, as if this explained it, instead of just the opposite.

The next week, a package arrived from Maine with my name on it. Inside was a note saying this was a late Christmas present, though in fact our family and the Dickersons had never exchanged presents in the past, beyond the occasional set of pot holders from my mother.

Only I received a gift. I knew even before opening it what it must be, the shape of the box was so familiar to me, as it was to any girl in those days who felt the way I did about Barbie.

Fashion Queen Barbie, in a strapless evening gown, with three wigs, each one a different color and hairstyle. My mother would disapprove of course, and did. "What is that woman thinking, sending a gift like that to a girl from a God-fearing family?" she said. Never mind that I was a little old for dolls.

"I thought you should have one of these," Val had written. "In my opinion, every girl needs at least one Barbie."

## *Dana*

# A Little Off

WE WERE LIVING in Maine at this point. The clam shack period, although the clam shack had become a vegetable juice stand, and that hadn't worked very well. And anyway, it was the off-season now, which was what had gotten George back into his songwriting again. In an attempt to bring in a little money, Val had put her mind to making one-of-a-kind greeting cards, and actually, the watercolors she was producing for these were beautiful. The problem came from the sayings she came up with, that she lettered inside each card with a special calligraphy pen. Every one was a little off.

*"Just because your life isn't going too well doesn't mean you can't dance in the moonlight."*

*"When the water freezes, sharpen your ice skates."*

*"Love is like a robin's egg. Blue. And it breaks."*

We had no money. Evidently Val had a few shares left of Uncle Ted's bubble-gum stock, which she'd been holding on to, but then she sold those. I remember because I came home from a job I had feeding our neighbors' animals while they were away on Christmas vacation—and there were all these bags on the floor of our front hall, of things she'd bought after the check came in: a jacket for my brother made out of the softest leather, and a lamp that reflected little flecks of light on the ceiling like constellations, and for me, a field guide to the birds of New England with a long-playing record as part of the set, so you could learn to identify birdsongs. In all the years of my growing up it was the only time a present Val gave me showed any sign of having been chosen with me in mind—me as I really was and not her idea of the kind of daughter she might have liked better.

Some people in our financial situation might have put the money in the bank, but after she'd taken care of a few basics like our electric bill, and stocked up on things like dried fruit and lentils, she'd bought all these presents. She had made a trip to Boston, in our old blue Rambler. "I thought I'd go visit a museum," she said.

She had evidently picked up some postcards in the gift shop though. The one I remember showed a woman sitting on a chair, wrapped from head to toe, almost like a mummy, with some kind of white fabric, sitting on a couch, propped on a bunch of pillows.

This was a woman who had so much money she hired a famous artist to paint her portrait, Val said. After she died they turned her house into the museum Val had visited in Boston that day.

When I asked her if she had a good time there, a look came over her, as if this was too hard a question to answer.

"It was too crowded," she said. "I left."

# RUTH

## Like Birds

SOMETIME AROUND JUNIOR high—around the time my father and I had our unlikely encounter with Val Dickerson at the Isabella Stewart Gardner Museum—the tradition of our annual spring pilgrimage to see the Dickersons ended. The next time I saw them was at our farm stand during strawberry season, the summer I turned thirteen.

I'd been out picking in the field that morning. With the weekend coming up—Fourth of July, our busiest weekend until Labor Day—I'd loaded up a bunch of flats on the back of the wagon hitched to our tractor to bring in to the stand, when I spotted my father out in back of the barn, talking to someone. It was an unusual sight, seeing him standing still that way, that time of year in particular. Even before I recognized who he was talking to, it was this fact that struck me—that anything would keep him from his normal watering and fertilizing. During his busiest season.

He was talking with Val Dickerson. She was wearing a very beautiful summer dress—sleeveless, with a cinched waist and a full skirt with lace on the pockets. Her hair, which I was used to seeing in a ponytail, was falling loose on her shoulders. She reminded me of Mary from Peter, Paul and Mary.

From the looks of things, Mrs. Dickerson was upset. She was moving her hands in the air. My father was standing very still, in his work boots and overalls, same as always, holding a sack of fertilizer he must have been carrying over to the truck when she'd stopped him.

She wasn't all dressed up like the last time I'd seen her, but she looked incredibly pretty. Noting this, I felt a small and surprising stab of protectiveness for my mother. My mother was more or less the same age probably, but had gotten a lot heavier in recent years, and her face—which had been firm and solid, like her body, when she was younger, seemed to have puffed out and sagged at the same time. Except for that one time Nancy Edmunds had put the hair dye on her—a mistake, for sure—she made no efforts to conceal the encroaching effects of growing older. At church they taught us not to care about the physical body, and that vanity was a sin, but still I thought it would make her sad, seeing Mrs. Dickerson looking so young and beautiful.

I didn't go over to say hello to Mrs. Dickerson, and there was no sign of Dana, who must have been at the farm stand, I figured, not that I felt a need to see her anyway. The person I approached, instead, was her brother, Ray, who was off in a far corner of the parking lot, juggling three different varieties of summer squash, or trying to.

I wouldn't normally have thought of speaking to a boy as old as Ray Dickerson—seventeen, probably—but he had waved. As always, just the sight of him brought on a warm feeling in me, unsettled but pleasurable at the same time.

"Leave it to my mother," he said, "to take a forty-five-minute detour off the highway to buy strawberries. She says yours are the best."

"I thought you lived in Maine," I said.

"We did. My parents are thinking of moving back to Vermont now. George tried selling clams and lobster rolls, and then these health food juices, but it didn't pan out. He's up in Burlington now, checking out some deal."

"You graduate this June?"

"One more year," he said. "Soon as I get finished with school, I'm taking off for California. Where the action is."

I had heard about this, a little. San Francisco. At youth group, the minister had made us all pray for strength to resist the temptations of sex and drugs, as promoted in the rock-and-roll music that was coming from some place called Haight-Ashbury. The fact that Ray Dickerson might be headed there filled me with respect.

"You got taller," he said. Ray himself was well over six feet now. His arms, tossing the Hacky Sack, had a wild, birdlike grace. I knew what my parents would have said about his long hair, never mind the eyelashes—*looks like a girl*—but he didn't, remotely.

I was afraid he might know what I was thinking, so I studied the berries in the flat I was holding. He stretched a long arm over the box and picked up a particularly red and juicy-looking one, which he popped in his mouth, stem and all. A thin stream of juice trickled out the side of his mouth, as if he were a vampire.

"You know what would be cool," he said. "If people fed each other strawberries out of each other's mouths, like birds."

I must've just stood there. Nothing that ever happened in my life before had prepared me for this.

"You know your face is red as a strawberry now," he said. "What're you afraid of?"

"I was just bringing these in," I said. All I could think of. Deep down, in that place between my legs that sometimes got damp when I drew my pictures in the barn, I felt a strange and thrilling current run through me.

"Like this," he said. He had popped another berry in his mouth. He leaned down, low enough for his mouth to meet mine—not so difficult, since I was tall too. He placed his hands on my shoulders and pressed his mouth against my own. I tasted the berry juice on his lips. I opened mine to receive the fruit.

This is what happened when Adam met Eve, I thought. Here comes the devil.

# *Dana*

# Strawberries

I ALWAYS HAD an interest in growing things. I liked gathering seedpods and taking them apart. I started beans in plastic containers left over from my mother's yogurt projects, and though I was probably only five or six at the time, somehow I knew, without anyone explaining, that you should not only poke holes in the bottom for drainage, but layer the dirt you put in. A little sand on the bottom. Richer soil on top. Don't overwater, but it's important not to underwater either. The worst thing you can do to a plant on a windowsill is give it just enough moisture that the roots come to the top and bake in the sun.

And there was more. I started avocado plants from the pit and got a sweet potato vine sprouting. I put in morning glories, and catnip, and sent away one time to a company that advertised you could grow your own peanuts, but they must not have been talking about Vermont when they promised you'd be eating nuts come harvesttime.

I had this idea once of making a playhouse using real live sunflowers for the walls, and I persuaded George to buy a packet of sunflower seeds for me that I planted in a circle and watered all that summer. We moved right around the time they were finally getting tall and about to flower, so I never got to put my idea in action, but it would have worked. After we left, I always wondered what that circle of sunflowers I'd cultivated would have ended up looking like by the end of the season. I was going to tie the stalks together at the top, so they formed a kind of flowering teepee, and put a chair inside, where I could go and read my biographies of important people in history. But by that August we were long gone, on to the next place.

I loved manure. Years later, when I said that to Clarice—the woman who became my love, she looked at me like I was crazy, though later she came to know me so well she understood what that manure signified for me—nourishment for the soil, food for growing things.

"I love the smell of it, even," I told her—not the greenest manure, but once it's aged to the point you can pick up a clump of the stuff in your hand. (This also offended Clarice at first.)

A lot of people don't appreciate good manure, no doubt. Sometimes, on walks, if we were going through a pasture where cattle grazed, I'd bend over and pick up a clod of the stuff and work it over in my hand, scattering the bits as I went. I liked to think about all the things that went into this particular piece of manure: grass, grain, seeds of other plants, chewed up and passed out through the cow's intestine, to start the process going all over again. When you think about this, it's a beautiful thing, I told Clarice. Eventually she understood.

It was as much a part of me as loving women, and not men, the way the sights and smells and, most of all, feelings concerning the cultivation of crops—the rituals of planting and cultivation and harvest—were hardwired into me. Other than George's interest in growing a little pot, back in our Vermont days in particular, it was certainly nothing passed on to me by George and Valerie. Though maybe, I used to think, I'd picked it up at Plank Farm, on those strawberry season visits of ours. Usually around the time of our birthdays, Ruth's and mine.

The fact that we did this at all was strange enough, considering Val's dislike for Connie Plank, and George's inattention and lack of interest in just about anything not directly related to his own get-rich-quick projects. Though in later years, George didn't accompany us on these excursions, any more than he accompanied us other places. The one who took us to Plank Farm was Val. Some force pulled her back to that farm. Once we were there, I felt it myself.

For Val, I think it had something to do with Edwin Plank—about as unlikely a person as you could imagine for her to connect with on the surface of things. In the later years, she appeared to develop a surprising interest in Ruth, too—as if she both wanted to know more about her, and didn't at the same time. As for me, trips to Plank Farm were about the land, and my talks with Edwin.

There was this one time we stopped by, on one of our moves—having gone out of our way to do so, as we always did. It was Fourth of July weekend, and we were headed to Maine, meaning the traffic was terrible—the weather hot and humid, no air-conditioning in our old Rambler, with boxes of our possessions stuffed into the seat between my brother and me and a crate of my mother's paintings and art supplies roped to the roof. George had gone on ahead of us, having gotten a call from some guy he'd met in a bar sometime back, who owned a bowling alley and needed a person to take over on short notice while he took his wife to Boston for cancer treatments. God knows why, he thought George and Val might be good candidates.

It was a Friday afternoon when we pulled up at the stand, and the parking lot was full. Val had gone off—to buy strawberries, she said. My brother was in his own world, as usual. He was smoking a lot of pot by this point so he was no doubt high at the time, though my mother never figured that part out.

Ray only had a year of high school left, and I knew he was marking time till he could leave us and head out west. I did not expect that once he'd left we'd see much of him anymore, and it made me sad, recognizing how eager he was to get away. We had grown up in the same house, with the same two parents—two people who never should have had children in the first place—though we were such different kinds of people we'd dealt with that situation in completely different ways. I worked my after-school babysitting jobs to save up for college, nose to the grindstone. Ray drifted.

Still, I worshipped my brother, and the thought that the one relative I really loved would be going away left a terrible emptiness. Whatever else separated us, we were bonded in one powerful way, like a couple of shipwrecked sailors stranded on an island in the middle of the ocean, the sole survivors of our parents' upbringing. Once he was gone, there would be nobody around who could understand, and it was hard to imagine what force other than the death of one of our parents—and not even that, maybe—might be enough to bring him back home. That summer, as his departure grew imminent, I lived in fear of the day he'd leave me alone with them. I knew it was coming.

The day we'd driven to the Planks for the strawberries, he stayed in the parking lot playing Hacky Sack. I made my way over to the barn, and beyond that, to the rich green, strawberry-dotted expanse of acreage that constituted the farm that had passed down through generations of Plank men, ending up with Edwin.

I'd been here before over the years, those times Edwin took me aside and showed me some interesting thing like how to cut the eye out of a potato to get a new plant started or how to pinch the extra leaves off a tomato plant, but this was the first time I'd ever gotten to explore the farm on my own. I was thirteen years old, and I felt myself pulled by some force real as gravity, only this one took me out over the fields—past strawberries, past spinach and broccoli, through cauliflower, eggplant, chard, peppers, into corn.

The stalks came only up to my waist. The season was still young. I studied the ears of corn, just starting to form, the way the soil had been mounded up around the base of the stalks, the bean plants between them. Nobody had taught me about this yet, but I think I understood by instinct that the planting of beans in among the corn must have had something to do with balancing the chemical content of the soil—the beans providing nutrients the corn might have depleted.

I looked up to the sky, gauging the time. Noon, or close enough. The day was hot, but the sun felt good on my skin. I was far enough away from everyone that I could peel up my shirt, exposing my stomach and my small flat breasts. The memory of Jenny Samuels still haunted me, the soft ripe fruit of her body against the hardness of mine. I lay down and dug my fingers in the soft, loose soil, wrist-deep. I breathed in the smell. I fell asleep, as if I'd been born in this spot, or had been buried here.

It was the sound of a tractor working its way through the rows that awakened me. Then the engine cut out, and I heard the familiar voice of Edwin Plank.

"That you, Dana? Your mother's been looking all over creation for you."

I pulled down my shirt. The tall, sunburnt form of Edwin in those old overalls of his stood over me. He was smiling.

"You know something?" he said. "I've been known to catch a few winks here myself."

I could have been embarrassed but I wasn't. "Hop on," he said, indicating the tractor. "I'll give you a ride."

That's how he brought me back to the barn and the parking lot, where my mother and Ray were waiting with the strawberries. I remember thinking that was the best ride I ever took.

"Too bad you and Ruth missed seeing each other," Mr. Plank said. "She must have gone up to the house."

"That girl's really grown up since we saw her last," Val said. "You must've seen her, right, Ray?"

"Yup," said my brother. "She gave me some strawberries."

# RUTH

## The Hardball Stage

MY FATHER LIVED by the weather, which meant the rest of us did, too. We kept a rain gauge just outside the kitchen door that my dad checked every time a little moisture fell. Every night, except when he was haying, he made sure to be back at the house for the evening newscast, though what he really wanted to hear was the weather—our local Boston weatherman, Don Kent (Don to my father), who in those days before advanced technology stood beside a big blackboard on which he scribbled the high and low temperatures for the day, and what we had to look forward to during the week ahead.

The summer I turned thirteen, we knew—even before my July birthday—that we were in trouble. Back in April, with early plantings in the ground and no rainfall for ten days, my father and the hired boy, Victor Patucci, had started the laborious process of irrigating, just to get the seed germinated, and by May, when there had still been no rain, every crop on our farm looked stunted and dry.

Mornings in the barn, I no longer heard my father whistling, and late afternoons, looking out the window from my room, or from the hayloft in the barn where I'd be sitting on the swing drawing, I could see from the bent-over look of his back, and the way he stopped to check the sky now and then, that my father was weighed down with worry. Nights when he came in from the fields, a dark mood hung over our kitchen table. When we said grace at dinner, nobody mentioned rain among our prayers. Nobody had to.

Strawberry season came with the lowest yield we could ever remember. The night of my birthday, a light shower fell over our farm for a few minutes—nothing more than that. My father came in from checking the rain gauge shaking his head.

"Barely enough to settle the dust," he told my mother, as she passed the potatoes. "If we don't get rain soon, I don't know how we'll save the corn."

One of the reasons Plank Farm had survived all these years where others failed had to do with the fact that we had three irrigation ponds—the most of any piece of land around. But by July, they were so low you could see scum forming on the top, and the mud around the edges had cracked and dried.

Now we were all called upon—even my reluctant sisters, even our mother—to assist with the irrigation pipe. I could remember times in summers past when it felt fun, squishing through the mud in bare feet. But that summer, all joy left us, as we spent day after day shifting pipes to their different locations to keep the crops alive, holding the muddy aluminum pipe as high off the ground as we could, especially in the cornfields, so as not to break the stalks, coming in past dark with the muscles in our arms so sore they throbbed.

Even with all our work, the crops were a disaster that season. Not just the strawberries, but the tomatoes and broccoli and beans, the cucumbers. Our yield was down 50 percent, which left no money for all the repairs my father needed on the barn and the tractor and, more significantly to me, for back-to-school shopping and the giant set of oil pastels I'd been longing for. The seed company that always gave us credit in the past sent out a letter that October to say that in light of the unpaid bills, they could no longer sell us seed stock for the coming year without cash up front or on delivery.

Then came November 22. My mother was cooking fudge for the annual church bazaar. My father was off in the back field, clearing away the last of the cornstalks. My sisters were at school but I had stayed home that day with a cold. My mother must have had the radio on. I heard a cry from the kitchen, of a kind I never heard out of her before.

"I have to go get your father," she said, setting the fudge on the counter. Just at the hard-ball stage, where as even I knew, a person had to keep stirring.

After, they came in the house together and told me the news. "God must have a plan for him," my mother said, but that didn't make any sense.

That night we said a prayer for the Kennedys. The pot of half-finished fudge sat on the counter—the only time I ever remember my mother leaving a dish out that way.

We all watched the funeral on television. I remember my mother, sitting on her chair in front of the round screen of our black-and-white Zenith, shaking her head as the cortège made its way down Pennsylvania Avenue, the camera cutting in with shots of Jackie and the children in their funeral clothes. Even though Jackie Kennedy was a Democrat, not to mention a Catholic, my mother loved her, almost as much as she loved Dinah Shore. Possibly the one topic she and Val Dickerson would have agreed on—Jackie Kennedy.

"That poor woman," she said. "What's she going to do now?"

"They're millionaires, Connie," my father said. "They've got a mansion on the Cape and servants and the whole shebang. No danger those children won't have clothes on their backs."

UNLIKE US, WAS WHAT I was thinking. What with the drought that summer before, and the interest payments on the loan my father had to take out to buy seed stock, and a sick cow that ran up a bill with the vet, my father sold his prize Model T that we'd kept in the barn to take out on special occasions for Sunday drives. For Christmas, our parents had told us, we could each choose one item of clothing from the Montgomery Ward catalog: a sweater or a skirt.

What was the person with the sweater supposed to do for the bottom of her outfit? my sister Sarah wanted to know.

"Mix and match," our mother said. "You girls are close enough in size you can trade off." As was so often the case, her remark excluded me. There was no way any item of clothing purchased for my sisters—even the oldest—would fit my own long-limbed body.

The next year was better, but other difficulties presented themselves now. It used to be that the kinds of produce we sold at our farm stand were not available at places like Grand Union and the A&P, but now all the big chains had started selling more unusual items of the sort a person used to have to visit Plank's to locate—varieties of lettuce besides iceberg, interesting melons and fresh peas, and because they bought in bulk, they sold them cheaper. A person who shopped at the supermarket could also find items we didn't carry, like pineapples from Hawaii and blueberries before the local season.

No flavor in those, my father said. But people didn't seem to notice that. What had happened to people's taste buds, he wanted to know. Too many frozen dinners and artificial flavors. No one appreciated the real thing anymore.

## *Dana*

# Vicarious Living

IT WOULD HAVE been hard to say who Val loved more, Jackie Kennedy or Jack. She loved Jackie's style and her ball gowns, how she redecorated the White House, her interest in art. But to my mother, JFK was the perfect man—strong, handsome, charming, and rich.

Valerie spent her life making up imaginary romantic scenarios. To her, I think, those seemed to her more important, in the end, than real love—and the fact that the prince of Camelot had probably not managed to remain faithful to his wife longer than a day did not seem to bother my mother. It was image that interested Val, more than substance—and for image, nobody could top JFK. I'm not sure she ever fully recovered after the shock of his death.

All the rest of that November, and beyond, she barely got out of bed. It was the only time in her life that I can remember when she didn't pick up a paintbrush.

"She'll snap out of it," George said. My brother and I just looked at him. Val was not the kind of person who snapped out of things, any more than she snapped into them. Once an idea or a feeling took hold of her, it stayed.

George was gone most of that winter. He had this idea for a game show and thought if he could just get a meeting with those people in Hollywood whose names he'd picked up watching the credits of *What's My Line?*—Goodson and Todman—they'd eat it up.

He'd driven out to Los Angeles early in December. We'd get postcards every week or so, about movie stars he'd spotted and great restaurants on Sunset Boulevard, but no mention of a meeting yet.

"I'm getting my ducks in a row," he wrote. "In this business it's all about who you know."

Who that might be in his case, he did not say.

My brother resented that George had gotten himself to California before he, Ray, managed that. In Ray's way of looking at things, he'd come up with the idea of California first—northern, not southern, in his case. But west was west. It seemed unfair that George would have driven there without him when he was clearly much more of a California type.

Ray was seventeen at this point, washing dishes at a restaurant near our apartment, saving up for his getaway. Rare as it was for Val to think about our futures, she worried that if he didn't go to college, he'd be sent to Vietnam, but Ray said no way was that happening. He'd intended to take the SATs but missed the deadline when he forgot to put a stamp on the envelope with the check. After that he decided he didn't need college anyway. Ray probably believed he could charm his way through any situation, and so far this had proved true.

FEBRUARY BROUGHT THE ARRIVAL OF the Beatles in America, which perked Val up a little. All around me, at school, girls were going crazy over them. The only difference of opinion about them focused on which of the four was cutest. Paul was the clear favorite, but a lot of the girls in our class loved John, too. The rebels tended to go for George or, if you were a little weird, Ringo.

"Who do you love best, Dana?" my home ec partner Angie O'Neil asked me, shortly after their first appearance on *Ed Sullivan*. "Let me guess: George? Or Ringo."

I could have said none of them interested me. I could have shocked her totally and confessed that my secret crush at the time was Honor Blackman, who played the beautiful crime-fighting anthropologist, Mrs. Cathy Gale, on *The Avengers* and wore skintight catsuits that I sometimes pictured myself unzipping and peeling off her, as if she was a banana.

"George," I said, playing it safe.

"That's good," she said. "Because I love Paul." She said this as if we were actually in the running for snagging one of them to be our boyfriend. This way we weren't in competition.

"I love their English accents," she said. This held true for Honor Blackman too, so I nodded in agreement.

If Val had taken more of an interest, she might have spent more time over my high school years exploring the question of why I never had a boyfriend. Boys called me up sometimes to get the math assignment, and sometimes for advice concerning girls they liked. I had good relationships with boys, actually. I think they understood, whether they articulated it to themselves or not, that in many ways I was like one of them.

"Do you think Lorena likes me?" a boy I was friends with, Mike, asked me one time, while we were doing a biology assignment together. Cutting planaria in half and watching them regenerate.

"Possibly," I said. I liked Lorena, too, was the truth; and I imagined it might be mildly exciting, discussing her together, though I was not about to reveal to Mike or anyone else the nature of my interest in Lorena.

"She has the most incredible body," he said. The fact that he would say this to me—a girl who had the least incredible body—seemed almost like an accomplishment to me at the time. I had done that good a job of freeing myself from any kind of female identity that would have left a person like Mike to suppose this observation might have hurt my feelings. Which it did not.

"Well, Cassie Averill is pretty hot, too," I said.

"Cassie's not as pretty as Lorena," Mike said.

"But she's got the best tits," I said. I had listened to my brother with his friends. This was how I learned how boys talked. If Mike thought it was odd, hearing this kind of remark from a girl, he didn't let on.

"You think they're bigger than Lorena's?" he said.

"No contest. I've seen her in the locker room."

He was setting a planarium on a slide now, but that wasn't why he sighed. "If only you could sneak a camera in there for me," he said.

"Yeah, right."

"You think Cassie likes me?" he asked me. This was a boy for you, ready to change his allegiance on a dime. One mention of a pair of 38 Ds and he'd forgotten all about the girl with the 36s he was obsessed with one minute earlier.

"Didn't you see her looking at you in history?" I said.

"Now that you mention it, I'm asking her out."

"Just promise to give me the details," I said. "I'm counting on you."

I lived vicariously in those days, listening to the stories of boys I was friends with, talking about things they got to do with the girls I had crushes on, and then listening to girls I had crushes on talking about things they did with boys I was friends with.

I was always falling in love, was the truth, but nobody ever fell in love with me. I was born in a girl's body, with a boy's desires, and because this was 1964, and nobody talked about these things, I supposed I was the only person on earth who had this problem.

# RUTH

## Letting Go

When my father was a boy growing up on the farm, he told me once, he and his brothers had longed for a rope swing over the deepest of their irrigation ponds—the same one where, years later, he and I would share our afternoon swims. But at the time, none of the existing trees around the pond was tall or sturdy enough to hold the rope. They needed a better tree.

There was a young oak tree growing alongside one of the farm ponds, but that tree was never substantial enough during my father's boyhood to hold a swing or the boy who would be clinging to it.

Then, with his brothers grown and gone, my father started a family of his own, and finally the tree was sufficiently tall and strong to support a boy holding on to a rope. The only problem was that no boy had been born.

After I came along, my father had given up on the dream of a male heir to the farm, but he had held on to the dream of the rope swing. The summer I turned eight he'd put one up.

My sisters never tried it once. They were afraid of water. But all that summer and every summer after that I made my way down to the pond in the late afternoon or early evening, and with my farm chores finished, I'd wait by the barn for my father and head across the field with him and Sadie to swim.

I'd have my suit on already. He'd unfasten his overalls and take off his T-shirt, so all he wore were his cotton boxers. Then he'd grab on to the rope and take a running leap over the water before splashing down.

As much as I wanted to share the pond with him—I, and I alone, the one other swimmer among our family of Planks—I could never bring myself to jump off the swing, into the pond. I could hold the rope and swing out over the water. It was the letting-go part that scared me.

Then one summer, right around the time I turned fifteen, we had a heat wave so brutal that even after the sun went down the temperature never dipped below ninety, and just getting dressed and brushing your teeth started feeling like more effort than it was worth. Even my mother gave up her daily routine of baking bread and putting beans on the stove, since all we cared about eating were Popsicles anyway.

One day she went to the doctor in Concord—"a female problem," was all she said about it. My sisters had gone along to do some back-to-school shopping, but at the last minute I decided not to accompany them. It was just too hot.

So I was there on my own at the house. It was a Monday—the day we kept our farm stand closed.

I had always wanted to draw the human figure, but never having had a real art class, I'd never gotten to work from a live model. Now the idea came to me—maybe it was the heat of the day that inspired me—to strip naked in front of the mirror and draw myself.

I went up to my room—the room I shared with my sister Winnie—and peeled off my clothes. I sat on the floor in front of the full-length mirror with my drawing pad in front of me and started to sketch.

Here's something I've learned over my years of drawing the naked human figure, though this was the first time I did it. There is something about the act of studying an unclothed body, as an artist does, that allows a person to appreciate it as pure form, regardless of all the kinds of traits traditionally regarded as imperfections. In a figure drawing class, an obese woman's folds of flesh take on a kind of beauty. You can look at a man's shrunken chest or legs or buttocks with tenderness. Age is not ugly, just poignant.

That day—my awkward, lanky fifteen-year-old body folded in front of the mirror in that impossible heat—I saw myself not as a girl who was too tall or too thin, a girl whose breasts were small, neck too long, hips boyishly narrow. I saw myself as a work of art, imagined a picture of me, as I was that day, hanging on a wall in a museum, and the idea was not shameful but exciting.

I studied myself more closely then, one inch at a time—the lines of my collarbone and my ribs, the curve of my calf muscle, and the muscles in my arms hard from a summer of hoeing potatoes and stacking hay bales. I traced the bridge of my nose and the way my nostrils flared at its base over my surprisingly wide mouth. In the past, I had often stood in front of the mirror looking critically at my features, but now I saw myself as an artist would, imagining how the painters whose work I'd studied in books at the library would portray me on the canvas—Picasso and Matisse, also Vermeer or van Gogh or El Greco and Rembrandt—and when I did that, I became something I'd never been before, an object of beauty.

I imagined then how it would be to look at my whole self—not just my face—with the eye of an artist. I considered my toes and my fingers, and my belly, and my thighs. Shame left me then, replaced by fascination and excitement. I became a student of my own body, and to the artist in me, my body became beautiful.

I don't know how long I sat there this way, but I filled up many pages of my pad. Hours may have passed, though it was still light out, and I knew my sisters and my mother would not be home for another few hours at least, and that my father would be out on the tractor until sunset, cutting hay. Flushed not only with the extreme heat of the day, but from my afternoon of drawing myself, I headed to the farm pond for a swim.

Normally I wore my swimsuit at the pond, but that afternoon I let my uncovered skin feel the water. When I came up for air, I could hear the slow grinding sound of my father's tractor over the other side of the hill and the lowing of the grazing cows. Just above the surface of the pond, a little cloud of bugs hovered, the wings of one catching the sunlight in a particular angle that made it beautiful as a jewel, and I could smell the fresh-cut hay.

*Remember this moment*, I told myself, though only in my head. Young as I was, I knew that I was witnessing a kind of perfection that a person might experience only a handful of times in her life.

I climbed out onto the shore and scooped a handful of mud from the edge of the pond, slathering it over my body until I was nearly covered. Then I climbed back on the rope swing and let myself fly out again over the water, higher than I'd ever gone. Then I let go of the rope.

# *Dana*

# The World on a String

IT DIDN'T EXCUSE George's absences and lack of attention that this was so, but I think he actually believed every one of his big ideas was going to make our family a killing. I never knew a person to possess so much optimism in the face of constant defeat. He just never gave up and he didn't understand anyone who behaved differently, people like my brother, for instance.

For Ray, just getting through a day sometimes was hard. To look at my brother, you would have thought he'd have the world on a string. Handsome and funny, charming and athletic: girls loved him, and even teachers gave him second chances when he screwed up. When he was feeling good, he was Master of the Unicycle, sailing down Main Street in whatever town we lived that year as if he was the mayor or maybe the king.

But other days—and there were more of these as he grew older—he would stay in bed till noon, or I'd see him leaned against a tree somewhere, chewing on a piece of grass, or playing the same eight notes on his harmonica, over and over.

"Your brother's sensitive," Val said, though to me it was more than that. To me it sometimes seemed as if my brother was missing a crucial layer of skin other people had that allowed them to get through the day when he could not. The time his junior high school girlfriend broke up with him. "You just don't give me any room to breathe," she said. Ray didn't come out of his room all weekend, and I could hear him through the walls, not simply crying but moaning.

Then he was fine again—not simply fine, but fantastic, though there was also a bitter edge to him. "I'll probably jump off a building one of these days," he said to me once, up in his room. "Knowing me." He was playing me an album he'd just bought, by The Doors.

"Jim Morrison," he said. "There's a guy who understands. Him and me, we'll probably be dead before we're thirty."

"Stop it," I said. "I hate it when you say things like that."

"Let's face it, sis," he said to me another time. We were watching television, and they were showing scenes from Vietnam, images of Vietnamese people standing next to a burned-out village, naked children crying. "The world's a pretty crappy place. Everybody's out for themselves, when you get down to it."

"How do you expect to get anyplace in life with that negative attitude of yours?" George said to Ray. "You must have inherited that from your mother."

"And where exactly has this positive attitude gotten him?" Ray said, but not to George. Always to me. George would have left the room by that point. He was the type who delivered most of his big statements on the way out the door, before you had time to offer a rejoinder, not that I would have. That was my brother's specialty.

More than once, George spent a bunch of money—three or four thousand dollars, probably, which would have been everything we had at the time—pursuing a patent for one of his inventions. Each time he was more hopeful than the last.

When the letter came from some lawyer he'd hired, to inform him, regretfully, that someone else had already thought up his idea for the electric cat food dispenser, or the all-in-one egg-breaker-and-scrambler that he'd just finished spending a year of his life developing, he'd read the letter out loud to Val with a tone of pride in his voice. For him, the big news was not that his invention was dead, their money wasted, but that the existence of this previous patent served as validation of his good instincts and brilliance in thinking it up in the first place.

"I knew I was onto something with that one," he said, concerning the egg scrambler. "One day, Dana, when you're standing in your kitchen and your hubby says he wants scrambled eggs for breakfast, and you don't feel like messing up a bowl and a fork at the same time, so you take out your scrambler, you can think of your old Pops."

"We'll think of George, as we watch the checks go to Mr. Got-There-First," said Ray, from over at the card table that served as the place we did our homework and ate our meals, in between times George used it for his desk in whatever house we occupied that year. "What good does it do to have a great idea if nobody ever pays you for it?"

As for me, none of that mattered so much. I was still stuck on the part of the story in which I was portrayed as having a husband, a person who would expect me to make him scrambled eggs. Even then I knew I'd never marry. Not a man, anyway. But I kept quiet about this, as I did about most things.

"This is your problem in life, Ray," George continued. "You keep measuring success with dollar signs. That's only one way to look at things."

This was not true even at the time, and later, my brother turned out to be a person with about as little interest in dollar signs, or dollars either for that matter, as anyone I knew. There would come a day when he was basically living in a refrigerator box, as much as I can determine it. But at the time Ray actually wanted to go to college. He might have done what I did, and work three jobs to pay for it, but Ray was never one to push hard for things if they didn't come easily. Maybe that's what happens when a person's as handsome and smart and funny and charming as he was. If good things don't drop in their lap, they let it go or maybe even start blaming everyone else but their own self. Whereas a person like me learns early that she's going to have to work for every single thing she gets.

Ray was good at everything, but one of his special talents was basketball. In those days, a person who stood six foot two was considered tall, and unlike a lot of people his height, he also had grace and speed. Whatever town we moved to, he'd end up playing center on the team and being the star, not that our parents ever attended a game. Basketball wasn't their thing, they told him.

Then partway through the season he'd stop going to practice. The coach would give him a warning, and when that didn't get results, another.

"Don't you think you'd better start going to practice?" I asked him one afternoon when he showed up back at home and I knew he was supposed to be working out with the team.

"They need me," he said, laughing. "Those guys aren't going to kick their best player off the team just because I don't want to spend a beautiful afternoon practicing foul shots I could make in my sleep."

That Friday night they had a big game against their number one rival team. Though it was winter, with the temperature below freezing, George and Val were never ones to provide rides, so my brother and I rode to the game on his bike, with me on the back, holding his gym bag against my chest. The truth was, I worshipped my brother. I would have jogged alongside him before I'd miss a game.

When we got to the high school, I went in the front, to the gym, while Ray went around back to the boys' locker room. Alone in the bleachers, I found myself sitting next to a bunch of girls around my brother's age.

"My brother plays center on the team," I said. "You probably know him. Ray Dickerson." Just saying his name, I felt proud.

He emerged from the locker room a few minutes later, wearing his regular clothes and carrying his gym bag.

"Come on, sis," he said. "Let's get out of here."

Too many missed practices, the coach had told him. He was out.

"Watch, they're going to lose this game big-time," he told me. Not that we stayed around to find out.

# RUTH

## The Old Ways

WE SAW VERY little of the Dickersons through my high school years. The Christmas letters stopped, and with no address to send them to, my mother no longer mailed the Dickersons our annual card and gift of homemade pot holders to replace the previous year's set.

But strangely, as uncomfortable as it had been all those years hearing my mother's regular musings—"I wonder what Dana Dickerson's doing right now?"—the fact that she had grown silent on this topic now struck me as worse. To have had in my life for as long as I could remember a person my mother spoke of as my birthday sister, and then to have her disappear from the landscape of our family's life as swiftly and dramatically as if a tornado had touched down and carried her off, left me more than ever with an attitude of resentment and dread concerning who she had been in our lives.

And then there was the other part: that I still thought about her brother, and that day in the parking lot.

I had a couple of boyfriends in high school. The first—unlikely as it seems to me now—was Victor Patucci—who had been working for my father since he was fourteen or so, for a wage that probably wouldn't have done much more than keep him supplied with hair cream and flashy hubcaps.

He was a long way from the figures who populated my dreams—poets and singers, artists. Never one to display any particular interest in farming, or anything to do with rural life, Victor appeared to have only one clearly identifiable passion at the time: for his car—a 1962 Chevrolet Impala that announced his arrival at Plank Farm a good three minutes before he pulled up behind the farm stand, just by the sound coming out the back, and the music—the Tijuana Brass, Mitch Ryder. He seemed to have a particular fondness for "The Ballad of the Green Berets." I knew this because every time it came on, he stopped what he was doing and recited the words along with Sergeant Barry Sadler.

But Victor had one thing going for him with me: he took me away from the farm—more important, away from my mother, and at the time, that was enough to justify the relationship, though where he took me was not anyplace I wanted to go.

Every weekend night, sophomore year, Victor drove the Impala to the parking lot over by the feed store—a place I associated with my father, which made me feel even more uncomfortable than I would have felt anyway. Sitting there in the car with this boy, receiving his attentions to my body as passively as a cow, it was as if my father might be watching me, seeing those rough, awkward hands of Victor Patucci, fumbling with the buttons on my blouse and squeezing my breasts as if he were not so much fondling them as milking me.

Even then I understood what prompted his ardor, or at least his selection of me as the person he'd chosen for his weekend makeout sessions: he wanted to take over the family business. At age nineteen he'd already set his sights on someday running Plank Farm and—as he liked to tell me—bring our operation into the twenty-first century. The old ways of farming were dying out, he said.

"Let's face it," he said. "Your old man's a dinosaur. If you guys want to keep this place going, you need a guy like me to make it happen."

In the summer of 1967, Victor approached my father with a proposal for increasing revenues at the farm stand. He'd make a weekly run with my father's pickup to the North End in Boston, the markets around Faneuil Hall, and bring back produce they sold there, cheap. That way we ourselves could sell our customers those items like mangoes and pineapples, and bouquets of hothouse roses from Chile, and those carnations they sold at the big flower market, dyed green or purple or blue—colors not found on the petals of any real carnation.

The day our dog Sadie died may have been the only time ever that I'd seen my father look sadder than he did the day he finally agreed to Victor Patucci's plan. I stood with him in front of the house that morning, as he sipped his coffee in the first light of day, watching Victor head out with the truck to bring home the imported fruits and vegetables for the purpose of reselling them at Plank's.

"No farmer should sell another man's crops," he said, kicking the dirt.

"It's just till things get better," I told him, though we both knew things were only likely to get worse.

"Arrogant little pip-squeak, that one," my father said, watching Victor disappear down the road. He had an uncle in the produce business in the Italian part of Boston, he'd told my dad. You wouldn't believe the prices we could buy tomatoes there.

Not Brandywine. Not Big Boy. Not Glamour or Zebra.

"These days it's all about moving stock, Ed," Victor had told him. All of the other workers called my father Mr. Plank, but to Victor, my father was Ed.

"I thought it was about putting good food on people's tables," my father said, walking back to the barn.

IT WAS A CURIOUS THING, Victor's obsession with taking over our farm, despite an almost total lack of interest in anything to do with farming. He laid out his vision for me one night at the A&W in Dover. It was time to have sex, for one thing. And to nail down plans for our future.

"I've been thinking," he said. "You could be Mrs. Victor Patucci."

Disregarding all the other reasons I might not have wanted to spend my life in the company of a person whose idea of a fun night out was a few hours at the dog racing park, I explained to him the way things worked in the legacy of the Plank family. Our land and farm were traditionally passed down to the oldest son. In the absence of a son, it seemed most likely that my oldest sister, Naomi, who was engaged now to her future husband, Albert, would take precedence, and if not, there were three more sisters and their future mates in line ahead of me.

Victor had thought of this, of course. As he had correctly observed, Albert had already announced his intention to become a gym teacher—having reluctantly given up his original and highly unrealistic aspiration to play for the NBA. Sarah, the only other sister to have hooked up with a clear candidate for a husband, had chosen a person equally unqualified and poorly suited to farming—a boy named Jeffrey who had one leg significantly shorter than the other, was currently at college pursuing a degree in accounting, and had made the disastrous mistake, on the occasion of his one and only visit to our home, of announcing that he liked to sleep late, preferably till noon.

"Your family's going to need a man around to run things," Victor pointed out. "I don't even mind keeping the name the same as it always was, though once we have a son, to hand the farm down to when you and I reach retirement age, I'm thinking it would make sense to change the name to Patucci's."

Just nineteen years old, my boyfriend was already planning not only the takeover of my father's land and the sex of our future children, but retirement.

I BROKE UP WITH VICTOR just before the start of my senior year.

I had a few dates after that, but the only other boyfriend I had all through my teenage years—the one who took me to our prom—was one my mother found for me at church. Roger was deeply religious, planning to become a minister, and never touched my breasts or any other part of me besides my hand, which he would take in his now and then, when a particular part of the church services we attended together stirred him.

My mother thought Roger was perfect, and I suppose my willingness to go out with him spoke to the desire I continued to register, to please her—impossible as this task remained. That stretch of months when I'd dated Roger probably came as close as any in which I succeeded in this, though the cost—namely, all those hours in the company of Roger Ferlie—had been high. I took comfort in the fact that my father himself expressed disdain for this boyfriend. It was always my father who understood me. Where my mother seemed to have me confused with some other person.

"The boy's a wimp, Connie," he told my mother. "I don't want to see our daughter going off with a person that would put on a pair of loafers to pick tomatoes. I'd like to see him fix a hay baler or deliver a calf. After he got up, that is. Round about supper time."

I had told Roger about my desire to attend art school in Boston and work as a medical illustrator or an art teacher. He said he thought it was important for a wife to be home with the children, and leave it to the man to work. When I broke up with him on prom night, after we spent the evening playing checkers because he didn't believe in dancing, he said he would pray for me.

"Good riddance," my father said, when I told him the news. My mother was heartbroken. This was the first time in years that I heard her reflect, again, on the whereabouts of Dana Dickerson.

"I wonder what your birthday sister's doing right now," she said, seemingly out of the blue. "I wonder if she's thinking about settling down. You girls are almost eighteen now. For all we know, she could be engaged and thinking about starting a family of her own."

Saying this, a look came over her face. We all knew that more than almost anything besides going to heaven, our mother looked forward to becoming a grandmother. With five daughters, it seemed like a good bet this would happen, but it hadn't as of yet, and young as we were still, she was impatient for that, and particularly vocal on the subject of our future childbirth experiences.

I DID NOT THINK ABOUT having babies, in those days. But I thought plenty about sex. To me, the definition of sex was Ray Dickerson.

Almost five years had passed since that day in the parking lot when Ray passed me the strawberry with his tongue, but I had reenacted the scene in my mind a hundred times. More probably. Then I created additional variations.

I imagined the two of us in a room somewhere, alone. He would be naked. I was drawing him.

There is a kind of artwork I liked to make in those days—a form I teach my students in my art therapy groups—called contour drawing. The idea is to keep your gaze solely on the object or person you are drawing, rather than on the paper. You move your hand holding the pencil along the contours of the form you intend to represent—a vase of flowers, a coffeepot, or in the case of my particular fantasy, the naked body of Ray Dickerson—without ever lifting the pencil off the paper.

This means that what you create is a single line that spools out over the page, like a tangle of string, only what it represents is, in its way, a rendering of the subject. The image you make is likely to be wildly distorted, but one that may possibly do a better job of suggesting the thing you're drawing than if you had labored over your drawing pad, checking yourself at regular intervals, erasing lines and measuring the spaces between things for strictest accuracy.

In my dream, Ray Dickerson was posing naked for me, but he had explained the rules. I was forbidden to touch him, permitted only to look. At first I had no problem with these restrictions. I was standing at a table, fully clothed. I moved a number two pencil over the paper, though my gaze never left Ray. He had a beautiful body of course. And then there were those eyes of his.

The trick to making a good contour drawing is for the movement of your hand, and the speed or slowness with which it moves along the paper, to duplicate as closely as possible what your eyes do as they make their way over the form you are drawing. In my dream, when I got to the area below Ray's waist, the place where his pubic hair began—and beneath that—I started to feel my body stir and my face flush.

At this point, my dream became a little vague. I'd never actually seen a man's naked body before, though in the front seat of Victor Patucci's car, nights after our root beer float, I'd touched one.

Those times, I never wanted to. Now I did.

ALL MY LIFE I HAD been a good daughter, or tried to be. My dream self was very bad. The person I was at this moment was nothing like the girl my mother imagined me to be. The girl I was, really, possessed dark longings of a kind my mother would have said only the devil creates. Now, in my dream, I held up my portrait of Ray Dickerson, and leaned in closer to study it. I pressed my lips against the paper.

"Good job, Ruth," he said to me, reaching out his arms. "Now come on over here."

*Dana*

# Ship Coming In

THE LAST PATENT George pursued, to my knowledge, was for something called the Talking Guitar Tuner. This one was designed for anyone who really wanted to play the guitar, only they were tone deaf—both of which applied to George. He had constructed this machine with some kind of tuning fork mechanism inside and a minicassette with a woman's voice that registered the notes of the string you were trying to tune and said things like "That's just a little high" or "You've almost got it now. Just turn the knob a little in a counterclockwise direction." Of all the ideas he ever had, he told Val, this was the best. "Keep your eye out the window, Valerie," he told her. "Because this man's ship is coming in."

Shortly after my graduation from high school, George and Val made what turned out to be their last move together, to St. Pete Beach, Florida—a location George chose for them on the theory that living in a warm climate was better for the creative process. Still waiting for the big payday on his invention, George returned to songwriting. He'd heard a new country duo on the radio—one of those couples who enjoyed a single hit and disappeared as quickly as they arrived on the scene. But something about the way their two voices wove together (combined, he said, with the inspiration of those nightly sunsets over the Gulf) got him writing again.

In spite of the instructional tapes, he'd never really learned to play guitar, but he took it out anyway and started strumming chords. For one afternoon, he sat on the porch at their beach apartment (a row of plastic flamingos in the postage-stamp yard, courtesy of Val) working out a melody and lyrics, which he got Val to type up for him.

"I met this guy at a bar with great contacts in Nashville," he said. Val and I made no comment.

George mailed off the tape, along with a single sheet of paper containing the lyrics, to someone he'd heard of who worked in a place called Music Row.

# RUTH

## Mission to the Moon

AT THE SUGGESTION of my art teacher, I had applied to art school in Boston. Without telling my mother, I had filled out the application, along with the ones to which she'd given her blessing: nursing school in Manchester; the state university where my father and I had traveled that time to see the prize bull; the state teachers' college up north. "You could be a teacher," she said. "Until you settle down with kids of your own."

For the art school application, samples of my work were necessary. My father helped me put these together, borrowing a camera from his older brother, driving the film to Concord to have the images made into slides.

"You know what we should do with the extras?" he said, when he brought them home the week after, waiting until my mother wasn't home (not an accident) to take them out and study the images.

"We should send a few of these to Val Dickerson. Her being an artist and all, she'd appreciate them."

I didn't think we even had the Dickersons' address anymore, but evidently my father did.

That April—the time of pea planting and spinach, which was how we measured time around our farm—the envelope arrived from Boston. I'd been accepted, and better yet, awarded a scholarship. We'd already heard from the other places that I was in, but now we had a good case for my choosing Boston.

"We'll tell her over dinner," my dad said.

"What if she doesn't go along with it?"

"I can convince her," he said.

SO I WAS GOING TO art school in September. That summer, I weeded the strawberries and worked more hours at the farm stand than usual to make up the money I'd need for books and supplies—which would be more, my mother pointed out, than if I were attending a so-called normal school.

All summer, I didn't take a day off. Even my mother spoke of how hard I'd worked. More than the other four girls put together she said, with a certain wonderment.

Sometime in early August, a man stopped by the farm stand in search of cheese—a product we sold, thanks to the Wisconsin connection. "I need a big hunk of the stuff to put on the back of my motorcycle," he said. "I'm headed to Woodstock."

I didn't know what he was talking about. Working as hard as I had those last three months, the only news of the world beyond our farm that had filtered through had to do with the upcoming Apollo mission to the moon. But now the man was explaining to me—as if I'd been living in a cave—about the music festival coming up in a few days. The biggest and best ever. He began naming the artists who were due to sing there. Just about everyone. (Though not my idol, Bob Dylan.)

"You're around eighteen, right?" he said. "You should go. Someday your grandchildren will ask you about it, and you can say you were there."

"My parents would never give me permission," I told the man as I was ringing up his cheese, and a bag of fresh plums from a bushel I'd just picked that morning.

"Baby," he said. "If you have to ask permission to go to Woodstock, you shouldn't be there."

WE SNEAKED OUT IN THE night and caught the bus from Concord. My sister Edwina came with me. Winnie and I hardly ever did things together like this, but she was going through a rebellious phase and this seemed to qualify as the kind of thing a person would do if she wanted to get the message across to her parents that she was no longer a good Lutheran churchgoing girl.

The Greyhound company got us as far as Albany, New York. From there it was easy enough to hitchhike that weekend, particularly if you were a couple of young girls unaccompanied by a boy.

By the time we got to Woodstock, there was a steady caravan of cars and Volkswagen buses heading in the direction of the festival. Two minutes after I stuck out my thumb, a carload of guys a few years older than we were picked us up. I thought about what my mother would say if she saw them. My father would observe that they needed two things: a bath and a job.

"She your best girlfriend, huh?" the driver said to me as we climbed in the back, nodding in the direction of Winnie.

"We're sisters," I told him, scrunching up my legs—a problem I had with riding in the backseats of VW Bugs even when they didn't already have five other people in them.

"You sure don't look like sisters," he said. "You might want to have a talk with your mom. Or the milkman."

"We don't have a milkman," Winnie said. "We grew up on a farm with our own cows." All of my sisters were unusually earnest, literal people, with virtually no trace of a sense of humor. Winnie was possibly the most severe case.

"I'll take the short one," said his friend. "The joker."

My sister gave me a look. They were passing a joint around. She didn't take it, but I did.

The closest their car could get was a couple of miles from where the festival was happening—some guy's farm, the boys had told us. I tried to imagine my father saying, "Sure, you want to have a music festival for a few hundred thousand hippies? Come on over." Evidently this Max Yasgur was a different type of farmer.

Once we got out of their car and started walking, we left those boys. It had started to rain, and they had found some girls better suited to partying. I had on clogs and my sister, Weejuns. We had worn our bell-bottoms from Penney's but we didn't look like people who belonged there.

"I never should have let you talk me into this," Winnie said.

"If you don't like it you can go home," I told her, though I was having second thoughts myself. But we kept on walking.

In the end, we found a place to lay out our stuff about a half mile from the stage, next to a family with a baby and a couple who were dancing in a way that seemed to have no connection to the music. The woman's shirt was off.

The rain was coming down harder now. The PA system blared announcements about what to do if you were having a bad acid trip, and where to go if you went into labor. Someone said Santana was onstage but it was hard to know from where we sat, there were so many people standing up, and the main sound we heard was the generator.

"I need to go to the bathroom," Winnie said. "I think I'm getting my period." She was crying.

After she left, I started to walk around in the mud in between people's blankets. I had taken my shoes off in hope of keeping them from getting ruined, though I figured the damage was probably done.

"Hey, beanpole," someone called out. In automatic reaction, I looked over, though the voice was nothing like my father's. A random guy. It had not occurred to me before, the nickname was obvious.

Seemingly from nowhere, a girl put a small orange pill in my palm. "Try this," she said. Things started to look twisted, like what happens when you draw with a ballpoint pen on Silly Putty and start stretching it. The sound came in on waves, so beautiful I felt like crying one minute, then like screaming. Up on the stage, Santana was singing "Evil Ways."

"I love you," someone called out.

"I love everyone," someone else yelled.

I was soaking now, and covered with mud. A lot of the people around me had taken their clothes off, not just their shirts either. It was the first time I had ever actually seen a man's naked body, not in a painting in a book or one of the statues at the Isabella Stewart Gardner Museum. People were slathering mud on each other's skin, marking their faces as if it was war paint, massaging the mud into the women's stomachs and breasts, including some who were pregnant.

For the first time in my life, I felt homesick. I thought about my parents—my father in particular. I imagined him heading out to the barn with his coffee to begin his day, whistling "Oh What a Beautiful Morning," then wondering why I hadn't shown up to help with the milking. Going in to look for me, finally, and finding the note on my bed from the night before. I pictured him calling to my mother.

"The girls are gone, Connie," he was saying. "Winnie and Ruth."

It may have been the effect of the orange pill, but I started crying. I had no idea anymore how to get back to the spot where my sister and I had set up our sleeping bag. I looked at the sky. Hard to tell what time it was, due to the rain, but I was guessing my mother would have the beans on to cook. We were into corn season now. Worried as they'd be about us, they might or might not eat tonight.

I sat down on the muddy ground. When I pictured coming here, I had imagined I'd make drawings of people. I had actually stuffed a sketch pad and some colored pencils in my backpack. As if this might have been a sketching trip.

I was crying when I heard the voice. "Ruth Plank. I don't believe it. Of all the people."

For years his long, handsome face had featured prominently in my middle-of-the-night fantasies, lying in my bed at night, or weeding the lettuce, but now that I saw him in the flesh it took a minute to place this person, he was so wet—clean shaven unlike so many of the men here, but with hair down his back. Ray Dickerson.

"You grew up," he said. He took my hands and pulled me out of the mud so I was facing him. We were almost the same height.

"Got any berries?" he said. Smack on the mouth he kissed me.

THERE IS NOT MUCH POINT going into how things went the next two days. I have heard enough people describe their acid trips—the unearthly colors and sounds, the love that filled them, not only for their fellow human beings but for the ant crawling up their leg, each blade of grass. I have heard, more times than a person need go into, about the miraculous transformation these individuals experienced, in which the meaning of life was revealed and life as they'd known it ended, the mind-blowing sex. In my case, all of this occurred over the course of the two days I spent with Ray Dickerson—all but the sex part. The consummation, anyway. Strangely enough, considering everything that was going on around us, he did not enter my body, though we did just about everything else.

Partly it was the rain, and the mud, and how many people were around all the time. Even stoned out of his mind at Woodstock, Ray was a romantic, with an oddly old-fashioned streak, and so was I.

"I want to be alone with you," he told me. "I want to lay you out on a bed of moss and rub oil into your body. I want to massage you."

These were not the kinds of things a girl like me grew up hearing people suggest. The strange thing was, they were all the pictures I had in my head too. Being with Ray Dickerson was like being with a male version of myself. I was looking in a mirror and seeing who I would have been, if I'd been a boy. I loved this person.

The drug seemed to invest me with whole new sense, another way of taking in the world. Everything was intensified, a little like what happens when a person holds a magnifying glass over a piece of grass at just the right angle so the sunlight hits it, and the grass actually gets scorched. Over those days I discovered new colors different from any in the rainbow, and sounds that seemed to have been created by instruments from another planet, frequencies undetectable until now. My skin vibrated with sensation. I was inside the heads of people around me. I knew what they saw and what they were feeling—Ray especially. I entered his brain.

AT SOME POINT OVER THE course of those two days I thought about my sister, and wondered, briefly, what happened to her, but I didn't feel guilty. Guilt seemed to be one of the emotions the LSD had wiped out, and anyway, I had understood since we first set out on our trip that what she'd wanted to get from coming here had nothing to do with hanging out in the company of her little sister. Maybe she was dancing naked with some guy, too, though I doubted it, and in fact I was right. Shortly after taking off for the latrines that first day Winnie had found a family whose little girl was freaking out from the crowds, and she hitched a ride with them as far as Buffalo, where she called the boy she'd been dating for the last year and a half, Chip, to come get her.

In a rare moment of imagined closeness we'd shared on the bus coming here, she'd confessed to me that she found Chip boring and unattractive (an estimation with which I concurred), but Winnie's Woodstock experience evidently provided the turning point in their relationship. Within a week of her return from the festival they were engaged, and a year later, they got married. Hers was the first grandchild presented to our mother, nine months after that. Charles III. The spitting image of his dad, pimples and all.

With Ray, deficiency of sexual attraction was never an issue. All those years I'd spent dreaming about him—passing strawberries between our mouths, lingering over his naked body as I sketched, imploring him to let me touch him. Now I was finally able to do that, and my hands couldn't leave him alone. His on me, the same.

What happened afterward is still hazy to me. The festival ended, of course, and slowly then, like refugees from a bombed-out country, we made our way out over the ruined, rutted, garbage-strewn fields of what had once been Max Yasgur's farm. Farm girl that I was, no longer high, I found myself wondering how they would ever restore this piece of land, if anything would ever grow in this place again. Hard to imagine crops taking root here, though having been there, I have no doubt that children were conceived in significant numbers that week.

I left Woodstock a virgin, however. Out on the highway, where streams of bedraggled celebrants stood with their thumbs out, and vans covered with flower stickers and muddy streamers crept along the road in a strangely subdued fashion, not unlike a cortege, Ray said good-bye with an abruptness that stunned me.

"I guess I'll see you sometime," he told me, getting into a car with a sign on the front that said, simply, "West." The same person who had covered my body with kisses just hours before took off as if he was headed to the 7-Eleven for a quart of milk. In the absence of any other destination, and knowing that in three weeks I was due to enroll at art school in Boston—my life's dream—I waved to him and called out "Peace." But afterward, on the bus, I wept.

When I got home the next day, my parents said less than you might have thought about my absence. Partly this was due to Neil Armstrong's moonwalk, which everyone was still talking about. There was also a worrisome infestation of corn borers, and my mother's delirious absorption in the news that Winnie and Chip were engaged. Most of all, I think, she was reluctant to consider what I had been doing all those days I'd been away. Best to pretend they never happened.

## *Dana*

# Escape to Canada

SHORTLY AFTER MY brother left home, the fall of 1969—destination, San Francisco, Haight-Ashbury—the first letter showed up at our house from the Selective Service. Ray had not registered for the draft, of course—as he had been required to do, years earlier—but they had finally found him, despite our many moves.

George never paid attention to the details of life—speeding tickets from his many road trips, pursuing one big idea or another, or the fines and threats that followed us from one address to another. He was in Hollywood when the notice came for my brother, but wouldn't have paid any attention to it, anyway, and Val was little better equipped to deal with such things. Reading the letter from the draft board, she had looked momentarily anxious, but she was a woman who lived her life as if she had no power to affect the outcome of anything.

"I wouldn't begin to know how to find him," she said to no one in particular, tossing the letter in the trash, with so many other friendly or less than friendly reminders of unpaid bills. "Somewhere on the West Coast is all I know."

The letters continued to arrive. Then came a phone call. With his December

30 birthday, Ray had come up number three in the draft lottery; his status was now 1-A. He was requested to report to the draft board within two weeks or he would be considered in defiance of the federal government.

"What can I say?" Val said into the receiver. "If I knew where to find my son, I'd be talking to him myself."

It was the summer of 1970. For the fifth year in a row, I'd been working a waitress job (and a second job, nights, at a lab) saving money for college, living at home. By now—with the war escalating, the number of dead soldiers up around forty thousand—Ray was officially listed as having violated the law, and there was a warrant out for his arrest.

Sometime that August, we finally heard from him. Although we'd never passed on any news—not knowing how to do so—Ray must have figured out his status by now.

"I'm heading to Canada," he said when he called. "You probably won't see me for a long time."

"How can we find you?" I asked him. Different as we had been all our lives, I adored my brother. I couldn't imagine my life without him.

"I'll be in British Columbia, probably," he said. "A guy I know is headed there. Maybe I'll become a fisherman."

I tried to picture my brother on a boat. It wasn't exactly the ship we'd all been told was coming in all those years. He didn't seem like the fisherman type, though if you'd asked me what type he was, I'd have been hard-pressed to answer. He was the type who could make the most amazing hook shot anyone ever saw a player execute and then stop showing up for practice right before the playoffs. He was the type who would read out loud to me, one entire book of the Tolkien trilogy, every night for a solid three months, then never again. He was the type who could lean against a tree all day, making up the most beautiful songs on the harmonica but, when someone asked him to join their band, shrug and say he didn't really know how to play.

"You need to call us when you get there," I said to him. "I need to be able to find you."

"The whole idea is to *not* be found," he said. "The whole idea is disappearing."

"If you go away, I won't have anyone," I said. I was twenty years old, but I'd learned a long time ago not to count on Val and George for anything but unreliability.

"You'll have the same person that you always had, Dana," he said. "Yourself. The only solid one of any of us."

Then he was gone. Unlike George, who went away for long periods, Ray did not send postcards detailing his exploits, with hopeful progress reports, and lots of exclamation points, promising that success was a 99.9 percent sure thing. Once Ray went to Canada that was it.

"You'll be able to look them in the eye when they come knocking at the door and say that you haven't seen or heard from me," he'd said, just before hanging up. "It'll be the truth."

He was right. A man in a military uniform did come looking for my brother. He handed Val a paper informing her that Ray was now officially listed as a felon, for failure to report to service in a time of war—and failure to report his whereabouts was also a felony. That paper she did not simply throw away. She burned it.

Nights back then, if I wasn't working, and the television was on, and a report appeared about Vietnam, I'd watch Val shake her head, as if she found some odd comfort in the gaunt and haunted-looking faces of other women's sons, in their helmets and flak jackets.

"At least he's not there," Val said, when footage appeared on the television screen, of villages in ruins and soldiers dropping out of planes into the jungle. I had never seen Val display so much concern for my brother as she did when he was no longer around to witness it.

As for me, I dreamed of disappearing to some other place too, though for me the dream was college, that I'd been saving up for since I was in junior high. In my mind I saw a woman in a long dress coming toward me with her arms open. I didn't wear dresses myself, ever. But I liked girls who did. I saw her rubbing my shoulders and stroking my face, in a way I'd never known my whole life. I saw myself running my hands through her hair. We were in the country someplace, with nobody around but the two of us. The clearest picture I could form of what it would look like: that spot of soil I'd lain in that day on Edwin Plank's farm, with the sun on my chest and the taste of strawberries on my lips, breathing in the perfume of fresh-cut hay.

# RUTH

## Drawing from Life

FRESHMAN YEAR AT art school, we did a lot of figure drawing. I had always been good at drawing from life, from all my days spent in the barn with my sketchbook.

Now we had a nude model every day—sometimes male, sometimes female. I found that I felt no desire for these naked male models. I approached the human body as clinically as a doctor might a patient on the operating table. Whether my task that day was to portray a hand or a vase of flowers or a man's naked body didn't make a difference. The important thing was to do it well.

Which I did. Two weeks after classes started, my life studies teacher pulled me aside. "You've got a real talent for the figure, Ruth," she told me. "I'm putting you in my more advanced section."

I took classes in color theory, too, and a survey course in art history, and a class in printmaking, but it was life studies I loved best. I drew all the time now, and on weekends I spent hours at the Museum of Fine Arts, sitting on benches copying the great drawings of the Italian renaissance, and the life studies of Michelangelo and Raphael and Botticelli. That spring, a drawing I made of my roommate—a girl from Texas whose interest was in large, nonrepresentational abstractions—won the prize for the best student drawing in a school competition.

My mother, hearing this news, and always dubious about the cost of my education, wanted to know if this award came with any money. My father drove down to attend the exhibition, and afterward he took me out to dinner in the North End, to a restaurant recommended to him by the one Italian he knew in New Hampshire, his longtime employee, Victor Patucci. Married now, with a baby on the way, it appeared that Victor must have given up his old ambition to take over Plank Farm and was resigned to running the greenhouse operation instead.

"These people they get for you to make pictures of at school," my father said. "They don't mind taking off their clothes and letting all the students gather round and take a look?"

"It's art, Dad," I said. "They're getting paid. Nobody sees it as a big deal."

"Times sure have changed," he said, cutting the spaghetti up into short pieces with his fork, the way we'd done on the farm. "Back in my day, they made such a big deal about all of that, it made you a little crazy. If people could have talked about it and not acted like the whole thing was so sinful, maybe we wouldn't have gotten into so much trouble."

"What trouble was that?" I might have asked, but I didn't.

The drawing award I won did, in fact, come with some money, but only a hundred dollars. And my mother wasn't totally off base expressing concern about finances, because even with my scholarship, keeping up with tuition payments—never mind art supplies—was starting to feel impossible.

I saw an ad in the *Phoenix*. *"Artist wanted. Must demonstrate strong ability with the nude. Minimum wage now, but strong prospects of future earnings for the right person."*

I called the number and made an appointment to go for an interview in Jamaica Plain, practically at the end of the subway line. My roommate, Tammy, was worried the guy I was going to see might be some kind of sex addict, running a prostitution ring or trafficking in female slavery, but I wasn't concerned.

One of the good things about being six feet tall is that men tend not to mess with you.

As it turned out, the guy who'd run the ad wasn't remotely seedy. Josh was small and skinny, not much older than I, though his hairline had already begun to recede. He wore thick glasses and, judging from the books on his shelf, appeared to favor Beat poetry and Oriental philosophy. Even before he opened his apartment door I could hear the music inside: Marvin Gaye. Where most of the people I went to school with were listening to Bob Dylan and Neil Young, or Joni Mitchell, or Linda Ronstadt, Josh Cohen was strictly an R & B guy.

A copy of *Everything You Ever Wanted to Know About Sex (But Were Afraid to Ask)* sat on the table, next to a bong.

"You know how many copies this book has sold," Josh told me. "Millions. The guy who put it together is set for life.

"The thing is," Josh said, "this book just proves there's a readership for more of this stuff."

"But they already bought that book," I said.

"Does your mom only own one cookbook?" he said. "Does she read only one story?"

Just thinking about my mother, in this particular setting, was jarring. And in fact, though she owned several cookbooks—most of them put together by women's groups at Lutheran churches, for some fund-raising bazaar or other—she was a perfect example of a woman who did read only one story. The one she believed to have been written by God. But I saw his point.

"I'm looking for an artist to work with me on creating an alternative sex manual," he said. "My budget's limited on the front end, but if I like your work, I can give you a share in the back end of the profits."

Josh came from New York. His father worked in the fabric trade. He knew how to sell like my father knew how to plant corn. Second nature.

I took the job. For the first time in my life since around age six, I did not spend the summer working in the fields and the stand at Plank Farm. Instead, seven days a week, I took the train out to Jamaica Plain to sketch pictures of men and women, also hired by Josh through ads in the *Phoenix,* engaging in an amazing variety of sexual acts.

I worked on the book—*Sexual X-tasy*—right through Labor Day, when I delivered the last drawings. Most of the drawings focused only on the bodies of the lovers, but the final image I created—my pièce de résistance—featured a man and a woman in a hippie-style kitchen (a good-looking loaf of bread on the table, herbs hanging in bunches from the rough-hewn beams). They were having a good time on the kitchen counter.

The sum total of my earnings, from the hundred and twenty-seven erotic/instructional drawings I created for the Josh Cohen project, came to one thousand two hundred and seventy dollars. To explain my absence from home, I had told my mother I'd gotten a job that summer at Filene's without thinking that this would lead my sisters to inquire about whether I got an employee discount and if so, could they come down and do some shopping with me? I had never seen them more interested in anything I'd ever done up until then.

Ironically, I spent my summer with people who wore no clothes at all. From midmorning to well past dark, I sat on a hard wooden chair, sketching sex acts, but back at my little studio apartment near Central Square, I was alone, though now and then some man would try to get me to go out with him.

I always said no. I could not get Ray Dickerson out of my brain.

## *Dana*

# Gone

I ENROLLED IN college. Of all the places my family had lived, the one I felt most connected to was New Hampshire—the state of my birth, the only place we'd ever actually owned a home—so I chose the state university there. The University of New Hampshire was also known for its agriculture department, and that was my interest from the start. The college was less than an hour's drive from Plank Farm.

I studied biology and soil chemistry, plant science, animal husbandry. For the previous two years I'd worked weekends and summers as a waitress, which gave me enough money for the first tuition payment. For the rest, I was counting on working my way through.

For my scholarship job, I got to work in the experimental barns. Among my responsibilities was labeling and cataloging various sperm samples of the seed bulls—a task for which my years of attempting to maintain order among the yogurt cultures in the chaos of my mother's kitchen had prepared me unusually well. I was swiftly promoted to the more responsible position of specimen collector—an art not without a certain element of danger. And I got to work in the

Small Livestock barn, the place where I discovered my particular love of goats.

I was happy working in the barn. I loved the lowing of the cattle in the evenings, nights I worked late, and the soft, rhythmic sound of their chewing at the trough as I cleaned their stalls. When I was done with my work for the day—having locked up the pens, labeled my vials and set them in the appropriate racks in the cooler, changed out of my overalls and back into my khaki trousers to head back to the campus, I was aware of a heightened appreciation for everything around me.

Riding my bicycle over to the dining hall, or the dorm, I often found myself whistling the way I remembered Edwin Plank used to do.

"I love the world," I said out loud one evening, riding home from the cattle barn.

I had not thought anyone was listening, but a woman pulled up alongside me on a bicycle of her own.

"Me too," she said. "It's a surprisingly rare trait."

She looked to be about my age, though later I learned she was several years older. Clarice took exceptionally good care of herself. Anyone who imagines that just because a person is a lesbian means she's unattractive never met Clarice. She had long curly hair tied back with a flowered headband, and though she was biking, she wore dangly earrings that swung as she pedaled and set off her long, elegant neck. Her nails were polished in some pearly shade—something you didn't often see on a person at the Ag school.

She was an assistant professor of art history at the university. I remember thinking that this was good. I had no interest in taking art history courses. She would not be my teacher, at least not in art history, anyway.

"I love riding at this time of day," she said. "There's something about the quality of light on the fields. Did you ever see the work of a painter named Turner?"

I could have told her my father once bought a painting that was supposed to be a Turner—one of his many ill-advised lunges at the elusive brass ring. I held my tongue.

"English painter," she said. "Nineteenth century. He was all about light on landscape."

"I'm in the Ag school," I told her.

"A woman farmer," she said. "We don't have enough of those. Did you grow up on a farm?"

"Not really." I hesitated. I'd never been able to explain, really, where or who I came from. "My mother is an artist, I guess," I said, and her eyes lit up at that. "And my father is . . .

"Gone," I told her. The most accurate word to describe George, probably.

Hers too, she told me. Or at least, not speaking to her. "My parents didn't approve of certain choices I made for my life," she said.

She had jumped off her bicycle now so she was walking next to me as we spoke. She told me her name then. I had already studied her rear end on the bike seat. Now I could see her strong and elegant calves.

"Do you have plans for dinner?" she said.

It was not a difficult decision, forgoing the dining hall.

We talked most of the night. Until we stopped talking, and when we did, that was good too.

# RUTH

## Make Love Not War

I DIDN'T HEAR from Josh Cohen for a long time. I had almost forgotten about the *Sexual X-tasy* book project when I got a call from him the next spring.

"The demand has been fantastic," he said. "My dad's ordered a second printing."

A second printing was news to me. I hadn't even known about the first one.

"How many copies is that?" I said.

"Fifteen thousand and counting."

Rather than trying to find a publisher for his book, Josh had decided to print and market it on his own with the help of his father, the fabric salesman. Evidently they were advertising our little sex manual in places like the Exotic Sex sections of newspapers, and at music festivals and antiwar rallies. The pitch was simple and direct: "Make Love Not War—and Here's How."

Production values on the book were a little iffy, but you couldn't beat the price: $2.99. My cut in the profits, ten cents a book.

That April Josh sent me a check for two thousand dollars. The next month came another thousand. By summer, I had paid off my college loan and had enough money to cover the following year's tuition. Thus far I'd made more money than my father cleared in a summer working our farm.

It had never occurred to me, when I was making the drawings, to ask Josh how my drawings would be presented, but now that I finally got my hands on a copy I discovered my name on the title page: *Text* (such as it was—mostly just names he'd thought up for the positions) *by Josh Cohen. Illustrations by Ruth Plank.*

I kept the book a secret, especially from my family, though I agreed to attend a convention in Arizona with Josh over the next spring break. Two separate hotel rooms, and he paid my way.

The convention turned out to be a show featuring early-model vibrators and sex toys and the kinds of things they sold at head shops in Harvard Square—pipes and crystals and belly-dancing apparatus. One dealer was selling vaginal speculums. A lot of people were selling massage oil and candles, some in interesting anatomical shapes. The people who came were older than we were, but still reasonably young—in their late twenties and thirties mostly. More women than men. Feminists, lesbians, hippies, and artist types.

"You did these pictures?" a man asked. He held out a copy of the book for me to autograph. "You've got real talent, man. Now tell me, do you actually know how to do all these moves yourself?"

The strange thing was, I had tried none of them. I was twenty-two years old by this time—living on my own as an art student in Boston—and I was still a virgin. The main sexual experience of my life—virtually the only one—had taken place during the time I spent at Woodstock with Ray Dickerson.

"I have a boyfriend," I said, just to get rid of him.

"Too bad," he told me. "I wanted to take you to the desert and fuck your brains out."

## *Dana*

# The Half of It

THERE HAD BEEN no explosive moment in which Val and George announced they no longer loved each other. There was no big, traumatic day when George packed his bags and drove away. The truth was that George was always driving away. He went on trips so often it was hard to say where he lived anymore, or which were the destinations, and which the trips. For as long as I remembered it seemed George had been disappearing. So when he disappeared for good, it was a long time before I even noticed.

He had gone to Nashville with a bunch of song lyrics in his bag, and a few demo tapes he'd made on our reel-to-reel recorder. One was the love song he'd pictured George and Tammy singing together.

My mother got a few postcards from Nashville, then one from Austin, telling her that Nashville was no longer the place for country music, Austin was. Then a card from Nashville again, to say he had a meeting with a big star coming up, though he was not at liberty to say which one. Then he was calling from Portland, Maine, to say he'd caught a ride north with a musician buddy from Florida (Florida? Who made music in Florida?) and could I meet him for dinner there.

It was the first time in a year that I'd actually seen George, and possibly the first time ever that he'd sought me out. The moment we sat down in the restaurant, the reason became clear.

"The thing about music demos these days," he said, "is that a person just can't get away with anything less than professional-quality sound anymore. What I need to put my work over the top is to hire a class-A producer and a few good studio musicians to record my stuff, so I can get it in the hands of the right people. I'm thinking a thousand dollars would set me up. I know you've got some money saved up for school, but you won't need it all till next year. I was hoping you might help me out in the meantime."

I looked at him across the table in the restaurant—the Western-style shirt, his face brown from (I guessed) a tanning parlor. As recently as three days earlier, when I'd gotten his message, I'd allowed myself to feel a small, slim hope that maybe there was more to our relationship than I had known.

"My father actually wants to have dinner with me," I'd told Clarice. "I know I shouldn't even care, after all the times he let our family down, but I can't help it. I'm happy."

"That's good," she said, her arms around my neck. "Just watch yourself. I don't want you to be hurt."

Now George was reaching for his drink. "I'd pay it back in three weeks," he said. "Four weeks, tops. First check I get, I'll sign it over to my little girl."

I set my fork down. I had ordered chicken but all appetite had left me now. George took a bite of steak.

"That's not who I am," I said. "Your little girl. I never was."

"I know, I know. You're all grown up," he said. "Where did the time go, anyway? I can remember when you were just a baby."

"Can you really?" I asked him. "Because I can barely remember you. You weren't around that much."

"I was working on deals, honey," he said. "It's not easy, supporting a family. Let me tell you."

"Tell me what?" I said. "You never took care of anything. You left Val to do it, and she wasn't much good at the job either."

"That's probably why we raised such great, independent-type kids," he said. "You never had the world delivered on a silver platter. One thing I wanted my kids to take from me was self-reliance. And look at how you turned out. You know how to do your own thing, that's for darn sure."

I looked at him hard then. "Whoever was responsible for how I turned out as a person," I said, "it wasn't you. If I turned out OK, it wasn't because of you. It was in spite of you."

"Listen," he said. "I'd say I did OK by you, under the circumstances.

"Your mother—" he began, but the sentence went no place. "Your mother was doing her own thing too," he said, finally. "You don't know the half of it."

"Whatever Val did or did not do," I told him, "at least she stuck around." I got up from the table.

We never spoke again.

# RUTH

## An Anatomy Thing

My mother and Nancy Edmunds came to stay with me for the weekend. They were part of a quilting group—my mother's one non-church-related activity, besides our farm. There was an exhibition of quilts from Appalachia they had heard about that they wanted to see. It had been Nancy's idea to make a weekend out of the trip—drive down, take in the quilt show and maybe Filene's basement, or the Freedom Trail, have a seafood dinner down by the water, and stay over at my place. Nancy could sleep on the couch and my mother would bunk with me.

This was to be the first time in the nearly two years I'd lived in Boston that my mother visited my apartment there. She had not come down when I first enrolled, or for the show in which my drawing had won the prize. At the prospect of her visit, I felt a combination of irritation and excitement. After all this time I had never gotten over the longing to please her, and disappointment every time I fell short.

We were at the fish restaurant, eating dessert, when Nancy brought the subject up. "We heard you published a book. That's quite an accomplishment."

I studied my slice of pie, unable to speak. At no point during the past few hours I'd spent with my mother had her behavior toward me seemed any different than usual. Friendly, but remote.

"Not exactly," I said, my tongue suddenly dry. "I was just helping a friend out. How did you hear about it?"

"A customer at the farm stand," my mother said. "Some young woman buying a flat of pansies. She wanted to know if we were related to this artist that did some drawings for a book she had."

"What kind of book is it anyway?" Nancy asked. "We haven't seen a copy yet."

"Sort of an anatomy thing," I told her. "They thought I'd do a good job because of my work in drawing class."

"All my girls showed talent in that department," my mother said. "You should have seen the Snoopy pictures Naomi used to make. They published one in the paper."

For once she did not mention Dana Dickerson. It did not escape my mind, of course, that for once my mother's lack of interest had served me well. She never again asked about the book, though Nancy brought it up a time or two.

"Don't forget to bring a copy home one of these days," she said.

When I didn't, no one pursued it.

# *Dana*

# Good Fencing

FOR THE FIRST time in my life, I was happy. I had graduated from UNH with a bachelor's degree from the College of Agriculture. I was living in Newmarket with Clarice, who was teaching full-time at the university. I felt guilty not to be doing my share of paying the bills, but she said not to worry, things balanced out. I had a big vegetable garden in the back that fed us all summer, and when fall came, I filled jars with dill beans and pickles and beets, and my homemade tomato sauce. Every night when Clarice came home from work, I had dinner waiting and candles lit. Nights on our bed, I massaged her beautiful shoulders, her fine, narrow back, tense from all those hours grading papers. I never got tired of looking at her lovely, intelligent, kind face.

"You're so beautiful," I told her. I couldn't help myself. I told her every day. "I love your body," I said.

"I feel the same way about you," she whispered, though we both knew how far I was from beautiful—my body was like a tree stump, my face square and forgettable. I imagined the potato Edwin Plank would have pulled out of his pocket to represent me: pale, round, and plain. Where Clarice's hair tumbled down her back in a lush golden mass of curls, mine was thin and spiky, chopped close to my neck as a boy's.

"To me, you are beautiful," she said, stroking my cheek.

I had a plan. I wanted to find a plot of land in the seacoast region, close enough to the university that Clarice could make the commute easily. Not a lot of land like Plank Farm, just a few acres on which I'd grow specialty vegetables like the unusual greens that were starting to come into fashion now as an alternative to iceberg and romaine lettuce. And I'd started thinking about raising goats.

I had some money saved up. It wasn't a lot, just a few thousand dollars. Mostly, when I looked at property, which I had begun to do, everything was way out of my range. "Why don't we wait to go see this property until your husband can join us," real estate agents said, when I asked them to show me a listing. When I said I wasn't married, they'd close the book.

One weekend I drove to Eliot, Maine—just over the New Hampshire border—to check out an item I wanted to buy Clarice for her birthday. It was an antique brass bed advertised for sale in the *Pennysaver.* I knew Clarice had always wanted one.

The man selling the bed must have been in his late eighties. His wife had recently died, and after sharing that bed with her for sixty-three years, he couldn't bear to sleep in it anymore.

Fletcher Simpson had lived in the house all his life. It was a tiny place, just two bedrooms (one for him and his wife, the other her sewing room, since they'd never had children). There was a screen porch and a perennial garden and out back—beds with rhubarb and asparagus and every kind of herb, and three kinds of berries. He'd planted a plum tree to mark their fiftieth anniversary.

I told him this was just the kind of place I dreamed of having someday. I had the feeling it would be all right to talk plainly, so I said I was looking for a spot like this to live with my girlfriend and raise goats and start a cheese-making operation. We'd have a farm stand maybe—just a small one. The kind where you leave out bouquets of zinnias with a jar next to them for people to put in their money on the honor system, and they do.

"How much you want to pay?" he said.

I told him I had saved up thirteen thousand dollars. Even back then, 1974, this wasn't much.

"I'll tell you what," Fletcher said. "You pay me that, to be my stake for the move to Florida. Take good care of my dog, and on the first of every month send me a check for a hundred dollars. Keep this between you and me, and leave the government out of it."

Six weeks later he'd signed over the deed and Clarice and I moved in. We helped Fletcher pack up first, then drove him to Boston to put him on the plane for Fort Lauderdale. We promised to send him regular reports about his beagle, Katie, which we did.

We never had to move the brass bed, of course. It stayed in the same spot, where we slept in each other's arms every night, with Katie snoring at our feet. Summers I ran the fruit and vegetable operation—with the zinnia bouquets, as planned. That was Clarice's department.

All year round I tended the animals, and I set to work studying the art of making goat cheese, which was not yet a fashionable item, though it became one. All my university courses in animal husbandry had not prepared me for the realities of raising goats—milking a new mother goat, or the smell of a male goat in rutting season, or getting the curd just right on a wheel of Tomme—but I learned quickly. Within a couple of years, we'd been written up in *Yankee* magazine. People started buying our cheese by mail order, and restaurants as far as Burlington and Portland featured it on their menus.

Goats are wonderful animals: intelligent, affectionate—funny even—though if you don't keep good fencing up, you can forget about your raspberry crop. I learned that lesson the hard way.

At the university, Clarice was on what they called "the tenure track." She kept her private life to herself, so I did not attend faculty cocktail parties, which was fine with me. We had few close friends. All we really needed was each other.

We were the happiest couple I knew.

# RUTH

## Bones and Teeth

AFTER MY MOTHER had given birth to her fifth daughter, it became clear that for the first time in ten generations there would be no male heir to inherit Plank Farm. One of my father's brothers was childless. Another, like him, had only girls. The last brother fathered a son—a boy they had started talking about as the possible inheritor of the farm, though Jake Plank had never seemed remotely interested in the idea.

As things worked out, it never came to that. Three days after landing in Vietnam, at the age of twenty, Jake was killed by friendly fire near an army base in Da Nang. All that remained of the next generation then were daughters, and not a one of us in possession of sufficient enthusiasm for the farming life to fight as hard as would have been necessary to overcome the gender problem.

Of the five of us, I was the only one with any interest in the farm, but for me, that had less to do with farming than with spending time with my father. I wanted to make art, not grow corn.

When my sisters and I were little, everyone was too busy to think much about the family legacy. Just getting through the days, and then the seasons, was all my father could manage. But as he got older, you could see the problem weighing on him. And Victor Patucci, out in the equipment shed, oiling the tractor, or going over the orders for fertilizer and seed, like a fox prowling the henhouse, licking his chops.

This became particularly evident as our financial problems grew more severe. Although my father had always maintained the Yankee tradition of paying cash and avoiding debt, by the time I left home he and my mother were taking out a loan every winter just to make it through another season. By 1973, the year I turned twenty-three, we had a mortgage on our property of more than fifty thousand dollars.

I was living in Boston at the time, working for a graphic design firm (and still, amazingly, collecting the occasional check from *Sexual X-tasy*), but I came home one fall weekend to help sell pumpkins a few days before Halloween.

Once again we'd been experiencing a drought, and though it was past the season for worrying about crops, my father was still keeping his eye on the rain gauge and not liking what he saw. In among the dots of orange where the pumpkins lay, our fields had seldom looked so dry.

It was around sunset, and you could tell the weather was changing. Black clouds had gathered over the horizon. The cows, back in the barn, were making restless sounds. Right after his old friend Don Kent, the weatherman for WBZ, my father looked to the cattle next to tell him what was going on meteorologically.

My mother was just clearing away the dinner dishes. Winnie was over, to work with our mother on a crib quilt for the daughter of a woman from church who'd just had a baby. Our father had settled in with the paper, expressing displeasure with the news. He'd voted for Richard Nixon, but after Watergate he observed that he'd never trusted the man.

At first I thought someone had fired a gun in the yard. Then came the sound, like an explosion. When the second crash came, we knew it was thunder. I stepped out on the porch just in time to see a lightning bolt strike the barn. A minute later, there was a burning smell, and smoke curled from the roof.

"Edwin, get the hose," my mother screamed. She was dialing the emergency dispatcher.

I'd never seen a building burn before. This one was engulfed in flames within minutes, the lines of the roof no longer visible beneath the tongues of fire. My father had pulled his boots on—no time to lace them—racing to the barn. After thirty years of fighting fires on other people's property, nobody had to tell him what a barnful of hay looked like when a spark got to it.

The hoses were coiled next to the baler. Even if we could have connected them up in time, there was no way of getting to them; the heat was too intense. And beside the hoses sat our precious Massey Ferguson, its tank filled with gasoline, and a second gas can beside it.

By the time we got to the barn, the flames had reached the stalls, and they were lapping up the walls toward the roof. All my life I'd lived around cows, but I'd never heard them moan as they did now, with the flames devouring them. The air was filled with the cries of burning cows and the sound of our own voices, screaming and shouting, and the smell of burning flesh. In the blazing darkness I saw the swing in the loft outlined in flames, spinning like a lasso from a rafter as it crashed to the ground, and with it, our weather vane.

My sisters' husbands came running—first Andy, then Chip and Steve and Gary. We were hauling anything we could find in the kitchen that would hold water—our canning kettle and mop buckets, the coffee percolator, but it was an effort as pointless as spitting on the flames. They had reached the sky now, where a full harvest moon hung like a medal. Even the leaves of the maple next to the barn were burning. The line of scarecrows my father had built to attract pumpkin customers blazed like a parade of Vietnamese villagers fleeing a firebomb attack. In the bizarre way fires traveled, the sign I'd painted that afternoon—BEST PUMPKINS AROUND! PICK YOUR OWN!—remained untouched, but beside it, a row of diapers belonging to my sister Winnie's baby flapped, burning, in the deadly breeze. Beside our old Dodge truck, my father stood like a man witnessing the end of the world. Which in a way he was.

Finally the fire trucks were there, and the hoses shooting a wide, powerful spray, but by the time they arrived it was too late to save our barn, or anything that had once resided there. Cows, tools, equipment, cats. Gone.

The whole thing was over by midnight, though the embers continued to smolder for two days after that. My mother, the one who did best at functioning in the face of crisis, suggested that we harvest the pumpkins ourselves and take them down the road to a neighbor's place to sell. Nobody would want to come to Plank Farm now for a fun outing with children. Only to deliver casseroles and sympathy.

We had insurance, though not close to enough as it turned out. One of the cows had actually escaped the blaze—an old milker named Marilyn, whose stall was closest to the one open door. Ignoring the firefighters' words, my father had run in the barn to free her moments before the main beam crashed down. Of the rest, all that remained were a few bones and teeth. My mother dealt with those. My father, though he didn't weep, could not have handled the sight.

In the spring we rebuilt, in a fashion. To economize, and to get the new building up as fast as possible, my father chose a prefab metal barn structure Victor had located, with a laminate roof to replace the old wood barn that had stood on the property since my great-great-great-grandfather Gerald Plank first raised the beams with the help of his neighbors in 1857. It had been a day his wife had recorded in a letter to her mother.

"Once the last beam was in place," she wrote, "the men descended the ladders for a meal of cornbread and beef stew I and the other wives prepared. All but my own fine husband, who, as tradition would have it, secured a young sapling to the highest peak. It will remain there a few seasons, I reckon, but the barn itself I expect to be standing long after Gerald and I are safely returned to the soil."

We bought another tractor of course—a used Ford 8N, purchased at auction. "This one won't have to last us so long anyway," my father observed quietly to my mother when he brought it home—a sorry comedown from our shiny red Massey Ferguson. "It's not like there's another generation of Planks standing at the ready to take over this place."

He replaced our tools, and bought a mower, but the fire marked the end of the days of fresh milk and cream on the table from the cows my father spoke of as "our girls." My father didn't have the heart for that part again, he said.

A week after the fire, my father received the first call from a developer—a conglomerate out of Nashua that had got wind of the disaster and evidently judged this as good a moment as any to make an offer on our place. The Meadow Wood Corporation was looking for land to construct communities of tasteful yet affordable homes in rural areas close enough to hospitals and shopping to provide an attractive climate for housing the coming generation, the man said—a two-tiered project that would begin with homes for growing families and eventually include assisted living and a twenty-four-hour care facility. They'd be more than happy to send a representative to come and talk with our family about a possible sale, terms highly attractive, he assured us.

"Some nerve that guy had," my father said, after he set down the phone. "Barging into a family's private business at a difficult time, flashing his wallet."

Come January, he was making his order from Ernie's A-1 Seeds, same as always. But we all knew if something didn't change, there were only so many seasons left before they had us.

# PART II

# RUTH

## A Universe of Three

AFTER MY GRADUATION from art school—a ceremony attended by both my parents, for once—I stayed on in Boston. I was working for a design firm but making my own paintings, too, on nights and weekends. Certain things I missed a lot about our farm—the smell of the barn, the taste of fresh peas eaten raw, right off the vine, the night sky as it can only look when no other light exists in any direction to diminish the brightness of the stars themselves.

Mostly, though, it was a relief to discover, after so many years, that the old sorrows I had known all my life—the chill wind of my mother's disappointment, my sisters' attachment to one another and distance from me—no longer stung as they once had. My father represented the one person in my family to whom I felt a deep connection—but even his tenderness and care seemed, sometimes, like a too-obvious attempt to make up to me what the others failed to provide.

"You have a special someone there in the big city?" he asked me once, when I was home for a weekend visit that May, helping to get the tomatoes planted. For my father—a man who generally confined his conversations with me to new varieties of corn, or the differences between the milk fat content of Guernseys versus Holsteins, or the progress of his attempts to create a new variety of supersweet early strawberry—this was an unusually intimate question.

"I go on dates now and then," I said, not so much opening the door to further discussion as closing it.

The truth was, the rare occasions in which I went out with men during those years were almost invariably uncomfortable experiences. Nearly every time a man suggested we go someplace together—to a movie usually, or dinner, or a beer in Harvard Square—I'd find myself counting the minutes until I could be back in my apartment again.

There was nothing so terrible about these men. There was just never anything that excited me, and in the absence of that I couldn't see the point of the whole thing. When they kissed me, I registered the feel of their lips on mine, their hands moving down my back or possibly over my breast, but with the detachment of a person drawing the scene more than living it. Nothing stirred in me.

I was a twenty-four-year-old virgin. The one person with whom I discussed this, oddly enough, was Josh Cohen. We didn't see each other regularly, but over the years since he had hired me to make the drawings for *Sexual X-tasy* we had developed a friendship.

Josh was wildly experimental. He told me about orgies he attended and weekends spent at hidden-away places in Vermont or Maine or upstate New York, where people walked around naked, moving freely from one partner to another—this being the days before anyone had to worry about the health implications of that kind of behavior.

As for me, the secrets of my own nature and yearnings were contained within the pages of my notebook. Even there, I had no interest in the kinds of activities Josh engaged in on weekends he drove his convertible to one of these spots, "to play," as he called it. Josh liked hot tubs filled with beautiful women and fit young Boston businessmen on the move, energetically climbing over one another like a pile of kittens in the hayloft. From what I gathered, avoiding all emotional attachment was the main objective. It held no appeal for me.

"Nobody who saw your drawings would believe you live like a nun," he said, one night when we were having dinner at a Cuban restaurant around the corner from my apartment. "You think up all these wild things people could do with each other. Then you never do them yourself."

"I never meet anyone who makes me feel like I'd want to," I said.

This was not completely true. There had remained, after all these years, a picture in my head—not even a picture so much as a feeling—of one man with whom I could imagine myself making love as easily as breathing. This was Ray Dickerson.

So I lived partnerless in Cambridge. My sexual experiences took place when I painted and drew. I didn't always create erotic scenes in my artwork, but when I did, it was as if I were not simply depicting but living them. I stayed up all night sometimes, painting, and when I finally lay down to sleep my body would be damp with sweat. Nobody saw these paintings but me. They were too raw for other eyes.

It was the fall, 1974. The first frost had come, and the leaves were turning. I remember this because I'd had one of my rare dates that evening, with a nice man who had taken me to see a movie.

This man, Jim, was an exceedingly decent man who seemed to like me a lot, for reasons that never failed to mystify me, considering how little enthusiasm I displayed toward him. I felt no desire for him and could never pretend.

Jim had walked me back to my apartment. I remember the dry leaves on the sidewalk, and thinking with a certain wistfulness of the maple tree in front of our house back home—where my father used to make us a giant leaf pile for my sisters and me to jump in. As we walked home, Jim was telling me something about the insurance industry—his chosen field—and how few people understood it properly. I tried to listen but felt my mind drifting.

We reached the door to my building. "I'd like to see you again," he said, moving toward me in a way I knew meant he was planning to kiss me.

"Could I come upstairs with you?" he said. "Maybe we could listen to music."

"I'm working tomorrow," I said. "I have to get up early."

I did kiss him, or at least, our mouths touched, though I felt nothing when they did.

It is one of the mysterious things I have spent years considering—how it can be that one person may have a way of touching you that can make your skin practically burn, and another (a much better man, perhaps, or at least a very good one who loves you as well and truly as any person ever has) may simply not possess a talent for that touch. And if he doesn't, none of the other things matter in the end. If a person doesn't move your heart, there's not a thing your head can do about that.

I could draw all these couples making love in a wide variety of positions, and Josh could end up selling enough copies to get him well on the way to where he eventually landed—a very rich man with his own publishing company, at the wheel of a 1987 Porsche heading to Esalen (he had moved to L.A. by this point) with a couple of former Playboy bunnies in the jump seat. Somewhere out there were a hundred thousand people who had evidently studied those pictures, or at least bought the book.

But in the end, the book does not exist that can tell a person how to make love, and, saddest of all maybe, no amount of love in a person's heart will necessarily instill in him the ability to make another person feel desire if it's not there. Either he touches you in a certain way, or he doesn't. This is not something you can teach anyone. I knew this that night on the doorstep with Jim when I told him good night, firmly expecting I'd never see him again.

Hours later, I heard the phone ringing. But I was in the middle of a dream. I let it go. Only the ringing resumed. Stopped for a moment. Then started again.

When a telephone rings in the middle of the night—and rings and rings and rings—you can only suppose something terrible has happened to someone in your life. So I threw off the covers finally and picked up the receiver.

"Ruth." That's all I had to hear to know whose voice it was. Ray. I had not laid eyes on him since the day he climbed into that van leaving Woodstock and rode away without even looking back out the window.

"Where are you calling from?" I said. I had seen Dana once or twice over those years, when she'd stopped by our farm. I had taken pains not to reveal the intensity of my interest in her brother but I had asked, as casually as possible, what he was doing, so I'd heard about Canada. The draft. Also the silence. Now here he was.

"I'm living on an island in British Columbia," he said. "I work as a carpenter. There's a few of us up here, who left when the army came after us. I keep to myself mostly though."

I can still remember how I felt, standing in my little apartment that night holding the phone. A current running through my body, a dam unstopped, water tumbling over rocks.

"I always hoped you'd call," I said.

"I was thinking you might come out here," he said. "It would be good to see you."

I knew enough by then to be cautious, but I felt only longing and desire. This was the only man who'd been able to reach me, touch me deep below the surface of my skin. He'd been able to walk away from me so easily. But he'd also come back.

That day I quit my job and my apartment, threw away most of the paintings I'd been working on except for a few I put into storage. I told my parents very little. I was going to see a friend in Canada, was all. Four days later I was on a plane heading west.

He was waiting for me at the airport in Vancouver. We didn't even say that much on the long drive north—an hour to the ferry at Nanaimo, an hour on the ferry, another three up north to Campbell River, and another ferry ride over to the island where he lived, Quadra.

He had his hand on my leg the whole time. I could feel his palm against the flesh of my inner thigh, warm beneath my skirt.

I did not ask him to fill me in on the particulars of what he'd been doing, how things worked for him in this place—certainly not his plans for the future or how I might fit into them. Sometimes he looked at me without saying anything. Mostly, driving along the highway, he'd stare straight ahead at the road toward the outline of the mountains against the horizon. Though I had never been to this place I had no doubt where we were headed.

That last ferry crossing was short. Ten minutes after we'd driven onto it, the boat pulled into the landing, and Ray started the engine on his truck. Slowly we rolled off onto the dock and past the town, which wasn't more than a few buildings—a post office, a grocery store.

It was another twenty-minute drive on a dirt road where we hardly passed a single car, to the point where he told me, "We're home."

No other houses within sight. No power lines or, as I later learned, running water.

That night, by the light of an oil lamp, he undressed me. What happened then bore no resemblance to any of the drawings I'd made for the book. For the first time, the eye that always seemed to be looking down at my life, observing it—drawing it, even—had closed, and I was simply Ruth, a woman inside her own body, exploring his.

I have no idea how long we stayed on that bed. Until morning, and long past. Now and then we'd fall asleep for a while. When we woke up, one of us would reach for the other, and it would begin again. I kept no track of time, or anything else.

IT WAS LATE FALL WHEN I arrived on the island with Ray. A few weeks later the first snow fell. A layer of ice formed on the spring where we got our water and Ray broke through it with an axe. Even with the fire going all day, the two-room house—uninsulated, with single-pane glass in the windows—was so cold there would be mornings I'd wake up and see my breath in the air, or frost on the blankets.

I cared about none of this. Or that we hauled our water from a spring a few hundred feet from the house. Or that money was so low we lived on rice and beans and peanut butter. In summertime, Ray had worked on construction, but there were no jobs for an unskilled carpenter on the island, once winter came.

I posted a notice at the general store, advertising art lessons. No takers. It seemed we weren't the only ones on the island with limited disposable income.

But we were rich in other ways. Outside the window we saw eagles sometimes, and always deer. We took long walks. He washed my hair and brushed it dry. Ray hauled water from the spring, heated it on the woodstove, filled an old iron tub, lit the candles, and bathed me.

Sometimes Ray would start a building project at our place—a wood-fired sauna with a stove made from an old oil drum, an art studio for me. He'd make a sketch, and sometimes we'd get materials together, or spend a few days hanging Sheetrock or planing lumber. But I learned early on that Ray's projects usually didn't get finished. We'd run into a problem and he'd get frustrated.

"I don't really need a studio anyway," I told him. "I like lying here drawing you." This was true. Something about the sight of him splayed out naked in bed reminded me of Christ on the cross. Those long outstretched arms, sinewy legs, and a certain expression that combined both pain and rapture. It was hard to say which one more than the other.

We spent a lot of hours on that bed. Ray had a low, drowsy voice, and he loved to read out loud to me. We went through all the *Lord of the Rings* books, and *The Chronicles of Narnia*, and *Dune*. He read me poetry—Yeats and Browning, Emily Dickinson, Edna St. Vincent Millay, William Blake. Sometimes, reciting certain lines, he would be so moved by the words he'd start to cry.

Even then, he was a fragile man. But at the time, this only made him more wonderful to me. Where my own father seemed so stoic it was often hard to know what he was feeling, every emotion that passed over Ray showed on his face. If he was happy, he might break into wild, crazy dervish dancing. When he was sad—and this was surprisingly often—he wept openly. Many years later I learned a name for this behavior, but at the time I called it honest and real.

We had this fight one time. I'd remarked to Ray about how he'd failed to get back to a man down the road who'd asked him to come and help put up his roof.

Not great money, but something at least. Only Ray had waited so long to stop by that the guy found someone else.

"I let you down," he wept. "I'm an idiot."

"You never let me down in the important way," I said. "How much you love me." In this area, it was true, I never doubted him. As I spoke my hands moved through his long tousled yellow hair, the color of mine—but where my own hung straight, his was a mass of curls I liked to bury my face in.

"I love your hair," I said. Then no more talk, only kissing.

We smoked a lot of marijuana. He wouldn't have had the money to buy any, but he'd planted a big crop the summer before, and unlike the rest of the plants he'd started, he had a successful harvest from those. Except for a handful of times—including Woodstock—I had never smoked before, and even now I didn't like the feeling of starting every day with a joint the way Ray did. But I liked how it felt getting stoned before we made love. And we made love all the time.

I asked if it seemed odd to him that I'd never been with any other man. He meditated a long time on my question.

"It's like you to be that way," he said. "You're the kind of person who can't do anything that isn't true to herself, and you had to wait until you were sure you had found your one true love on earth."

My one true love was him, of course. Same as I knew I was his—though in Ray's case, there had been no shortage of partners before me. Just not the right one, he said.

After all these years, it's still difficult to say this, but I believed at the time, as clearly as I knew my name, that Ray Dickerson was my destiny. I held nothing back, believing as I did then that we would be together always.

What he wanted, he said, was to create a relationship in which the two of us were like one person. When I hear those words now, the idea has an ominous ring, but at the time it seemed like the most idealistic and wonderful goal two people in love could have for themselves. No boundaries. Nothing unspoken. No inch of each other's bodies we did not know.

When spring finally came and the weather got warm enough, we spent our days naked, mostly—something you could do, living where we did, with no neighbors in any direction closer than a mile away. We swam a lot, in a lake down the road from our cabin, where nobody ever went. I had known for a long time—never not known, maybe—that Ray possessed a tendency toward melancholy and such acute sensitivity that it sometimes seemed to me that he was not meant for life in the world as we knew it. One day when we passed a deer hit by a car, lying by the side of the road, he had been so overcome he turned around and went back so we could put the body in the back of his truck and bury it. Another time, when I went into town without him and took longer than usual, I'd found him sitting on the cabin step when I returned, his hands raking his beautiful long hair.

"I thought you'd left me," he said. "I couldn't bear that."

He brought me presents: a kitten from a little girl he'd met in front of the food co-op who had a box of them to give away. A bottle of green drawing ink and a brush made from a lock of his own hair, tied to a piece of bone, a music box, and a pair of very delicate silk slippers that I suspected he may actually have stolen from the house of a rich woman he worked for briefly. He brought me a velvet purse, inside of which were shells he'd gathered on the beach for me, that he laid, one shell at a time, over the naked skin of my belly. One day he came back from town with fresh oysters, also gathered on the beach, with the plan of feeding them to me, but he couldn't get them open, so finally, after an hour of trying, he drove back to the beach to set them free again.

"They shouldn't die for nothing," he said.

He said we should invent our own language that no one else would understand, not that there was anyone around to listen to our conversations anyway.

"The government probably has its eye on me right now," he said. "On you too, just because you're with me."

KNOWING WHAT I KNOW NOW, it is difficult to describe what it was like, loving Ray. Years ago a recovering crystal meth addict spoke at my son's school.

She said that even after ten years clean, she still missed the way it felt to have that deadly substance in her veins. If she'd kept using it, she would have died. Still, life without the drug felt, sometimes, like a lesser thing. A sad though necessary comedown.

Listening to her speak in that auditorium filled with my fellow concerned parents, sitting next to my good husband with whom I'd lived at that point for close to twenty years, the image of Ray's face was all I could see, and a wave of grief and longing overtook me, so strong I had to cover my eyes. Even after all that time.

Back in our British Columbia days, the way I felt when he was in me was like no sensation I have ever known, and I could have swooned from the rapture of it. After a while of being with him, the simple act of his touching my hand would cause my pulse to change, bring heat to my skin.

He had made a name for all the places on my body he loved to touch, which was all the places on my body. He made me promise I would never speak these names to anyone but him, and in spite of everything else that happened in the end, thirty years later I never have.

Our lovemaking went on for hours, leaving me exhausted. I was too weak afterward to try and make friends, or make art, or even clean the house. All around us things were falling apart, but there never seemed to be any time to put them back together.

He sang to me, songs he made up—every day another different strange lyric and tune. Because he never seemed to rest, and I did, he would sit on the edge of the bed sometimes and play me to sleep with his harmonica—Gypsy-sounding tunes that invaded my dreams.

Many times he told me he wanted to have a child with me.

"Where would the money come from?" I asked. "How would we live?" I might be able to sleep in a frozen bed, with nothing but rice in my stomach, but I knew if we had a baby, I would want more for her. School, friends, a house with running water, cookies in the oven, birthday parties, a Christmas tree.

As we were living now, we hardly ever saw anyone but each other, though increasingly—on those rare occasions we'd drive to town to pick up supplies—I'd find myself looking for opportunities to strike up a conversation with someone. It didn't matter who, a different voice was all. And then I'd feel guilty, as if I had betrayed Ray, knowing what he had said to me a thousand times: that he would never need any other human being but me. Me and our child. A universe of three.

Sometimes I imagined what my father would think if he could see me in this place. I would picture his gentle, worried face—the expression he had when too many days had passed without rain, or one of the cows had milk fever, or deer had gotten into the corn, and the homesickness would come over me. I wanted to be with Ray, but I was missing parts of the world too. I wanted to believe there was a way to have them both—the things I had loved, and the man I loved more than anything—but I didn't know how to make this happen.

By the time fall came—close to a year now from when I had arrived on the island—Ray was talking daily about the two of us having a baby. He knew it would be a girl, he told me, and he even had a name for her: Daphne.

I had been using a diaphragm—a purchase I'd made right before flying to Vancouver, on my way to being with Ray. Now every time I took it out of the case, he shook his head. "What about Daphne?" he said. "Don't you want her to come live with us?" He said it as if there were a real person just outside our door, alone and shivering, in need of nourishment and rest, and I was denying her. Sometimes, when we made love now, it was as if the face of our unborn, unconceived child was pressed against the fogged-up glass, pleading with us to let her come in.

"I want to throw that thing away," he said. "I want to burn it." But I put the diaphragm in anyway. I could not see us as parents, responsible for another person besides ourselves.

Then, one November night we were lying in bed together—moonlight streaming in the window, slashing across the naked body of the man I loved—and I found myself talking to Ray about something that hardly ever came up with him, consumed as our life was in the present.

"All my life, I've had this feeling that I didn't really belong in my family," I said. "I love my father, and maybe I love my mother and my sisters, but they feel like some other species of being from me. I don't really know them. They don't know me."

"I am your family now," Ray said.

I knew this. But one person didn't seem like a family. You needed more than that.

"Let's make our family," he said. "We'll be our own tribe. That comes from us and no place else but here."

That night we made love without the diaphragm. "You are my family now," he said, his eyes burning into me. "The only one I need. We'll make our own good family."

I believe I knew the instant it happened that we'd conceived a child, and by the next morning I could feel it in my body. A few weeks later, I made him take me to the clinic in town to confirm this. From the moment I told him the news, Ray couldn't stop smiling. For me, there was the oddest mix of feelings: joy mixed with a clutch of panic whose origins I could not fully identify. Partly, I think, I was just so terrified that this might change everything between Ray and me. Nothing, not even a baby, was worth risking that.

But another worry plagued me too. I had loved the way Ray felt things so deeply, and how I could always make things right for him. Now we were introducing a child into our delicate, often precarious balance, and I couldn't help comparing the probable future to my own past. As lonely and frustrating as it had felt, growing up with my two quietly stoic parents, there had been a sense of comfort in knowing how strong my father was. When our barn burned down, when the crops failed, when my sister and I ran away to Woodstock, my father had remained steady as a heartbeat. An hour had never gone by in which I didn't know that whatever happened, he would take care of things. I tried to imagine how it would be for our baby, who would look to her father for strength and protection. And find a man less able to offer support than to require it from those he loved.

Thinking about my father as I was now, I registered a surprising impulse.

"I want to call my parents," I said.

All that year, I had told them almost nothing of what I was doing. The handful of notes and cards I'd mailed home—no return address—had said, simply, that I was living on an island in British Columbia and was happy.

Now I wanted them to hear my news, and the wonderful fact that the father of my baby was a man they'd known most of his life, the older brother of my birthday sister, Dana Dickerson. Our families would be truly linked in the way my mother always seemed to want.

We placed the call from a pay phone outside the clinic. I could hear the ringing, imagined the two of them in the family room, having washed the dinner dishes and watching television probably. Or my father would be reading, my mother doing a jigsaw puzzle or working on a quilt.

"It's Ruth, Daddy," I said, when I heard my father's voice come on the line. "I'm calling from Canada with news. Can you put Mom on?"

Then I told them. On the other end, after I'd said the words, only silence.

"Are you sure about this, Ruth?" my mother said. Not the excited tone I'd expected from a woman whose whole existence for the last ten years had seemed focused on the arrival of grandchildren.

"We got the test today," I said. "I'm six weeks along."

"That's really something, sweetheart." This from my father. From my mother, still, nothing.

"And Ray Dickerson. I guess this means you two have gotten reacquainted. You've been spending a lot of time together I imagine?"

"We live together, Dad. We've been together a year now."

Suddenly it seemed bizarre I'd let all this time pass without telling them.

"I need to think about this," my mother said, when she finally spoke. "It's big news. Complicated news. I need time to think."

I laughed. How much time did a person need to take in that eight months from now—right around when the corn came in, or started to—a baby would be born? How complicated was that?

We had no phone number to give them, but I told them our address. Next day came the text of a telegram, delivered to our rural delivery mailbox, announcing that my mother would be paying us a visit.

I might have expected this for the birth, but she was coming *now*. In three days. She had included her flight arrival information in the telegram.

We made the long trip to Vancouver to meet her plane, naturally. No way would I have expected my mother—a woman who had never traveled anywhere before, other than to Wisconsin, on a bus—to make the difficult journey alone to the island where we lived.

It was easy to spot her exiting the jetway—a small, stout figure with a determined look, like a soldier heading off to war. She was wearing her old gray coat, a scarf around her neck, a hat, her sensible shoes, and a pin in the shape of a flower on the collar. She was carrying her purse in one hand and a paper bag in the other that I knew contained a jar of her strawberry jam. Her arms, when she put them around me, had that old familiar stiffness, though after a year of Ray's touch, it felt even stranger now to be held by a person whose embrace conveyed less love than wariness.

I worried about what she'd think when she saw our home—not so much the woodstove because we'd had one of those on the farm, too, but the outhouse, the bucket sitting by the door that we used to haul water, the tar paper on the roof and plastic on the single-pane windows of the place that, in her eyes at least, would seem like nothing more than a shack. In the few days since receiving the news of her arrival and meeting her plane, I had raced around cleaning up, hanging curtains, taking down the drawings of Ray, naked, that covered our walls, and the poems he'd written for me, tacked in odd places around the house.

My mother barely spoke on the drive home—the two ferries, and the two endless stretches of highway in between, though I pointed out scenery along the way, and she nodded.

"Very nice," she said, her voice tight. "This is beautiful country. I'll give you that."

We had fixed up a bed for her in the corner of our living space I used for my art studio, the only other room in the house besides ours. I had set a bowl of shells I'd collected next to her cot and laid an Indian print spread over the thin mattress, along with as many blankets as we could find.

It was dark by the time we got home. Because the pregnancy made me so tired, I went to bed almost as soon as we reached the house. You never knew how Ray would act around people—sometimes charming, other times silent and morose—so I was relieved and happy to see how friendly he was being to my mother. As I excused myself, I could hear him boiling water for tea over the woodstove.

"This'll give our baby's future grandmother and me a chance to get to know each other better," he said, sounding like a person I barely knew.

From where I lay in our bed, I heard comforting sounds coming from the kitchen—mugs clinking, the honey pot being set on the table, the plate of cookies that I'd baked the day before laid out. I fell asleep feeling happy at the picture of Ray and my mother getting along so well, and dreamed of our baby.

When I woke up the next morning, everything was different. Although it was early, my mother was already dressed, her bag still packed, as if she were about to leave.

"We're going home," she said when I stepped out of the bedroom, my stomach still churning with the morning nausea.

"What are you talking about? We are home. My home."

"I'm taking you back to New Hampshire now," she said. "There's been a terrible mistake. Your father and I will take care of you now."

What she was saying seemed so crazy, I just laughed. Then it occurred to me that I hadn't seen her in more than a year. Maybe some swift and devastating form of dementia had overtaken her though she was only in her early fifties.

"I live here now, Mom," I said slowly. "I'm not going anywhere. I live with Ray. We love each other. We're having a baby."

"Ray agrees with me, you need to leave this place," she said. "A car is coming to take us to the airport."

Through the window, I could see the figure of my lover, but I'd never seen him looking like this. Though it was cold that morning—freezing in fact—he was sitting in the yard. His back was hunched, and he held his head in his hands. He was not weeping, as I had seen him do on numerous occasions. This was worse. He seemed stunned and mute, as someone might look after undergoing electroshock therapy.

"Ray!" I called out the door. "You need to come in here. My mother's saying crazy things."

The room was spinning. I had been nauseated before. Now I threw up. My mother went to the sink for a cloth and some water from our pail. Her old standby: cleaning up.

I tried to call out again to Ray. I opened my mouth, but no sound came.

Slowly then, like a man in a horror movie—a zombie, a character in *Night of the Living Dead*—he made his way into the house. I tried to meet his eyes, finding nothing. On the floor at my feet, my mother was still washing up. His face, as familiar to me as my own hand, had gone flat and blank. But there was something else. His beautiful long hair that used to fall down past his shoulders was gone. Chopped off. What remained stood up in short, uneven patches on his fine-boned skull. I could see a thin blue vein running through his skin, blood pumping.

"What's going on here?" I screamed. "Nobody's making sense."

"This never should have happened," he said. The voice of a dead man, if dead men could speak. "It's best for you to go."

"What's going on? Why isn't anyone saying anything?" I realized something now. He had never come to bed that night. Wherever he'd slept it was not with me. Not then, or ever again.

"One day you'll understand, this was for your own good," my mother said, gathering a few pieces of my clothing. "For now, you just need to come with me."

I reached for Ray. I pounded my fists on his chest, scraped his skin. I pulled at what was left of his hair.

"What did she do to you?" I screamed. "You've lost your mind."

No answer. It was as if Ray's soul had left his body, and all that was left was skin and bones and organs—all but the brain and the heart.

"I can't talk about it," he said, his voice flat and low. "You just need to go away now. We can't have this baby."

"What are you saying? This was what you wanted. A hundred times you told me so."

"I made a mistake. I don't want it anymore. I can't talk about this. Get out."

The world went dark.

SOMETIME EARLIER—BEFORE SHE MADE THE trip to Canada, probably—my mother must have arranged for a taxi to pick us up. Now it was parked in the yard. I could hear my mother's voice telling the driver, "You'll have to excuse my daughter. She's going through a lot at the moment."

I have the dimmest memory of Ray as my mother was leading me out to the taxi. He was lying on the bed, curled up, with his newly shorn hair sticking up in clumps, his face turned to the wall—but when I called out to him that last time, he had looked up and our eyes met.

"This isn't real," I said. "Just say something to me. Come and get me."

I can still see his ravaged face as he looked at me.

"What are you doing?" I was crying. "What did she say to you?"

He shook his head and turned again to face the wall.

I HAVE NO IDEA HOW my mother got me into that car. I have no memory of the journey back across the Campbell River Narrows, or the drive to Nanaimo, the second ferry, the final stretch of highway. For the first twenty minutes, I screamed and wept. After that, in all the hours of our journey, I doubt any words were spoken.

I know all kinds of things must have happened—checking our bags, presenting our passports—but how she managed to take care of this I have no idea. Somehow, my mother had a ticket ready for me. One-way to Boston.

———

I DO NOT REMEMBER THE flight, or my father meeting us at the airport, though he must have done so, or the long drive back to our farm (past midnight now, an early dusting of snow covering the field where a few leftover pumpkins lay unclaimed).

For all that first week back, I kept trying to reach Ray, but there was no phone number to call. No response to my telegrams. I even called my birthday sister, Dana, to see if she knew where he was.

"I have no clue," she said. "I haven't laid eyes on my brother in years."

He seemed to have vaporized.

And so when my mother came to me a few days later to say she'd arranged an appointment at a clinic, I simply nodded.

My sister Winnie came with us to Boston that day and sat with me in the waiting room while our mother remained outside. By this point I thought I must be losing my mind. I no longer fought any of it. Just watched, with horrified wonder, as if this were an episode of *The Twilight Zone*, but more terrifying than any I'd ever seen. Not just watching *The Twilight Zone*, but in it.

With my own hand, I signed the papers for what they called "the procedure," though it was my mother who filled them out.

My mother, a woman who believed that birth began at conception, had brought me to an abortion clinic. I, a woman who just seven weeks before had greeted word of pregnancy as the happiest news of my life, now slipped her feet into the stirrups.

I could only believe I had lost my mind. Then, for a while anyway, I did.

## *Dana*

# Stranger Things

AFTER CLARICE AND I bought Fletcher's place—now named Smiling Hills—I started dropping by Plank Farm more often. At first this was just because we lived reasonably close now. I'd be passing through on the way to pick up Clarice after her classes—nights she worked late, and I didn't like her to have to drive home alone—or it was strawberry season, or later, when the corn was coming in.

During the period of my animal husbandry studies at the university, I'd become fascinated with goats, and now we had established a small herd—a dozen, of a variety known as Adamellans, whose milk produced a particularly fine cheese. We kept just enough chickens to provide fresh eggs for the two of us, and because it had been a lifelong dream for Clarice, we bought her a horse, Jester.

We decided early on that our farm would specialize in only a few of the higher-end crops, and ones that didn't take up so much land—since, unlike the Planks, we only had a few arable acres. Partly because Clarice loved them, but also because they made sense for our locale, strawberries were my chief focus other than the cheese, and because I had never tasted better strawberries than those at Plank's, I went to talk with Edwin about starting my own growing operation.

Many farmers wouldn't want to share their expertise with a person who could be viewed as a competitor, but Edwin Plank had always been generous about sharing his knowledge with me. When I called him up to ask if I could stop by and discuss getting our beds started, he seemed not only willing to assist, but actually eager.

The basic concept of strawberry propagation was simple enough: as they grow, strawberry plants shoot out runners—little offshoots that live on after the original plant has petered out. These are called daughter plants. That's where you got your new stock: from the daughters.

Any farmer can tell you it's important to cut back the daughters. If you let them all develop, the bed will become too crowded, the plants will be stunted, and the berries will be sparse and small. To harvest a good crop of strawberries, Edwin Plank had told me, you must choose the five healthiest and best-looking daughter plants and let only those bloom and bear fruit the following season.

Most commercial growers rely on seed companies and nurseries to supply them with daughter plants every year, rather than going through the laborious process of selecting and propagating their own new generation of strawberry plants every year. But for our farm, I wanted to grow berries that were acclimated to our particular region—the New Hampshire and southern Maine coastal area, and to the soil conditions on the particular piece of land I was cultivating. It was for this reason—but also no doubt because I looked for any excuse to talk with Edwin Plank about our mutual passion for farming—that I'd set out to visit Plank's Farm that day.

"I've been waiting for this moment," he said to me, when I showed up that afternoon. As he led me out to the greenhouse, there was a kind of excitement to his step. Or as much of that as a person like Edwin Plank ever revealed anyway.

"I want to show you something," he said. "I've got a little project going that might interest you. With that university diploma of yours and all, you could be just the girl for the job of taking it over."

Although, unlike me, Edwin had never gone to school to study horticulture, he was an amateur plant scientist. Ever since he was a boy growing up on the farm, he told me, he was interested in the process of plant propagation.

Edwin had a natural understanding of how plants worked—the kind of education that didn't come from books or classroom lectures. "I don't believe I ever got over the kick of grafting a branch of one fruit onto another fruit tree," he told me. "When other boys were out playing ball, I was doing experiments with different kinds of soil conditions and fertilizers, to improve the quality and yield of the produce."

I'd been that kind of kid myself. I remembered a time my mother and brother and I had stopped by for strawberries—early July, as usual—when Edwin Plank had taken me out to the field where the corn was growing and explained how the ears are formed.

"The beautiful thing about corn, Dana," he had told me, "is how every stalk is both male and female, all in one plant. The tassels are the male part—the father, you might say—that forms the pollen. The way nature works it, the pollen from the male tassel lands on the silk, which is the female part of the corn.

"Each strand of corn silk is actually a hollow tube connected to the undeveloped mother cob. The pollen travels down the silk to the cob, where it forms a single kernel. Each kernel has its own silk attached to it. Someone up there thought of everything, because they even made it so the silk is covered with a sticky substance that catches the pollen. To make sure it doesn't just blow away."

What a person could do, if he wanted to have a little fun—"he or she," Edwin clarified, seeming to recognize even then, in my nine-year-old self, the potential of a future farmer—would be to gather the pollen off one variety of corn plant and sprinkle it over the silk of a different variety.

"You never know," he said. "You could come up with your own whole new strain of corn. Could be the best there ever was.

"Why, just last year I read about a plant breeder who came up with a seedless cucumber," he went on. "Son of a gun, if that wasn't a good idea I don't know what is."

Even as a child, I loved the idea of inventing a new vegetable or fruit. The funny thing was that all my life, George had been going on about his big ideas that were going to make us rich—new products that never existed before, or songs he'd write that would turn into hits, or amazing inventions. None of them ever felt real.

But as the two of us stood in the field that day—Edwin in his brown overalls, me in my shorts and Keds, munching on a bag of peas Edwin had picked for me along the way—I couldn't imagine anything I'd rather spend my time doing than collecting and redistributing corn pollen to see if I could actually succeed in doing what he talked about, starting a new breed of plant.

I was halfway through my twenties—and Edwin closing in on sixty probably—when he took me into the controlled environment of the greenhouse to show me his strawberry breeding project—undertaken in the greenhouse, he explained, to provide a controlled environment where the blossoms would not be cross-pollinated by the bees, as they would be out in the open. When a plant breeder was working on something like this, he told me, it was important to eliminate any variables that might affect the purity of the experiment.

"I don't show these plants to many people," he said. "You could say this is my secret laboratory."

For more than a dozen years, he told me, he'd been trying to develop a new strain of strawberry—sweeter and more flavorful than all the rest. The way he did this was to identify the best berries of every given growing season. First he'd mark the plant that had produced the tastiest, juiciest berries of the season. Then he would carefully dig it up, along with its daughter plants, and transplant them into a marked bed in his unheated greenhouse. The next spring, when blossoms began to develop, he'd carefully snip the stamens—the pollen-producing parts of the flower—off the blossoms he wanted to hand-pollinate, and discard them.

Then he'd pick several blossoms from the plants he wanted to use as fathers—the plants that had displayed desirable traits like large, attractive fruit or resistance to disease, and twirl them over the pistils, or the sticky female parts of the mother plants. His goal was to combine the best traits of the mother plants with the best traits of the father plant to develop a new genetic cross, a whole new variety of berry.

When the new strawberries formed and ripened from this cross-breeding experiment, he would select the largest and sweetest ones, then mash them and strain them to remove the seeds. He'd plant these seeds in flats in his greenhouse, and when they were large enough, transplant them to his special beds outside, separate from his other strawberry beds.

He would mark those plants, watch the fruit, test for sweetness, and if they were unusually good—which by and large they were—he'd do the whole thing all over again the following year, improving on the quality of his plants with every generation.

You could dig up the daughters and transplant them into a nearby bed, or one a thousand miles away. But each daughter plant was an exact genetic duplicate of the parent plant.

"What I've ended up with here," he said, indicating a patch of plants about the size of the bedroom Clarice and I shared, meaning not very big at all—"are probably the best berries you've ever tasted."

He didn't sell the berries from those plants. The plants and what they produced were strictly for propagation purposes. "But one day," he said, "I'd like to think the variety will be perfected to the point we can take some samples down to the university and show them to the experts."

I had spent four years with the university types who studied plant science, of course. They did their work in controlled conditions, handling the plants with gloves on, measuring things like sugar-to-acid ratios with highly technical equipment. But they weren't farmers like Edwin, born with the instinct for growing things.

"You know what I hope?" he said. "I'd like to believe that one of these days, you'll open up your Ernie's A-1 seed catalog and there'll be a full-page spread about this great new strain of strawberry plant they're offering, bred on a small family farm in the state of New Hampshire."

He was getting closer, he told me. But he wasn't as young as he used to be, and this was a job that needed some youthful energy and spirit. It might turn out that perfecting this new variety of berry would take more growing seasons than Edwin had left in him, he told me. So he wanted to know—would I be willing to take over the job of propagating the plants?

"You never know what could happen," Edwin said. "You could find yourself owning the patent on a brand-new variety of strawberry plant. Stranger things have happened."

Hearing this, I might have been reminded of George, perpetually waiting for his ship to come in. Except Edwin was nothing like George.

I said I'd love to work on his project, of course—moved by Edwin's willingness to trust me with his precious plants, the breed he'd spent so many years developing.

I thanked him for his faith in me.

"I'm not worried," he said. "I can tell what kind of girl you are."

So I drove off that day with precious cargo in the back of my truck: three flats of Edwin Plank's lovingly tended daughter plants—"my good daughters," he called them—headed for Smiling Hills Farm.

# RUTH

## No Love Lost

FOR SEVERAL WEEKS after I returned to my parents' farm from British Columbia—I cannot say home, because it didn't feel like home anymore—I stayed in bed. Only this time I was alone. It was not just Ray I'd lost—and the child we would have had—but my own self.

Ray had told me we were one person now. Then he sent me away. Who did that leave me to be? And there were all those other things he'd told me about our life together and the future we had—our destiny. I no longer knew what was real. If anything was.

A thousand times I replayed Ray's behavior that last morning, the day he cut off his hair and told me to leave. It never made sense, but part of me also knew that the man I had loved, and still did, was a fragile person haunted by demons I'd often glimpsed but never truly seen. Because of that—because of his unfathomable vulnerability and fragility, I forgave him.

But my mother had no such excuse. Whatever it was she told Ray that night—whatever the words had been that transformed my world in a matter of hours—I knew her to be a strong person, and one fully in control of her actions. What had happened was precisely what she'd intended.

I pleaded with her to explain. I began with rage and when that didn't work, I shifted to pitiful supplication.

"Tell me what you did to make him go away," I said. "I need to understand."

"Some things are better left alone," she told me. "He was not a well person. There are times when a parent knows best for her child. I would rather have you hate me than see you making a mistake that would ruin your life."

When I begged my father to explain, he turned away. "I know right now it feels like the end of the world," he said. "But there will be other times." Ever the farmer, that's how he saw life. You planted your crops, they flourished until frost hit, then winter came and they died. Then, came spring. There was no such thing as endings, only the endless cycle of the seasons. Every year a new chance.

Him, I forgave. My mother never. I could no longer speak to her.

In an odd way, this new hatred of my mother provided the impetus for me to finally get out of bed just so I could get away from her. When I could not bear another day of seeing her walk through my bedroom door with her tray of soup and saltine crackers, I pulled myself up and started gathering my things. I called my friend Josh, who still lived in Boston, and asked if I could stay with him until I found another place. He came to pick me up in his sports car the next day. He knew how to talk to people's mothers in a way that endeared them to him.

"Now there's the kind of young man you should be keeping company with," my mother might have said, in times past. "Even if he is of the Jewish persuasion."

She said nothing about Josh this time, however. Even my mother appeared shaken by what had happened in Canada. She had ruined my life all right, and gotten me home on the strength of her scarily powerful resolve and determination. But now that she'd done this, she too appeared depleted and exhausted.

She said nothing as I carried the box of my possessions down to Josh's car. I was taking almost nothing with me to Boston. I wanted nothing to remind me of this place.

"No love lost between you two, I guess," Josh said to me, as I set my suitcase in the backseat and climbed the stairs for one last look in my room.

"If I never see her again, that's OK with me," I told him.

I did one last thing before I left the farm that day. From under my bed, I had taken out my old junior high sketchbook with all the dirty pictures in it that I'd made back then, my thirteen-year-old's attempts at portraying the mechanics of all the other wild and forbidden combinations of male and female bodies that I'd thought up and put on paper when I was young. My thrilling early attempts at pornography.

All these years, the notebook had remained under my bed, buried in the stack of 4-H Club magazines and old issues of *National Geographic*. Now I carried it downstairs. I set the notebook on the kitchen table, next to the Bible my mother read every morning with her coffee.

No need to leave a note. She'd recognize the artist.

## *Dana*

# The Closest Thing to Heaven

THE TIMES CLARICE and I spent in each other's company on our little goat farm in southern Maine were the closest thing to heaven I had ever known. She wasn't much of a gardener. Nobody could be who cared that much about her fingernails. But she loved picking bouquets of flowers for our self-serve flower stand out by the road, and gathering eggs, and taking her horse Jester out on the trails behind our house.

We set up a chaise lounge for her in the shade, where she would stretch out, reading papers or preparing a lecture, while I worked in the strawberry beds or hauled goat milk in to the separator. Sometimes she'd come out to where I was working, with a glass of lemonade for me, or I'd take her something to look at—a bug I'd found, a piece of old china my hoeing had turned over in an area that must have long ago served as the dump for Fletcher Simpson's ancestors.

As a scientist, I kept meticulous notes on the strawberry propagation project—rainfall; number of blossoms per plant, and sweetness and color of berry measured on a scale from one to ten. For this, I enlisted the help of Clarice, to whom I presented my plates of test berries—each one labeled with a code number—for the purpose of determining which were the best plants to focus on for propagation of our new strain. I liked to sit at Clarice's feet while she placed each berry in her mouth, one at a time. I'd study her face as she sucked in the juice—the exaggerated expressions she'd make if a particular berry seemed to her worthy of particular merit.

"Oh my God, oh my God, oh my God," she would pant, or moan, as if the experience of taking this morsel of fruit were capable of inspiring nothing less than orgasm.

"No. No. No. No. No. Yes."

Afternoons, we took Fletcher's old dog, Katie, for a walk by the brook, looking for wildflowers if the season was right. Summers we swam in the pond down the road, no need for suits. In winter we snowshoed. Nights in our little kitchen, with a tape of Frank Sinatra playing, or Chet Baker, or Nina Simone—or sometimes Clarice's choice of Emmylou Harris or Dolly Parton—we danced.

There was nothing we lacked in life. Or only one. I wanted us to raise a child together.

# RUTH

## Risk Assessment

I ENROLLED IN grad school to study art therapy. My plan was to work with troubled people, using the tools of drawing to explore their experiences. I had enough savings from my unexpected book royalties to pay for a little apartment in Cambridge not far from where I'd lived before. My year on Quadra Island with Ray had taught me many things; among them was the ability to live on almost nothing.

All that spring and through the summer I took classes during the day. At night I fixed myself rice and beans or soup, or sometimes nothing more than a bowl of popcorn, and read, or drew, and listened to music, until it was time for sleep. I did not think of Ray, or at least, when thoughts of him came to me, I pushed them away.

No men entered my life. Men seemed to recognize something about me now that kept them away, and this was good news. I had no interest in sex, no interest in love. I worked, ate, drew, slept. Apart from Josh and a couple of women I knew slightly from my classes, I kept to myself.

I was walking home from the library one night—fall now, leaves on the ground, the kind of night that reminds you winter's on the way.

*The spring will be frozen over now next to our cabin,* I thought. *Ray will have to take out the hatchet soon to break through the ice.*

I wondered if he'd grown his hair back. I wondered what he'd done with the drawings I'd made of him, that we took down for my mother's visit, and the poems he wrote for me. If she had never come that day, we'd have a three-month-old baby now. Daphne.

"Ruth." I looked up to see a face I dimly knew but could not place. A pleasant face, though with the kind of regular, even features that were easy to forget.

"Jim Arnesen," he said. "We went to the movies together a couple of years back."

I remembered then. *Last Tango in Paris.* Marlon Brando and Maria Schneider and the butter. A picture of the two of them together came to me. Then it was not Brando and Schneider, but Ray and me. There was no such thing as sex that wasn't with him.

"You have time for a drink?" he said.

I shrugged. There was no particular reason to do this, but no reason not to.

At the bar around the corner, Jim told me what he had been doing since we'd seen each other last—selling life insurance without charging the usual commissions. It wasn't the most lucrative work, but he was proud to be a quiet outlier in a world of fast-talking salesmen.

"I never stopped thinking about you after that night," he said. "I might as well tell you. I used to walk by your place, hoping to run into you. Then I finally got up the courage to ring your bell and someone else was living there. For a few days I kept trying to figure out a way of finding you, but I didn't even know your last name."

"Plank," I said. "As in, piece of wood."

We started going out. He took me to dinner mostly, but also to the Museum of Science and Fenway Park, a place he loved. He was a lifelong Sox fan, he told me. The day Jim Lonborg—pitching on just two days' rest—lost the seventh game of the 1967 World Series had been one of the darkest in his life.

If that was what Jim called a dark day (my Jim—as I had begun to think of him), then he was lucky. There was some comfort being with a man for whom losing a ball game was the definition of trouble.

Sometime that winter—after a surprisingly long time in which all we ever did was kiss a little on my couch—we went to bed together. His lovemaking was, not surprisingly, similar to his kissing. Heartfelt and earnest, and utterly lacking imagination, inspiration, or danger. But I felt a tenderness for him that I named as love.

His professional specialty was risk assessment, and if there was one thing Jim Arnesen knew, it was how to play it safe. If there was another, it was devotion and constancy to me. He was steady as a metronome. Reliable as the postal service. I didn't need to know him long to understand: I could more safely place my trust in this good man than trust in my own self.

Right around my twenty-seventh birthday—strawberry season, Fourth of July weekend—he took me to Maine for the weekend at a bed-and-breakfast on the coast. I knew, as we set out on the highway, that he would ask me to marry him on this trip. It was never too difficult to predict Jim's behavior.

We had dinner at the B and B that night. Studying the menu, I'd noticed a familiar name. "All our greens are organic, and come to you from Dana Dickerson's Smiling Hills Farm." Apart from that one brief phone call to Dana the year before—my frantic attempts to locate her brother before the abortion—it had been years since I'd spoken with my birthday sister.

*Maybe she knows where he is now,* I thought.

*If she does, stay away.*

For dinner we had the prime rib. Afterward, Jim ordered champagne and made a gesture to the waitress that was probably meant to remain secret but wasn't. A moment later the crème brûlée arrived. Mine had a diamond on top.

It was not the corny romantic gesture that moved me. No scenario dreamed up by Jim Arnesen could have approached the kinds of scenes I'd played out on that frozen bed on my island in British Columbia with Ray Dickerson. But Jim moved me in a different way. Looking at him then, across the table—his eyes damp, his smooth hand stretched out over the white cloth, reaching for mine—I felt no roughness, no trace of danger or trouble, only kindness. This was a good man.

"I love you but I'm not in love with you," I said. That old line people come up with over and over, as if they've arrived at some profound revelation, when all they're really saying is they are feeling rational in a relationship, as opposed to crazy.

"That's enough for me," he said. "Just as long as you let me be in love with you."

"I'm a difficult person," I said. "I sometimes wish for what I can't have. There are things about me you wouldn't like so much."

*Pictures then of Ray and me. Fingernails on his back. The two of us covered in mud. A day spent on the mattress, dawn till dusk. No words but animal sounds.*

"I don't need you to be different from how you are right now," Jim said. "Unless you say no. That's the one thing I'd want to change. Say you'll be with me, and I won't need anything more."

A thought came to me: *I can make this man happy.* For all my extravagant expressions of wild love, that was something I'd never been able to accomplish with Ray Dickerson.

WE GOT MARRIED THAT FALL—A city hall event. Jim's parents were both dead and I did not invite mine, or anyone else. A few days later I did call my father—at an hour when I knew my mother would be at church—to let him know.

"I hope you'll be happy," he said. "I wish we could've been there on your big day."

It wasn't such a big day, actually, I wanted to tell him. I'd had a big day already. I needed no more of those. Only small ones from now on. Regular days for the rest of my life.

## *Dana*

# A Matter of Lifestyle

ABOUT THE ONLY source of tension between Clarice and me concerned Clarice's reluctance—unwillingness, in fact—to make our relationship known to her colleagues at the university. Though I would sometimes pick her up after class, I stayed in the car while I waited for her. When there were faculty events, I did not attend. One year—1983, I think—the seniors chose Clarice, out of the entire faculty, as an honorary member of their class. There was a dinner held at which she had been asked to speak.

"I want to be there," I said. "I think it's time people know there's someone who loves you so much." This, too, was an issue between us. In the absence of any sign of a partner, Clarice's colleagues in the department were always trying to set her up with one or another newly divorced or widowed man. She brushed off their efforts, but enigmatically, never telling anyone the reason she chose not to meet their most recent candidate for her affection.

"You don't understand how it works in my world," she said, when I pushed to attend the dinner in her honor. "It wouldn't be good for my standing at the university."

"Don't you work at an institution of higher learning?" I said. "Aren't people at universities supposed to practice open-minded thinking not only in the classroom but out of it? What about some student who may have been sitting in your humanities lectures all year, who is struggling with the knowledge that who she really wants to be with is a woman, not a man? What kind of message are you teaching her with your silence? There might be something else you could be saying, a lot more relevant to her future than the influences of the Italian renaissance on British architecture."

"I'm not at the university to make a political statement," she said. "I'm there to teach art history. That is where I work, and nothing more. My real life is here."

"Can't you integrate the two? I do." Even though the world I inhabited—of small-scale independent farmers, and bigger growing operations like Plank Farm—tended to be run by older people whose views on most things ran along conservative lines, I'd never encountered any problems at livestock shows or horticulture symposiums when I spoke of my partner and made it plain her name was Clarice.

The next year, 1984—just before my thirty-fourth birthday and Clarice's fortieth—Clarice was up for tenure, after more than a dozen years of waiting. The faculty in her department and a committee of higher-ups from the dean's office would vote on her appointment right around graduation time. With her popularity among the students and her recent publications in her field, it seemed clear to us both—even Clarice, though she tended to worry more than I—that she'd receive the promotion and the significant increase in salary and position that went with it. We had even begun planning the trip we'd make, a cross-country drive to Yellowstone Park.

"I know most people in my field would go someplace like Florence," she said. "But you know what I want to see? Herds of buffalo. And the Annie Oakley museum."

The previous fall I'd started volunteering at the school in our town, coming in once a week to work with the elementary-school kids on projects involving plants and animals. For me, this was partly about making connections and forming ties in the community where we lived and where—unlike my wandering family—I intended to sink permanent roots.

There was another aspect to my volunteering. I wanted children in our life. More and more, I longed to raise one with the woman I loved. I wished there could have been a way for Clarice and me to have one ourselves, and sometimes we even talked about it, but the idea did not seem feasible.

"If we got my brother to be a sperm donor for you," I said, only half kidding, "that would be almost the same as if you and I had done it together." Even as I said this I was aware of how totally different my brother was from me—not just physically but emotionally.

But even if we'd wanted to ask Ray to help us, there was another more concrete hurdle: I had no idea where my brother was. Some years before, Ruth Plank had called, looking for him, with the news that he had been living on an island in British Columbia. That was the last I'd heard of his whereabouts from anyone, including Val and George.

We decided that once Clarice was granted tenure at the university, we'd look into adoption. Back in those days most foreign countries would never consider two women, living together, as acceptable parents, but somewhere, we believed, we'd find a child who needed a home—an older one, maybe; that was fine with us. Till that day came, I looked for another avenue for having children in our lives. This was what prompted my decision to create what I called the Farmer-in-the-Schools program in our town.

I loved working with the children. One week we planted beans in paper cups; another time, thanks to a rare suggestion from Val, I taught them about yogurt cultures. We stuck celery ribs in food coloring and watched the color creep up the threads of the stalk, following the same path nutrients traveled. Just as I had done, long ago, I got every child to grow an avocado plant from a pit. In spring, I brought a baby goat to school and let the second graders hold him, then taste the milk his mother made, and the cheese made from the milk.

I often found myself thinking about the person who had inspired me when I was young, Edwin Plank. I liked imagining that one of the children in this school might one day elect to tend a piece of land and grow something on it. And that someday others might, because of our experiences together, keep a cherry tomato plant in a pot on their deck, or cultivate a little patch of parsley and basil. It was a small good thing for the world, I believed, that these traditions would endure.

Near the end of the school year, I invited the third graders to come to Smiling Hills for an end-of-the-year picnic. It was too early yet for strawberries, but Clarice made lemonade and gingersnaps, and we had an early crop of snow peas for them to munch on, and feed bags for a sack race. She wound daffodils around Jester's bridle for the occasion and let the children sit on his back and walked him around the field with them.

As always, I wore my blue jeans for the children's visit, though with a nicer-than-average shirt—fashion never being my interest. But Clarice, who had made a point of being home that day to share the party with me, had put on an old-fashioned-style dress with lace around the neck and a full skirt of a kind she understood that little girls would appreciate. All that morning she'd worked on putting together a scavenger hunt for the children, with clues to take them all around our property.

The children had been brought to our place by a group of parents who'd volunteered to chaperone the excursion. They were just getting out of the cars—racing toward the pen holding our baby goats—when I saw a funny look come over Clarice's face.

"I know that woman," she said, dipping her head in the direction of one of the mothers. The one she indicated was dressed in a pantsuit, with one of those pageboy haircuts, turned under with the help of a blow-dryer. It was the kind of hairstyle that always reminded me of a sorority sister, though she was in her thirties. Next to her was a little girl I recognized, Jennifer, who'd once asked me if she could have a couple of extra scarlet runner bean seeds to take home and plant.

"She's married to a man in my department," Clarice said. "Our impressionism guy."

"I guess you want to make a good impression then," I said, but she was clearly not in a mood for joking.

"I shouldn't have been here," she said. "It was a stupid risk."

"You're being paranoid," I told her. "Nobody's going to care."

We focused on the children then: a garden inspection; the scavenger hunt; three-legged races, followed by a snack. When the last car was pulling away, as we were standing in front of the house waving good-bye, Clarice reached for my hand.

"A very good day," she said, kissing me.

Two weeks later came the vote on Clarice's tenure. That evening she got a call from the department chair.

I was standing next to her as she took in the words, watching her face. I knew right away they'd denied her application.

"I'd like to know the reasons given for the opposition," Clarice said. Her voice was steady as she spoke, though knowing her as well as I did, I could hear what lay beneath the surface of her cool, even tone.

It had been, the department chairman explained, an issue of morality that concerned some members of the department, though not him, personally. One individual in particular had raised a question of sexually inappropriate behavior.

"With a student?" I heard Clarice say. "Was there any suggestion that anything ever happened with a student?" I had heard Clarice's stories concerning "fraternization" between male professors (married, more often than not) and undergraduates. These were rife, and tolerated.

There were no accusations involving students, the department chair assured her. The problem was more a "matter of lifestyle," he said. Though they would be more than happy to see Clarice continuing to teach her two humanities sections and her freshman art history survey, the consensus was that at this point in time, tenure was not an option.

After she put down the phone, we lay on our bed and held each other. She did not cry.

"It was my fault," I said. "You knew it all the time. I was wrong to think you should let people see our real life."

It was too precious, our life. Nobody should have been invited to witness it but us.

"At least they won't try setting me up with eligible bachelors anymore," she said.

She went back to work. We stayed home that summer, instead of making the Yellowstone trip. It would be too difficult to leave Jester and Katie and the goats, anyway, Clarice said. And the strawberries.

# RUTH

## A Family of One's Own

After my marriage to Jim, my love of making art seemed to disappear. The sorrow was gone but I missed the excitement I used to feel, walking into whatever odd little space I'd set up for myself to paint in. The urge to make pictures had left me.

I wanted to be a mother. If the dream of a certain form of passion was over for me, this was what remained—the hunger to create a family I felt truly part of as I never completely had with my own.

I told Jim that I wanted babies. He said that was fine, so did he, though most of all what he wanted was to make me happy, and if having babies would do it, he was ready.

So I took no diaphragm with me on our honeymoon to Cape Cod. And though our sex life already had a certain tepid regularity to it—our lovemaking taking place, typically, at every-other-day intervals—now, with conception in mind, we stepped up the level of activity.

Based on my experience with Ray, I imagined I'd become pregnant right away, so after six months had passed and it didn't happen, I started taking my temperature. I called Jim at work if the number on the thermometer spiked, and he—though diligent about his clients—raced home to get to work on this, his most important job.

Three months, six months, nothing. The memory of the pregnancy I'd relinquished preyed on me, of course. I couldn't help but feel that what was not happening now was punishment for my abortion, and for the arrogance of having ever supposed a woman could choose her moment for motherhood, the way a person would schedule a haircut or a dentist appointment.

A year after we'd started trying, we consulted a doctor. Though twelve months wasn't such a long time to wait, she did all the usual tests.

It turned out that Jim had a low sperm count. "You never know, it could still happen," she said. But she advised us that if we were anxious we should look into the alternatives: A donor. IVF. Adoption.

In the end, we found our daughter in Korea. I was just shy of thirty-three years old.

We flew to Seoul to collect Elizabeth from the orphanage. She was fourteen months old—found abandoned on the street outside the orphanage eight months earlier with nothing but a rag wrapped around her body and her umbilical cord still attached. No record existed of who her mother might have been. I'd be her mother now. That was what mattered.

They took us to a building where all the parents came to sign the papers and pick up their babies. All that morning we'd sat with the other couples on a long wooden bench, waiting for our names to be called, our daughter presented to us.

Every time the door opened, Jim and I leaned forward, ready to spring, but each time they called one of the other couples, until we were the only ones left. Then finally our turn came.

They took us into the room. At the far end, wrapped in a thin blanket, gray from many launderings, our baby girl was held out to us. Jim at my side, I ran to hold her.

She was perfect of course—smooth caramel skin, almond eyes, a thick thatch of shiny black hair, her mouth a rosebud. Placed into the arms of a strange woman she'd never seen before, our daughter did not cry or flinch, only stared at us.

She was, from the first, a person who seemed to accept whatever happened to her next with an air of quiet, noble dignity. She shared a crib with an eighteen-month-old named Ae Sook, who'd been abandoned like herself. The two babies had scarcely been parted for more than a few minutes since that day. They slept curled around each other, closer even than the narrow confines of their crib required. When one cried, so did the other. When one reached out a finger, the other took it.

Then the world changed for her. One day she was Mi Hi—Korean for Beauty and Joy—eating rice from a pair of chopsticks. The next day Ae Sook had disappeared, and Mi Hi was Elizabeth, on a plane to the United States, in the arms of a pale American woman who could not stop stroking her hair, and a kind-faced, anxious-looking man who said, when he took her gingerly on his own lap, "How are you, Elizabeth? I'm your father," as he handed her a saltine. Jim never spoke to a child any differently than he spoke to anyone else.

I looked down at our daughter. Her face looked serious—no smile, but neither did she reveal any sign of distress. Small as she was, she had no words for what she might be feeling, and even if she had, I could not have understood them.

Then we were at Logan Airport. Then in a taxi. Then opening the door to an apartment in Brookline, with a musical mobile circling above Elizabeth's new crib, playing "Rainbow Connection," and, outside the window, the lights of the city of Boston, the neon Citgo sign above Fenway Park.

We gave her pureed peaches and took her in her stroller in the Public Garden to see the swan boats. If she remembered Ae Sook, or the sounds and smells of the orphanage, or the arms of whoever the woman was who'd laid her in the box that day outside its doors, we'd never know. Whatever happened next, she did not protest. We were her family now.

After all that waiting, all I wanted was to hold our daughter, but she was crawling—would have been walking by now, only at the orphanage they'd kept her in that crib so much she was behind schedule.

All my life I'd kept a drawing pencil within reach, though for the last year or two, I'd barely sketched a single image. Now I drew Elizabeth until she grabbed the pencil from my hand. I walked with her for hours, through the streets of Boston, pointing out the names of things, lifting her out of her stroller when we reached a grassy spot. We tossed bread crumbs for the ducks, laid out plastic letters on her blanket, turned the pages of books, making the sounds of all the animals. Pond swimmer that I was—never fully comfortable in man-made bodies of water—I signed our daughter up for swimming classes at the Y. Nights when Jim came home from work, the three of us sat in the kitchen—Elizabeth in her high chair between us, Jim at one end of the table, I at the other. When I looked across the table in his direction, he was always looking at me, smiling. I mostly kept my gaze on our daughter.

It was a safe and cozy life we led back in those days—Jim at the office selling insurance policies, I at home full-time with Elizabeth. No sign of danger on the horizon.

I loved the routine of it, welcomed the demands of naptimes and diaper changes, feedings and walks, weekend excursions—just small ones, nothing elaborate—to the children's museum or the beach, a petting zoo. Saturday night was generally our time to make love—a brief interval that for me was more about affection and the appearance of regularity and keeping up the business of marriage than passionate desire, though the words my husband whispered to me in the dark were those of unending love.

When Elizabeth was old enough, I put her in preschool so I could complete the last class necessary for my art therapy degree, and so she would have other children to play with. This, too, like everything that came before, our daughter accepted with as little sign of disturbance as any other change in her young life so far.

I never minded being home with her. It had been stillness that was hard for me—clear, unspoken-for expanses of time that allowed me to remember things I preferred forgetting. Ray Dickerson, of course. And my mother, with whom I spoke now only on rare occasions by telephone, and saw twice a year—my

Fourth of July weekend birthday, and Christmas, when we made a brief trip to the farm where my parents lived to see them and my four sisters and their husbands on those subdivided parcels our father had carved out.

"There's a piece with your name on it, Ruth," he told me every time Jim and I drove up to New Hampshire. "It wouldn't be such a bad commute for Jim if you settled down here. I bet he could even get himself a bunch of clients up this way."

I missed living in the country. I did not miss my mother. There was no way I would place myself or my daughter within such easy reach of her.

But her power to hurt me had diminished now that I had made a family of my own. Though it seemed to me she had never fully included me in our family—and neither had my sisters—that mattered less now.

I was the mother of a daughter of my own, who bore even less resemblance to me than I did to the other women in my family, and still I could not have felt any more connected to her if my blood ran in her veins. Whatever it was that explained that hard place in my mother's heart reserved for me, I could not fathom. I'd given up trying.

## *Dana*

# Always Complicated

A CAR PULLED up at the farm one morning on a day we had our CLOSED sign up. Two women who looked to be in their fifties got out. It annoyed me a little that they'd come down the driveway in spite of our sign, on a rare day I was going to be alone with Clarice, whose semester hadn't started yet.

It was Connie Plank and a friend she introduced as Nancy. "We heard you were raising goats out here," she said. "We thought it would be a fun excursion to come say hello."

Seeing her there and hearing the oddly insistent tone of her voice, as if she was expecting something from me, I felt a momentary sympathy with Val, for all those times over the years that Connie had shown up this way, unannounced, at whatever house we might be living in at the time, with that air she always managed to convey, as if she was checking us out, to see if we were doing things she might disapprove of.

"I was actually just heading out," I said, not wanting to engage Clarice in this unwelcome visit. "But I'll show you around the garden for a minute if you'd like."

I showed her the strawberries first, then the goats and our cheese-making operation. I told her nothing of the strawberry breeding project I'd undertaken with her husband, and she didn't ask about much.

"My family were cheese makers in Wisconsin," she said. "You probably didn't know that."

No reason why I would have, but I shook my head.

"Cheddar," she said. "My father was one of the biggest suppliers in the Carr Valley for a while. He put us all to work. My sisters and me."

"Interesting," I said, wishing she'd leave.

"I hate cheese," she told me. "Just the smell of it. Bad memories, probably."

Once again, there seemed little to say. Now Connie's friend stepped in.

"It's just so interesting," she said, "the way you and Ruth were born the same day and all. It would be nice if sometime everyone could get together for dinner. Share all those memories."

I could have said "What memories?" but I didn't.

"Tell Ruth hello for me," I said.

"You two always loved playing with those dolls of yours," Connie said. "Though if you ask me, that Mattel company is sending the wrong message to young girls."

"I guess the message didn't take, in my case," I said, indicating my overalls and T-shirt. Though I could have added, if I'd wanted to shock them, that my girlfriend loved dressing herself up like a Barbie sometimes.

"Oh, you look just fine to me," said Connie. "Kind of remind me of my own younger self, actually."

This was not good news.

"I think my daughter's a little put out with me at the moment, if you want to know the truth," Connie said. "She doesn't come home much."

"She's probably just busy," I told her. "I don't see Val that much either." Though in my case, it was more than busyness that kept me from visiting, and I wouldn't have doubted that the same was true for Ruth.

"You know how it is with mothers and daughters," she said. "It's always complicated."

# RUTH

## Seeing Things Differently

I HAD COME back to the farm for a brief visit so Elizabeth could see her grandparents, I said. It was still hard for me to be around my mother, but I didn't want our daughter growing up without extended family and I knew she'd love the farm. That afternoon, my mother was baking cookies with her. My father and I had taken a walk over the fields. He wanted to show me the piece of land he'd selected to be mine and put in my name, if the day ever came I wanted it.

"I chose this one for you because it's closest to the pond, and for how the light hits the trees," he said. "And for the early morning sun. Since you're an early riser like me. You could have a house here someday."

"It's just too hard for me," I said. "Being around Mom."

"Your mother does the best she can," he said. "She sees things differently from you, that's all. But the idea is always to look out for you."

I kept on walking, saying nothing. I wondered if he knew what she had said to Ray Dickerson that day to make him close his heart. I'd never ask.

"After you left us that time," he said, "she found that sketchbook on the table. I reckon that was your idea, leaving it where you did."

"My drawings." The ones I'd made when I was young. When all I had needed to create excitement and joy was to pick up a pencil and draw, and I believed the only limits in a person's life were those of her own imagination.

"I thought those pictures might just give her a heart attack," I said. "Maybe that's what I hoped."

"Some things happened to your mother when she was young, too," he said. "They changed the way she looked at the world. The things some people might enjoy, to her, they made her afraid."

"I didn't ask her to agree with me. It just would have been better if she could have left me alone and just allowed me to be different."

"There's sometimes more to a story than you know, Ruth," he said. "A person might have their reasons for doing what they do, even the things that seem so hurtful. The things she did that you blame her for so harshly might have been done to protect you. It could even be they were done out of love."

"I'm sure she threw that sketchbook in the woodstove, anyway," I said.

"She saved it, actually," he said. "I have to admit that surprised me. She said you sure knew how to draw. She said you reminded her of Val Dickerson that way."

# *Dana*

## A Hard, Tough Place

AFTER CLARICE WAS denied tenure at the university, things changed. She had always been a fundamentally optimistic person, for one thing, and someone who saw the best in people. What happened when that committee judged her as morally unworthy to hold the position of full professor (though they remained happy to see her carry a heavy load of lower-level introductory teaching responsibilities) left her not simply angry but something painful to witness: bitter.

I had loved her softness and her open, trusting way of being with people, even though I was never that way myself. But there was a hard, tough place now in the woman I loved—a cynical edge, as if she was just waiting for the punch line of a joke, the moment when the clown would pop out of the box and yell "Gotcha," and anyone who didn't understand this was a sucker.

"I'll go to work," she said. "But all those years I spent staying late, talking with students, inviting them on trips to Boston to look at art with me—I'm finished with that. I'm strictly nine-to-five from now on."

I might have been happy about that, knowing it meant more time for the two of us, except I saw the effect on Clarice. More often than not now, I'd hear a sharp and brittle tone to her voice as she took off for work in the morning.

"Here we go again," she said. "How many more times am I going to haul out my lecture on Leonardo da Vinci?"

She came home weary, and when I asked about her day, her answers came in single syllables. She'd get off the phone from talking with a student and sigh. "Who do they think I am, anyway? Their mother?"

I again raised the topic of adoption, which she had dropped after the tenure episode. "You don't need a raise for us to afford a child," I said. "We'll work it out."

"I'm probably too old now, anyway," she said. I told her that was crazy. She was only forty-four.

"I don't know if I'm up for it," she said. "I've got this weird numbness in my fingers."

That part was real. She'd seen a doctor, who said the problem came from poor circulation, and advised more exercise. The numbness did not go away.

"We'd be great parents," I whispered, lying with my arms around her in our big brass bed. "There's a child out there who needs a home, and we could give her one. Or him."

"We'd probably be rejected for our lifestyle, anyway," she said.

# RUTH

## Taking Care

It had been one of the things that annoyed me about my mother, that she was always so maddeningly predictable. Then around the time she turned sixty, my father began to observe curious changes in her behavior. Always an early riser, who had gotten up at sunrise to fix coffee for my father and see him off to the barn, she began staying in bed until nine or ten, sometimes sleeping, sometimes just lying there. When my father or one of my sisters would ask if she was sick, she got angry.

"Can't a person take a rest around here without getting the third degree?" she said.

Her cooking changed. Foods she'd prepared all her life—baked beans and corn chowder, anadama bread, chocolate chip cookies, turkey pot pie—started tasting different, and then someone would realize she'd left out a key ingredient like salt or flour, or put them on the stove, or she'd forgotten a dish she'd left on the stove until the smoke alarm went off.

She repeated herself. She left things in odd places—her glasses, her car keys, even her purse—and when she couldn't find them she burst into tears.

One time she started out to the greenhouse to tell my father a salesman was there to talk about a new water pump. Halfway there she evidently forgot where she was going, and headed back.

"What was I supposed to do?" she asked the salesman. "It's all so confusing."

The moment we knew how bad things were came on Christmas, when our family had sat down to turkey dinner, and as usual, my father asked my mother to read the scripture passage. She opened the familiar Bible and put on her glasses, cleared her throat, and began.

But the words she spoke were gibberish. The family was too stunned and shaken to do anything but sit and listen until she finished.

The next week, my father drove my mother to the hospital where her doctor ordered an MRI. They found a tumor called a glioblastoma lodged in her brain. Inoperable. They told us she had six months to live. Eight at most.

At the point of my mother's diagnosis, Jim, Elizabeth, and I were living in Boston. Though we lived an hour's drive from the farm—an hour and a quarter, at most—I rarely called or saw my mother. I spoke to my father on the phone now and then—usually when I knew she'd be out at church. This was how I had learned about my mother's strange behavior and, finally, the reason for it.

An odd thing happened when I realized my mother was dying. I wanted to go home to the farm. Jim was traveling a lot for his insurance business, and I was working part-time, with Elizabeth in preschool. It came to me that we should return to the farm and care for my mother.

Until then, I'd never had any reason to contemplate my mother's death; her sturdy demeanor and unflagging good health had made her seem indestructible. Now I felt that time was slipping away, and I had to grab every second I could, in an attempt to make things right or at least (more accurately) understand why they had gone so wrong. And where always before she had seemed like such a powerful and frightening force in my life, the tumor revealed—for the first time—her frailty. She was no longer strong enough to hurt me as she once had.

When I moved back home, I intended to stay only a couple of months, to help my father and sisters take care of my mother. Once spring came, I could take Elizabeth out around the farm and let her do all the things I used to, back in the days I'd followed my father out to the barn—feeding the chickens, riding on the tractor. I told myself I was making this choice in large part for my daughter's sake—so she could know the farm, and her grandmother.

Now, though, I realized how much I'd missed my home. My father, the land, the farm stand. In an odd way I even missed my mother, as judgmental and cool as she'd always been toward me. As deeply as she'd hurt me.

She was sitting on the porch when I pulled up. Her hair, which had been dark brown when I'd last seen her, was all white. Her body seemed to have shrunk.

"Tall as ever," she said, as I approached, holding Elizabeth. She did not reach to embrace me, though she patted my daughter's head.

"Hi, Grandma," Elizabeth said. She had heard enough of my remarks about my mother to sense ours was not an easy relationship, and so remained, herself, protective and a little wary.

"What are you here for?" she asked. "I thought you were so busy with your job." Art therapy, working with emotionally disturbed children, mostly, and sometimes Vietnam vets and other PTSD survivors.

"All those years you took care of me," I said. "I thought it was time I did the same for you."

So I cooked for her and my father. I took her for walks. I gave her baths and I read to her. My sisters focused on the farm stand, and I stayed close by our mother.

My reasons, in the end, were selfish. I wanted the slate clean. I had to know, once she was dead, that I'd done my best. I didn't want the burden of feeling that I should have done more or differently.

Her decline came with alarming swiftness. Her face changed—this was the steroids—and though I tried to fix her hair the way she had always liked it in the past, she pushed my hand away, leaving a fine halo of thin white hair that spread out in all directions as if she'd put her finger in an electric socket.

I would have expected she'd want us to get her to church somehow, and I had enlisted Jim—who came up from Boston on weekends—to help me do it, but when I offered, she just shrugged.

"I've had enough of that stuff," she said, with a little wave of her hand. Sixty years of living by the Bible, as—her term—"a God-fearing woman." Gone in a flash.

THE TUMOR WAS LODGED IN the portion of the brain that controlled language and speech, which meant that my mother's words sometimes came out garbled, though never beyond recognition. But the harder part was this: the glioblastoma's steadily growing presence was affecting my mother's abilities to control her subconscious thoughts. This had the effect of removing virtually all inhibition.

Suddenly my mother, a woman who had lived her life with the strictest adherence to propriety, was making the most outrageous remarks. Only they weren't outrageous, actually. She was now simply stating, out loud, the kinds of things she must have been thinking all the time, but keeping to herself until now. One central theme of which was sex.

Once she was sitting in the kitchen with me while I fixed dinner for my father and her.

"How often does he like to put his penis in you?" she asked, meaning my husband. "Do you actually enjoy it?"

I might have worried how to respond, except there was seldom a need to. My mother kept on talking.

"I never liked the act of intercourse myself, but maybe your father wasn't doing it right," she said. "I always wondered what the fuss was all about. I bet that Burt Reynolds did some things differently, when he did it with Dinah.

"Don't get me wrong," she said. "Your father is a good husband. The only hard part was him wanting me to let him in all the time and pound away at me, like some old barn door slamming, when all I wanted was to be left alone."

Another time I was making biscuits, rolling out the dough and cutting the circles out and setting them on the tray to bake. Elizabeth ran through the room, in search of a peanut butter sandwich.

"It's good you never had to worry about her hanging on your breasts all the time," my mother said. "I never could understand women wanting to do that kind of thing."

Though I would have loved to be one of them, of course. If I had been able to give birth, I would never have missed nursing my baby.

"I never liked my breasts particularly," she said. "They just made trouble. But your father was always after me to let him do things to them.

"He could never get enough, you know," she said. "Your father. I suppose you know he was hung like a horse, as the saying goes.

"Then again," she said, her face darkening, "maybe it was my own father that ruined everything." This was my Wisconsin grandfather she was talking about, the one we never visited, news of whose death, when I was little, had been received with barely a response. I sat there holding my daughter, taking in my mother's words, feeling sick.

"I wanted to be a good wife to your father," she said. "In the beginning I even thought I might enjoy it with Edwin. But from the first time we did it, all I could think about every time we'd start was my father."

I shifted my daughter on my lap. I was holding her tightly, less because she needed that than for the measure of comfort it offered me. I wanted to ask my mother to explain, but I wasn't sure I wanted to know what she might say if I pursued the question either.

"They wondered why I never wanted to go back to Wisconsin until after he died," she said, sounding angry now. "Who would? If I never saw that fucker again, that would be too soon."

All those years of reading out loud to us from her Bible, never missing church, washing our mouths out with soap if we said "darn" or "hell." My new mother—the one I got when she was dying—had a mouth like a drunken sailor.

"Then he was dead, and I thought I could finally talk to my sisters about it," she said. "Rode the bus all the way to Milwaukee with my girls. Get to the depot, my sister says, 'Just one thing I want to make clear. We're not opening up any old Pandora-type boxes, Connie. Pop's dead and gone. We're leaving well enough alone.'

"I just wanted to ask my mother why she let it happen," my mother said. "A girl's mother is supposed to protect her."

I could have said plenty here. Did she think it was protecting me, going all the way to British Columbia to confront the one man I ever really loved and take me away from him?

How she had accomplished this I had never understood—how she convinced a man who said I was the love of his life, too, to say good-bye to me. How a woman who believed that life began with conception could have taken her daughter to an abortion clinic. This she had managed. God only knew how. Here was my last chance to ask her, but I couldn't.

Even now sometimes, as I was laying her naked body on the sheet and running the warm sponge over her skin to bathe her, memories would assault me, and I would have to fight the small, mean impulse to scrub a little too hard, or force the brush through her hair without slowing down to untangle the knots. The urge to inflict pain—registered, though resisted—came to me when I remembered my mother beside me in the waiting room, filling out the forms because I was crying too hard to do it myself. The nurse handing me the gown. Feet in the stirrups and my mother saying, "I know what's best for you."

I saw the taxi to the airport. The long flight home. Letters to British Columbia, returned unanswered, no forwarding address. Even when she was on her deathbed, I blamed my mother for this and burned to ask her, *How could you have done it?*

GIVEN ALL THE OTHER THINGS my mother said those last few months, it's surprising that she said as little as she did about Val Dickerson. For thirty years it seemed as if one of her main focuses in life had been this other family with the daughter born the same day as I, but at the end of her life, my mother seemed barely to think about the Dickersons, though one day and one only she spoke of Val.

"I do wonder what it would be like to have been pretty, like her," she said. "Men always nipping at her heels, no doubt. You can't really blame a fellow, if he wants to lift the skirts of a woman like that and give her a whirl. Those long legs and all that blond hair. Down below, too, no doubt. I suppose you're the same."

This was how it went with my mother now. An endless monologue whose contents made me get the queasiness you might feel turning over a rotting log and discovering a mass of slithering insects and worms—so long hidden from the light—scrambling out from under. For hours I sat beside her, grateful for those times my daughter came to settle in my lap, where she fell asleep sometimes. After all my mother's dark commentary on the human condition, it comforted me to hear the sound of Elizabeth quietly snoring in my arms.

"When all's said and done," she said, "what does it really matter, anyway? How long does the whole sex thing last? Five minutes? Ten maybe. The part that matters isn't getting the baby, it's raising her. That's what I did. More than anything in the world I wanted to be a good mother."

"You did the best you could, Mother," I told her. Even at such a moment, there was a limit to how much I could reassure her or pretend she'd done a good job. I could feel a tight, hard place in me that, even in the company of a dying woman, withheld the thing she wanted most to hear.

It was winter when her symptoms sent her to the doctor for tests and early spring when she was diagnosed—crocuses pushing through the last of the snow. By the time the lilacs bloomed her walking had become unsteady. "I hope I'm still around for strawberries," she said.

One of the things she asked me during those last weeks was if my birthday sister knew that she was sick. After so many years it still irritated me to hear her asking about Dana.

"We could call her if you wanted, Connie," my father said. He was sitting at her bedside for a change, drinking coffee, putting in a rare daytime appearance. It was hard for my father to see my mother this way. I would stand at the window sometimes now and watch him in the field, staying out even later than usual, circling the rows until the last rays of sunlight were gone. I knew he didn't want to return to the house. It was the only summer I never heard him whistling.

Nobody ever did call Dana Dickerson, but as it turned out, she came by anyway, just around our Fourth of July birthdays. My mother had hung on until then, though just barely. By the last couple of weeks she was sleeping most of the time, barely speaking anymore—which was a relief, given the kinds of observations she'd been making lately.

Dana was living not far away then, on a farm of her own, raising organic greens and goats. She maintained the ritual of paying a visit to the farm stand during strawberry season, even though she now grew strawberries herself, just to discuss issues of farming with my father, evidently. Speaking with one of my nieces out at the farm stand, she'd learned about my mother, and asked if she could come up to the house and pay her respects.

Dana arrived in the company of a very attractive woman. She herself dressed more like a man than a woman now. It was clear, seeing the two of them, that they were a couple.

I took this news in with a certain mean-spirited pleasure. Now that it was revealed that Dana Dickerson was a lesbian she had finally done something even my mother, for whom Dana represented everything that was desirable in a daughter, would surely find unacceptable. My birthday sister would no longer be the daughter my mother would have wanted. I wondered if my mother would be aware enough to understand.

They didn't sit down—Dana and this woman she had come with. They made no particular effort to conceal the fact that they were a pair. They were holding hands, as I recall. Dana was studying my mother's face. Her skin was stretched tight and her eyes were closed.

"You always raised the best strawberries here, Connie," she said. "I had to make sure Clarice got to taste them. My partner."

My mother opened her eyes and looked at the two of them—Dana first, then the other woman.

"You turned out homosexual?" she said. "Knock me over with a feather."

Here it comes, I thought: the moment I'd waited for all my life, when my mother would finally see Dana Dickerson as a flawed woman and appreciate, at last, the daughter she'd been given, me.

"I can't say I understand what you girls do, or how you go about it," she said. "But if you ask me, it makes a lot of sense. Who needs a man and all that complicated apparatus they're always showing off? I'm guessing you two have yourselves a nice, sweet time together. Softer skin."

Dana, though we had not prepared her for my mother's behavior, seemed to take her words with a matter-of-fact interest. Her partner, Clarice, stroked my mother's hand.

"We're very happy together," Clarice said.

"Well, isn't that nice," my mother said. "I'll take that to my grave."

One other group of people with whom we had only the briefest dealings over those last months were my mother's Wisconsin relatives. Her parents were long dead, but there were two sisters still living near their old cheese operation.

"We thought you'd want to know," my sister Naomi began, when she finally placed the call.

I did not hear the voice on the other end of the line, but the conversation was brief. When my sister put down the phone, she had looked shaken.

"Her sister said that was a shame," Naomi told me. "She said it was too bad but they were never close, and to send the obituary when it came out, for their scrapbook."

THE LAST TIME I SPOKE with my mother was the day she died. She spent almost all day sleeping by that point, but as I was sitting there—I was drawing her—she had opened her eyes. My sisters were making arrangements at the funeral home and my father was resting, so I was alone in the room when it happened.

"You were a good daughter, in the end," she said. "Not the one I was expecting. But things didn't turn out so bad."

She was buried in the family plot, which was set in a grove of birches behind the house next to one of our irrigation ponds. She had rows of Planks to keep her company—Plank men, and their wives, the children who hadn't made it through infancy or childhood, and the ones, like my father, who had grown up to tend the farm after their father's passing, and then passed it on to the next generation. Standing around the hole in the earth—it was a rainy day, early fall, hurricane season but thankfully there were no big storms this year—I watched my father sink his shovel in the earth and raise a spadeful of dirt to scatter over her coffin. One more planting, out of season. My sisters wept and I wished I could, but no tears came.

AFTER MY MOTHER'S DEATH, I told Jim I wanted to move back to the farm and build a house there, on that piece of land my father had been saving for me all this time. As usual, my husband went along with my wishes.

The place we built was nothing fancy—a couple of bedrooms and a little art studio for me, with a sunny kitchen that looked out over the irrigation pond where my father and I used to swim. I wanted to help look after him now, I told Jim, but there was more to it. My roots in that place had reached deeper than I'd known.

I got a part-time job running a kids' art class, and a second job as an art therapist in Concord, the capital, working with emotionally disturbed adults and men suffering from post-traumatic stress disorder, Vietnam veterans, mostly. Jim would keep his insurance business outside of Boston. Though this would mean an hour-long commute for him, he didn't argue.

We had a comfortable life, then. Our daughter loved being on the farm, and though my father had once commented how odd it was that first Americans went to Korea to fight, and the next thing you knew they were adopting babies there, he adored Elizabeth. She spent many hours doing chores with her grandfather, riding next to him on his tractor when he plowed, tending the hills of pumpkins and snipping the heads off zinnias. As he had done with me, so many years before, he taught my daughter how to renovate the strawberry beds after the season was over, selecting the five strongest daughter plants, spacing them evenly around the mother plant, like the rays of the sun, and letting them take root for the next season.

"Daughters," he told her as they dug. "Nothing better than a good daughter."

I worked long hours but I liked how I spent my days. Mornings I taught the elementary-school kids in town, making collages and clay animals and potato prints, which made it easier to locate patience for the men and women I worked with at the state hospital. It was a long way from my days as a young artist, working as I did now in a basement room in Concord, moving among the tables of people so profoundly depressed or damaged that in some cases I had never heard them speak.

But—maybe in part because they were unrestrained by the conventions of what was considered regular society—my clients at the mental hospital made beautiful things, painted with a kind of freedom and expressiveness you wouldn't find in a class of so-called normal people. A portrait of a woman made by one of my students at the hospital would not simply fill the paper but spill over its edges—eyes boring into you, colors applied with bold, slashing strokes that practically vibrated with feeling. One man in my group liked to paint portraits of baseball players from the 1960s, with all their statistics forming a border around the edges of the canvas. One woman only made paintings of babies; another made a self-portrait using matchsticks.

Many times, surveying the artwork of my students in that little class of mine, I'd imagine how it would be if their pieces were hung in some downtown New York City gallery—how critics might rave about them, the big prices they'd summon. Occasionally I'd feel a stab of something like jealousy that here in this sad little room, with a bunch of people so heavily medicated they barely spoke, and shuffled when they walked, art was being made of a kind I myself no longer seemed able to produce. Sometimes, truthfully, I almost envied my students their madness and their capacity to lose themselves in the art they made, as I once had. Perhaps the turmoil that afflicted them actually made them better artists.

Somewhere along the line—after I was brought back against my will from Canada—I had lost my passion for drawing and painting, or for anything else, with the exception of my child. But I was a good teacher, and there was a surprising amount of reward in that.

In my life at home there was less art than craft, I thought. Jim and I were good parents—kind to each other, devoted to our daughter. He worked hard taking care of his insurance customers and on weekends when we weren't occupied with Elizabeth, he played a lot of golf. We had settled into a life with each other in which virtually the only shared endeavor was our daughter, though he would have welcomed the opportunity to shower on me the kind of love we both gave to Elizabeth. I just didn't want it from him.

We lived less like husband and wife, it seemed, than affectionate brother and sister. I told myself there were worse things a person could say about her life than that.

## *Dana*

# How Things Happen

IN 1977 PRESIDENT Carter had declared an amnesty for all Americans who had left the United States for Canada and elsewhere during the Vietnam draft. For a while after I heard the news I kept hoping I'd hear from my brother, but no call came. I called Val to ask if she'd heard anything, but it was unlikely that my brother would have found her even if he'd wanted to because she'd moved so many times by then. She was in Virginia at that point, doing occasional portraits for rich people—of their children, mostly—and augmenting her income with greeting card designs. When I mentioned the amnesty, she seemed not to have heard me.

With the exception of that one odd period in which she'd protested the war, Val didn't pay attention to the news of the world, or news of her own children for that matter. The rare times we'd talk, it was usually about her painting and pottery or her yoga or some new eating regimen she'd hit on—vegan, macrobiotic. I told her about Clarice, though she asked no questions about our life together. Once, though—out of character, for a person who seemed so unaware of any individual besides herself—she told me she'd heard Ruth Plank was living on the farm again. Someone—probably Edwin—had evidently told her Ruth had gone to art school, and that interested her.

"Funny how these things turn out," she said. "You ending up raising goats. And Ruth's painting. Do you ever wonder how things happened that way?"

I hadn't, but now, thinking of my brother, I said, "I wonder if she's heard from Ray." I never knew the particulars but I'd been aware something had happened between them once.

"Your brother's off in his own world," she said. "I don't expect to see him again."

"You don't know that," I said. "Everything's changed now. He's free to come home."

"It's not necessarily the government's say-so that matters," she said. "It's what goes on in his own head. Your brother burned his bridges with us a long time ago."

"He could be married, for all we know," I said. "You could be a grandmother. I could be an aunt. Don't you want to know if he's got a family?"

"You know the funny thing?" she said. "He called me once from a pay phone somewhere in Canada. He said there was going to be a baby."

All these years, and this was the first I'd heard of that. "Then what?" I asked her.

"Then one more call," Val told me. "He said it didn't work out. He was crying. That was the last time I ever heard from him."

# RUTH

## Road Trip

IT WAS HAYING season when my mother died, and maybe because of that, my father had little time to grieve for her, though he must have thought about her plenty, all those hours on the tractor moving in circles, mowing the fields.

We were experiencing a low-rain summer again, so he was occupied all that July moving the irrigation pipe. He still did a lot of that heavy work himself, though often now my sisters' children helped out, along with his longtime worker, Victor Patucci—whose title was foreman now.

"Victor's always after me to retire and let him run this place," he said one night, coming in from the field after a particularly long day in which he'd stayed out, watering, until the last hours of sun were gone. "But there's something about that fellow that rubs me the wrong way."

As rough as things had been for my father ever since the barn burned down, he wouldn't have known what to do in the Florida retirement community whose brochure Victor showed him one time, or on the senior citizens' cruise to Bermuda. My father needed Victor, but he had never cottoned to Victor's ideas concerning how our place should run. Maybe it was true that we'd boost efficiency and increase profits if we cut back on all the little specialty items we grew and gave up on growing things like zinnias and peas—crops he loved, that weren't particularly profitable—to focus on volume and what Victor called "the entertainment factor" of the farm that could turn it into a real moneymaker.

But tending the land had never been just about making money for my father. Not even mostly about making money.

"If all we had to do was cultivate plants and we never had to worry about selling anything," he sometimes said, "life would be perfect."

But for Victor, the bottom line was profit. "He's a bean counter, not a farmer," my father said. "The only thing that fellow likes to see growing is his bank account."

If my mother had been alive, she would have sat with him all those nights after work, working on a quilt while she listened to his reports on how the corn was looking and what kind of a tomato crop they might expect. As it was, the evenings must have been lonely for him. Even with my sisters and me dropping by when we could, bringing dinners over, he came in from the fields so late that he ate most of his meals alone.

Come fall, after the frost, he was restless. Once pumpkin season was done, there was little work remaining, and he'd take walks along the road, throwing sticks for his dog, Sam, or spend hours playing solitaire. My daughter, Elizabeth, used to stop by and play hearts with him, but she was busy with homework most nights now, and on weekends she visited her friends. The other grandchildren were no different.

"I wish those darned seed catalogs would get here," he said, but it was only November. He had another two months to wait before they arrived and he could get to work on next season's orders.

Sometime in early December my father announced he was planning a trip. "I thought I'd pay a visit to Valerie Dickerson," he said. "Her being an old friend and all."

I hadn't seen Val for years, and didn't even know where she lived anymore, though it would have been easy enough to find out from Dana, and probably that's how my dad had learned she'd moved to Virginia. She was making pottery, he said.

"That's a long drive," I told him.

"I always liked a road trip," he said, though apart from those spring vacation pilgrimages to check up on the progress of Dana Dickerson's childhood, I doubted he'd ever taken one.

"When did you ever go on a road trip, Dad?" I asked him.

"There's my point. About time," he said. "I can take in some historical sights. See the country."

The day before he set out, he visited the barbershop in town instead of asking my sister Sarah to trim what was left of his hair. When I stopped by that evening to check on him, I noticed a small package on the table, gift-wrapped, with a ribbon.

"A person doesn't want to show up for a visit empty-handed," he said. He'd bought Val a pin depicting the New Hampshire state flower, the purple lilac.

He set out before sunrise. For once in his life, he did not wear his overalls. He was wearing a new pair of jeans, with the creases pressed, and a collared shirt with a tie. He had his usual L.L. Bean jacket, naturally, on account of the cold. Standing on the front porch to see him off, I kissed him good-bye and smelled aftershave.

He had made arrangements for us to take care of Sam for a full week, and my mother's African violets, figuring he might want to stay down in Virginia for a while, checking things out, particularly considering this trip constituted the first vacation he had ever taken in his life.

He was home seventy-two hours after he left. I heard his car pull up the road past midnight. He must have driven straight through back from Richmond, to save on a motel, but even so, given how long it would have taken him to get down there, he could not have spent any time at his destination.

The next morning I stopped by to ask how things had gone with Val. He was sitting with his coffee at the kitchen table, but he didn't want to talk about it much.

"How did she like the pin?" I asked. If he heard the question, he ignored it. He was stirring the cream in his coffee, looking out the window to the fields below our house.

"She got married," he said. "One of those fellows that trades in stocks and what have you. Suit and tie, the whole bit. You know how she met him? He hired her to paint a picture of his dog after he died. Next thing you know, they were hitched.

"They asked me in for lemonade," he said, "but I said I was on a tight deadline. Busy man, that's me."

My father was reaching into a drawer now for something, as he told me this. When in doubt, apply WD-40 oil to a hinge, one of his mottoes in life.

"She's still a beautiful woman, though," he said. "That part didn't change."

## *Dana*

# A Deadly Ticking

IN 1991, A food columnist for the *New York Times* picked up a wheel of our Tomme goat cheese at a farmers' market in Portsmouth and wrote a column about artisan cheese makers, with a picture of me and our best milker, Andromeda, next to the little flower stand Clarice still kept stocked with bouquets of flowers for sale on the honor system. Within a week our mail-order business had doubled. I told Clarice that come November, when our goats stopped producing milk for the winter, we should take a vacation. We could finally afford to visit Italy and see the paintings she loved. Eat fresh pasta. Drink wine with our lunch.

"You know what I'd really like best," she said. "To take that trip out west we always talked about. See some buffalo. The Grand Tetons. Yellowstone. I bet it's amazing in the winter."

But by fall she was having problems with her health. The numbness Clarice had noticed in her toes and fingers, off and on for a year now, was getting more pronounced, and so was the problem with her leg. I noticed it when we rode our bikes—the way she'd walk hers up the hills. She didn't talk about it, but I could tell she was worried.

We were making dinner one night when I handed her a bottle of wine vinegar for the salad dressing. She tried to open it and couldn't. The bottle slipped from her hands.

The doctor we went to this time practiced in Boston; his specialty was neurology. He ordered tests. When the results came back, he called Clarice.

"You should come in," he said. I would have accompanied her regardless, but he told her, "Bring your partner."

It was ALS, amyotrophic lateral sclerosis, a degeneration of the motor neurons of the central nervous system otherwise known as Lou Gehrig's disease.

Though neither of us was the type to follow medical news, we had both heard of this one. First would come minor motor control issues, leading to gradual paralysis of the limbs, followed by swallowing problems, then breathing problems requiring a respirator. Somewhere along the line even speech would become impossible. Eventually, the entire nervous system shut down. This was when death occurred, usually within three to five years.

"The brain does not lose capacity," the doctor told us. "Only the body does." Meaning Clarice would remain Clarice, trapped inside her body unable to move or speak, or scream.

He ran through a number of treatment options, but he made clear that none of them was designed to do more than manage the disease. This was a condition for which the diagnosis remained terminal. Later, he said, he could go into more of the particulars with us, but we probably needed to be alone with the information for a while first.

I drove home faster than usual, with a certain crazed thought that if we died now we could prove wrong the physician's assurance that ALS would kill Clarice. If we died now, I could die with her.

"Slow down," she said. "There's ice on the road." Her voice was steady. She put a hand on my shoulder.

The highway unspooled before us, all the long way home to Maine. I let myself pretend someone was chasing us. Lou Gehrig, rounding the bases, headed our way. If we could just get back to the farm—goats, dog, woodstove, brass bed—before he tagged us out (rules of the game jumbled here, like so much else), we'd be home free.

"Let's not talk about this until tomorrow," she said as we pulled up in front of the house in the darkness. "Let's go to bed."

FOR ALL THE TIMES WE'D made love in that bed, all the sweetness we'd known there, the two of us had never spent a night like that one.

She sat on the bed and let me undress her—something I'd done many times before, though this particular night the motions of unbuttoning her blouse, slipping it from her shoulders, unhooking her fine, lacy brassiere, all took on a different kind of meaning. I know she was thinking what I was: that soon the day would come when I would undress her every night, not for lovemaking only, but by necessity.

I got on my knees in front of her. I cupped my hands under her small, firm buttocks, pulling the zipper down, unzipped her skirt and slipped it around her hips and past them until it fell to the ground. Still at her feet, looking up, I rolled her tights down her thighs, her knees—she hated her bony knees, but I thought they were beautiful—and peeled them off her, as if she were some rare and exotic fruit over which layers of pod and leaf, skin and shell, must first be stripped away before a person could suck the juices out of her.

But not yet. First I massaged her feet—the place the terrible numbness had begun. One by one, I took her toes in my mouth. I used to laugh at her for her love of nail polish—the dozens of bottles that lined her dresser, along with all the other things she loved that had never mattered to me: combs, clips, rings, pins, ribbons, feathers. I loved to give her jewelry, though all I wore was a watch. I heard it now, the deadly ticking.

Suddenly every single thing about her was precious: her anklebone; the tiny scar from a childhood bike accident; the spot behind her knee where, when I moved my tongue a certain way, laughter came out of her, in the voice of the little girl she must have been once, and became again when I touched her there.

Still in my dress pants and sweater—city clothes—I laid her on the bed as a person might lay a child who fell asleep in the backseat after a long car ride home. Her body had gone limp, as if she was trying out how it would be in the not-so-distant future. It was like she was practicing a new way of being, so unlike her old familiar self that used to climb all over me, caressing and kneading, wrestling and scratching, licking, kissing, biting, stroking, kissing more.

"Come back to me," I whispered to Clarice.

"I never left," she said. "I'm always here."

One inch at a time—one centimeter—I made my way over her body. At certain places, well known to us both from other nights and days, I lingered.

"Remember this?"

"Nova Scotia."

"Acadia National Park. Camping in the rain."

"The night we brought the rototiller home."

"New York City. The Monet show. Our hotel after."

I had taken my clothes off too now, so I could feel her skin against every inch of me, and most of all, so she could feel mine. All the small gifts we took for granted were departing. We counted all the places we loved: fingers, elbows, ears, neck, belly. We counted them one by one, as a tourist might the great museums of Paris or the rock formations of Yosemite.

We did not speak, or feel the need for words, and this too served as some kind of small comfort. Even when words are gone, I wanted her to know, I will hear your voice. When you can no longer speak, neither will I. (Though just the opposite happened, it turned out. More than ever, when we reached that point, she needed words from me. It rested with me, then, to speak not only for myself but for her, too.)

I kissed her all the places that men, making love to women, are unlikely to think of or notice. Not simply her breasts and nipples, but under them. The little hollow spot above her collarbone, where, if she were lying down, and it was raining, the rain could actually collect. I had measured once—the scientist in me, again—how much liquid that place could hold. On Clarice, with her fine bone structure, it would hold a bottle-capful, almost. First pour it in. Then drink.

I kissed her earlobes, forehead, the fold between thumb and forefinger, and all the other folds between all the other fingers too. The base of the spine, and each bone over it. Elbow, wrist, belly button, armpit.

"Never put deodorant there," she used to tell me, even though I worked long hours in the sun and came in sweaty, days on our farm. "I want your real smell on me."

Now I drank in hers.

Only after honoring all those other places did I visit the one where we always ended up. The dark, hidden spot in her where treasure lay. I lingered there longest of all. Far away, I heard her voice—a low purring first, then a sound like newborn baby animals rooting for mother's milk. Then moaning.

Hours had passed since that terrible moment in the doctor's office, and still we had not yet wept over his news, but now the two of us could cry. The sound of our voices filled the house then. The voice that came out of me—out of us both—was one I'd never heard before and never want to hear again.

It was a pure, clear animal wail—two voices, raised in a single long cry that filled the night and went on a long time.

Then we slept.

# RUTH

## The Darnedest Thing

WE FOUND OUT Val Dickerson had died from a message left on our answering machine for my father. He was living on his own, more or less, but the forgetfulness he'd been experiencing for a number of years had now reached the point where a caretaker was needed to spell us in between the hours each of us put in babysitting him. If you left him by himself now, there was no telling what he would do. He might go out to the barn and start up the tractor, never mind if it was winter and the ground frozen. Or he'd head out to the greenhouse and decide this was the day to get a few dozen flats of Early Girl tomato seedlings started. One late November day, long past frost, I found him wandering in the cornfield.

"I don't understand what happened," he said. "The Silver Queen has disappeared. We should have had twenty rows here. Someone's been robbing us blind."

Of course he no longer farmed by this point. Though the title to our now heavily mortgaged farm still belonged to my father, a couple of years earlier we'd leased our land to Victor Patucci.

The afternoon the message came saying Val died, he had been watching television. It was the early days of Oprah, for whom he seemed to possess a surprising affection.

"That girl may be a Negro," he said. "But she sure makes sense."

I was unloading groceries when I pushed the blinking message button—surprised that anyone would have called. After my mother's death, my father no longer attended church or got involved in community affairs the way he had for so many years. Most of his friends, if they weren't dead, were old, like him. Those who could spent the winters in Florida.

The voice on the machine was unfamiliar. He introduced himself as David Jenkins, the husband of an old friend of ours, Valerie Dickerson. He was calling from Rhode Island.

"I thought you should know, Valerie passed away suddenly last weekend. She wasn't sick. I found her in her art studio. She must've been painting when it happened."

I set down the carton of eggs I'd been holding, shaken not so much from the news of Val as I was by the way just hearing her name had conjured a memory of Ray. I saw his long hair falling over me. I could almost taste strawberries on my tongue.

I was long married by this point, and unexpectedly pregnant with our son, Douglas—a full ten years after we'd adopted Elizabeth. But even then, a week and a half away from my due date, with my back sore and my ankles swollen and my cheeks splotchy, just thinking of Ray Dickerson caused my face to grow hot.

Jim and I had been married almost sixteen years. The night Doug was conceived had been the first time we'd made love in close to a year, and we'd never conceived a child even when we were trying hard, which was probably the reason I'd felt no need for birth control.

After all our efforts to have a baby when we were younger, I had assumed it would never happen. Punishment for the abortion, I secretly believed. And here I was, pregnant for the first time at age forty-two, I said. Pregnant for the second time, actually, but that was something I never spoke of.

Now came the news that Val Dickerson was dead. Thinking about her and about Ray made me forget about my father, who was sitting in his chair a few feet away from the answering machine, facing the television. What roused me was a faint, not quite human sound coming from his chair, like an animal in distress.

I looked over at my father then, hunched in his chair, the afghan my mother knitted long ago covering his thin knees. For the first time in my life—the death of my mother no exception to this—I saw my father crying.

As well as I could for a woman at my stage in pregnancy, I knelt in front of him and put my hand on his.

"I'm sorry, Dad," I told him. "I guess you heard the message. You remember Val, right?"

Watching his face, I saw that this was a ridiculous question, though there were plenty of people in our life—my sisters' husbands, for example, and the grandchildren, including our eleven-year-old, Elizabeth—whose names he no longer knew. But the news of Val Dickerson's death had evidently touched a place in him where memory remained, like a patch of soil the tractor has missed, where a few dry stalks of last summer's crops still stand in their withered rows, the soil not turned over.

"She was some kind of woman," he said, fingering the afghan. "Tall."

"One time they drove all the way from Vermont to buy strawberries," I said, still thinking about Ray. As much as the news appeared to have shaken my father, it had produced a strong effect in me, too. "And then there were those crazy trips we used to make to visit them. All those hours in the car playing I Spy and looking for license plates of unusual states, all for a few glasses of lemonade and a cup of instant coffee. George was hardly ever there and I never got the feeling Val was all that happy to see us."

"Your mother never got along with Valerie Dickerson," my father said. The words came out with surprising force.

"But she always wanted to stay in touch. It was the darnedest thing."

He was silent. On the TV screen, Oprah had put her hand on the shoulder of a woman who had just announced she had an eating disorder. "Let it out," Oprah said. "It feels good to talk about it."

"I WONDER WHAT DANA DICKERSON is doing now," I said. Only after I said it did I realize that this was the very remark my mother had always made—one I'd always hated for the message it conveyed, that the life of a girl we barely knew merited so much more interest than my own. Now here I was doing the same thing.

"She liked making pictures," my father was saying. He had taken a handkerchief out of his pocket. He blew his nose. "She had a nice smell about her."

"Remember Ray?" I said to him. I had not spoken of him for years but here in this room, with a man for whom past and present had melded into one thick fog, it seemed I could safely speak the unutterable name. Some part of me wanted to say it out loud, just to feel the sound of it in my mouth. With my father as he was now I could have said anything.

*He fed me strawberries with his tongue when I was thirteen.*

*We lived in a cabin in Canada once. I thought he was my destiny. We were going to have a baby.*

"Yellow hair," said my father. "Too bad you didn't know her."

LATER, I CALLED VAL'S HUSBAND, David. At the point she died, he told me, she had been living in Rhode Island, where she had settled with this new husband, the businessman with the golden retriever portrait. At the time of her death she was teaching yoga and taking night classes at the Rhode Island School of Design. She must have been close to seventy by this point, I figured. Hard to imagine, of the woman who had always seemed to me so young and beautiful.

Given what I gathered from the last news I'd heard about Ray, years ago—that there was no news, actually, that even his sister didn't know his whereabouts—it appeared unlikely he'd be at the funeral, and this was a relief. On the one hand, I longed to see him again. Still, if I allowed myself to imagine he might actually show up at the service, I hated the thought of Ray seeing me as I was now. Some women look beautiful, pregnant, but I only looked fat.

In the end, I couldn't attend the funeral as I'd planned. That morning, the contractions began. By afternoon, I was in labor. But my sisters made the trip.

## *Dana*

# Bound to Leave

AFTER WE GOT the news about Clarice, nothing else seemed to matter. I milked the goats and filled the cheese molds with fresh curds and kept the strawberries weeded and picked and the farm stand stocked, though I gave up on those bouquets of zinnias we used to sell by the side of the road. It was too much effort, and what was the point?

As for Clarice, she pretended for a while that nothing had happened, and since she wanted to inhabit the state of denial for a while, I let her. Soon enough it would not be possible.

I marched along then, keeping up a show of normal life. When the call came from Val's husband in Rhode Island—a man I barely knew—to say Val had died, I had been typing Clarice's notes for a humanities lecture. Her fingers no longer worked well enough to do this herself.

I would not have expected the news of Val's death to hit me hard. By the time she died, Val had been so nearly absent from my life for so long that her complete departure from earth was not likely to make much of a difference, or so I believed. I'd go to her service, of course—relieved that there was someone else now to take care of the arrangements—but Val was less like a parent to me than a distant and frequently maddening acquaintance. Though we were never close, I had made a point of calling her once a week, but I hardly ever visited.

The last time I'd seen her she'd seemed the same as ever. She was a little vague and dreamy, preoccupied with her artwork as usual. When I'd mentioned our goats, she responded by telling me about a class she was taking at RISD extension in raku pottery and a trip she and David were going to take to Quebec.

Then she was dead, and once I got the news, a surprising thing happened. I was hit by a strange and terrible wave of grief, for all the things we'd never got around to talking about. My relationship with Clarice, for starters.

I never pictured her having a hard time with that. Val was not the type of person who would have been shocked by the idea of two women loving each other. If anything, I might have risen in her estimation for the originality of my choice in a partner. One of the things that always bothered Val about me was, I suspect, what she took to be my conventionality, my complete lack of an artistic spirit.

My not being an artist was true enough. But keeping to convention was never my problem, as Clarice could have attested. If you wanted conventional, you didn't have to look any further than the five Plank sisters—the oldest four, anyway, who, to my great surprise, showed up at Val's service, held at the yoga studio.

I had told Clarice about that old "birthday sister" routine Connie Plank had insisted on promoting all those years and the uncomfortable and pointless visits their family used to make to see us. And now here came the Planks again, marching into our life as if to reassert a connection I'd never understood in the first place.

These were women who believed in following the rules all right. They filled the better part of a whole row at the yoga center in nearly identical navy blue suits, each with a strand of pearls around her neck. All of them wore their hair in roughly the same short, neatly blow-dried style. Their bodies were the same shape, more or less—short and thick around the waist, with surprisingly large and well-developed calves, for women who did not appear to spend time in a gym.

All those other times, occasions I stopped by the farm stand, the only Planks I'd seen on those visits had been Connie and Edwin, and occasionally Ruth, so this was the first time I'd seen them since we were children. Now when I did, what I registered first was how out of place they seemed in a roomful of Val's yoga students and artist friends—how unlikely it was that they'd be here at all, with Tibetan prayer flags fluttering over their heads and a tape playing Native American flute.

I wore pants to the service. (Dress pants, topped by a nice blouse and a suit jacket.) The Plank women looked like they stepped out of the pages of a Talbots catalog. But if you stripped away the surface things—makeup, clothes, jewelry, wedding rings—it became clear: the four sisters bore a startling resemblance to me.

I was not the only one who noticed. Clarice, spotting them coming in, had assumed these must be relatives of mine I'd mysteriously failed to mention in our many years together.

"They're Planks," I said. The only one missing was the only one to whom I bore absolutely no resemblance whatsoever, Ruth.

OVER THE YEARS, VAL HAD compiled a list of songs she wanted to have played at her funeral. She had the unexpected foresight to entrust the list to her husband, and now the number was so great the musical selections alone took over an hour.

After the flute music came Neil Young's "Cinnamon Girl" and Van Morrison's "Brown Eyed Girl" (though my mother's eyes were blue, I knew she felt the words applied to her) and Paul McCartney and Cat Stevens and Jackson Browne. Mostly these were very romantic or sentimental songs celebrating some woman or other who possessed traits my mother must have seen as similar to her own, but there were other surprising musical selections too—Etta James singing "I'd Rather Go Blind" and James Brown, singing "I Feel Good," followed, strangely, by a selection from Enya.

The musical prelude went on for nearly an hour—long enough for the four Plank sisters and me to study each other, which we did.

Because of how we were seated, the sisters' primary view of me was of the back of my head, and I could practically feel the combined gaze of four pairs of eyes. I turned around when I could, pretending to scan the room for some relative or another, but each time I found myself staring at a Plank sister who was staring back at me.

There were two shockers for them to absorb, only one of which was my being seated next to Clarice, who had an arm around my shoulders. More troubling no doubt was the sight of my short, solid, and utterly familiar build, my square and startlingly recognizable face.

Back when we were younger, we might all have seemed like a bunch of interchangeable girls—Esther, Sarah, Naomi, Edwina—even Ruth, who had not yet started shooting up to that dramatic height that earned her the nickname of Beanpole. Back then our similarities in appearance might almost have been chalked up to age, dress, and the sweatiness of a summer day that made everybody's face red and their hair stick to their faces. It would take another few decades for the resemblance to become what it was now.

Given how long the music went on, I had ample time to consider what this meant. I found myself scrolling back over the years, pulling out odd images of those intermittent but invariably disturbing times our two families' lives intersected.

I thought about Edwin Plank, who always stood in the background, as if his role on these occasions was nothing more than that of family chauffeur. Still, I had always been drawn to him. A thin, tall man, he would get down low to the ground when he spoke to me—which he did in an authentic, grown-up voice, not the baby talk so many adults use when talking to a child.

Edwin Plank may have been the first person to notice my interest in plants. One time he inquired about the sweet potato vine I'd been growing on our windowsill. He studied the leaves on a rosebush my mother had been struggling with, commenting that it needed more nitrogen, and we should pinch the suckers while we were at it. It was he, I now remembered, who had shown me what I might do to increase the height and sturdiness of some sunflower seedlings I'd started, taught me how to renovate a strawberry bed, and, later, trusted me with his precious daughter plants—the result of his years of meticulous crossbreeding of strawberry varieties.

As I sat there at Val's funeral, more pictures from the past came back to me. What I saw in every remembered scene—whether it was playing Barbies with Ruth, buying strawberries at Plank Farm, or talking about corn with Edwin—was a shadowy figure, always somewhere in the background, unable to take her eyes off me. The only other person in my life, possibly, besides Clarice, who had looked at me with so much love and longing. Connie.

IT WAS ON THE DAY we buried Val that I realized the truth: Val Dickerson had not been my mother. Connie Plank was.

Connie, who—whenever she saw me—went for me like a bird dog. Went *at* me, a person might have said, her embrace was so fierce and smothering. Connie, who practically demanded to see my report cards, and inquired about my religious education, who sent my mother so many letters imploring her to get me baptized that finally Val had written back with the lie that the rite had been performed. Connie, who brought gifts to me (always me, not my brother): the Junior Bible, and a small paperback book called *Way to Inner Peace* by Bishop Sheen, and—the year I turned twelve—a locket in which there was room for two photographs. One of the oval frames remained empty. In the other she had inserted a tiny photograph of herself.

Considering how long the musical buildup took, the actual content of Val's service, as laid out in the xeroxed program, appeared blessedly brief—a reflection and meditation from her husband and one of her yoga students, followed by remarks from anyone who wished to speak.

I was feeling shaken, not so much by the fact of Val's death than by the sight of the women I suddenly realized must be my sisters. I took out the piece of paper with the statement I'd prepared about Val's love of beauty, her dedication to her painting.

"My mother loved art," I said. (For this occasion, at least, I would refer to Val as my mother.) What I did not add was that whatever love might have been left over for me had been largely overshadowed by a feeling I got from her all my life, that I had disappointed her. I always felt that I was not the daughter she had wanted.

And I wasn't, of course. For the first time, I understood why I'd always felt that way. It finally made sense. The person who should have been sitting here in the front row was not myself at all but Ruth.

After I was finished speaking, David asked if anyone else present wanted to add a few words. At first no one moved. And then one of the Planks—Edwina—walked to the front of the room.

"My sister Ruth is having a baby today," she said, unfolding a piece of lined paper. "She asked me to read this."

It was only a handful of sentences. I pictured Ruth writing them, in the early stages of labor perhaps. I wondered if she knew already what had become clear to me within that last hour.

"Our families met when Dana and I were born at the same hospital on the same day," she read, a little stiffly. "And you might not think that would form the basis of any particular bond. But if I'd never met Val, growing up, I might never have known a woman could be an artist. Because she was one. And that made me believe I could become an artist myself."

Edwina refolded the paper and took her seat. It seemed that the service was finished, with nothing to add but a brief Sufi prayer. But a gaunt figure I had not noticed before, who'd been seated in the back, rose and moved toward the front of the room now. It took me a moment to realize who this was.

More than twenty years had passed since I'd seen Ray. I might have supposed that after all this time of what had no doubt been a difficult life, those good looks of his that made women love him wherever he went might have disappeared. He was certainly thin, with a deeply lined face—a suit jacket that looked as if it might have been purchased from a thrift shop, with sleeves that ended a good five inches up his long, thin wrists. His hair was as short as an inmate's.

It didn't matter. Even now, Ray was a handsome man, but it was something else that struck me, seeing him again after all that time: the old flair and charm that I—the stolid one, the one lacking all capacity to impress anyone by any other means besides sheer hard work and constancy—had so admired and envied in my dazzling older brother. I would not have expected him to smile as he spoke, but when he did I saw the flash of surprisingly white teeth, and those eyelashes people always used to say should have been mine instead of going to a boy.

He told a story about the summer we'd packed up and moved to Maine to take over George's friend's clam shack on roughly twenty-four hours' notice.

"When we got there, it turned out the place had been condemned by the health department," my brother said, shaking his head. "All clam digging in the Gulf of Maine had just been suspended due to red tide, which inspired Val to turn the place into a takeout smoothie joint, selling fruit drinks and vegetable juices. Not much market for those yet, as it turned out. I guess you could say she was a woman ahead of her time. So George lost his shirt on that venture, as usual, and my mother just kept painting pictures. She wasn't really cut out to be the mother type, if you want to know the truth. Though she could make fantastic yogurt."

This was meant to be a funny story, and you could make out a little ripple of uneasy laughter, but the group quickly fell silent after my brother finished speaking. Mostly what his words conveyed was how directionless our family had been, how lost.

You were never sure, with Val and George, where you were or how long you were going to be there, or where you were going next or even who you were. In my case, anyway, I was right to wonder. For over forty years, I'd gotten it wrong.

When Ray was finished speaking, he just stood there for a surprisingly long time. Then he reached into his pocket, and for a second I could almost feel our small, uncomfortable group considering the possibility that my brother might be one of those postal worker shooter types. Who knew? He might pull out a gun.

But it was a harmonica. He started playing "Shenandoah"—sad, slow, and sweet. He cut it off abruptly, right in the middle, in the part where, if a person was singing, the words would be "I'm bound to leave you," which may or may not have had any significance. Then he put the harmonica back in his pocket and returned to his seat.

After the service was over, I scanned the group, looking for Ray. At first I thought he must have stepped into the men's room, but when he didn't appear I understood. Once again, my brother had vanished.

I felt bereft then. Whichever woman I called my mother, both were dead now. Any chance I might once have had to understand our story was gone. Gone, too, the brother I adored. Clarice not gone, but going. And George had never been there for me at all.

It was only then, oddly, that the other fact hit me: there was one parent left, and that was Edwin Plank.

I felt a small surge of joy. I had no mother, but for the first time in my life, I had a father.

# RUTH

## Losing Ground

MY SISTERS SAID very little to me about Val Dickerson's funeral. But they told me Ray Dickerson had been there.

Two days earlier I had given birth to my son, Douglas, who was nursing at my breast even as we spoke. An odd time for a woman to be inquiring about a man she'd last seen almost twenty years ago, a person might have said, but still I asked.

"So how was Ray?"

"He looked thin," Naomi told me. "A little odd. But he always was."

I asked if he still lived in Canada. If he was married. What he was doing. But they had no more information to offer. Dana was sitting with a woman, they said. The two of them were holding hands. But, as they'd just been saying, the Dickersons always were strange.

Looking back, I now believe, they must have discussed among themselves what it was like seeing Dana Dickerson. But my sisters and I were never ones for sharing stories, and there was plenty else on our minds at the time, anyway.

For a long time now, the farm had been in financial trouble, but another worry overshadowed that of our growing debt. Our father's Alzheimer's had progressed to the point where it was getting increasingly difficult to care for him at home. Esther had made an appointment for us to go check out a nursing home.

Another group of developers was after us now to sell our land, and though their best offer still fell far short of what my sisters and their husbands believed our place to be worth, I was the only one of the five of us who remained adamantly opposed to a sale. Diminished as he was, our father was alive, and we all knew where he would have stood if he'd been able to hold his ground, but these days he spent his time watching television, or just sitting in his chair looking out the window. That brief moment in which he'd been so stirred by news of Val Dickerson's death represented a rare example of anything approaching coherence.

"If they took a vote tomorrow, you know how things would go," I told Jim, after the most recent offer had come in from the Meadow Wood Corporation. "My sisters can't quite bring themselves to move our dad off the land while he's alive, but once he dies, they'll want to take the money and run."

"Maybe it's for the best," my husband said. The idea to move back to the farm, full-time, after my mother's death had been mine, and though he'd gone along with it, he'd never been a country boy. The commute to Boston had been getting to him, and it would only get harder now that we had a second child.

"Esther and Sarah want to buy side-by-side condos in Florida," I said, of two of my older sisters—one divorced now, one widowed. "Naomi and Albert want to move closer to the grandchildren in Las Vegas. Winnie and Chip have their eye on one of those giant RVs the size of a Greyhound bus, so they can drive around the country staying in Walmart parking lots and visiting casinos. It may actually be a good thing Dad's out of it, so he can't understand what's happening."

"Your sisters have a right to their lives," Jim said. "Frankly, I wish this place didn't take up as much of ours as it does these days. I'd think you'd be happy for the money and freedom too. You could start painting again."

"I've got a new baby and an eleven-year-old to think of," I said. "I'm not about to run off and rent a studio somewhere and try being a painter. And there's my father to take care of."

"Your father needs to go into a home. Your sisters are just being practical."

"He loves this farm. I do too."

"Maybe if you weren't so occupied with the farm you'd have a little more time for our relationship," Jim said, quietly.

"People with new babies aren't exactly the most romantic couples around," I told him. "That's normal."

But I knew the truth. We weren't that way before the baby either.

# *Dana*

# Close to Perfection

FOR AS LONG as Clarice and I were together, I told her everything that happened in my life, same as I believe she did with me. More than that, I told her all that I was thinking and feeling. It was a superstition, almost, to never leave anything out, as if once either of us started doing that a small but insidious division might develop between the two of us that could only grow wider.

Her diagnosis changed everything. Now, when I thought about the future, and the prospect—the certainty—of a life without her, I kept my grief to myself, and because grief was now the dominant emotion in my world, the old closeness we'd known changed. No less love existed between us—only more, if that was possible. But I went through my days with her like an actor, playing the part of a happy person.

She needed it, I believed. She had made a clear, unspoken choice to proceed, as long as possible, as if things were the same as always, and because I would do anything for her, I went along with the act. But the cost for me was great.

I wept only when alone—in the barn, generally, milking our goats, and overseeing the cheese, jobs that allowed my brain room to pursue thoughts and images and memories, of which there were too many.

I saw us, on a trip we'd made two years back, to Mount Desert Island, in Maine, picking blueberries and feeding them to each other and making towers of flat stones, balanced one on top of the other. And I remembered how it was later, in our tent, when a thunderstorm hit, clinging to each other for warmth.

I thought about the dream we'd had, and then abandoned, of being parents together, and imagined Clarice pregnant—Clarice, who loved the prospect of pregnancy. I had loved the thought of her pregnant breasts, her full round belly.

Early in our time together she had told me how, when she told her parents that she loved women, her father had set her belongings in the front yard of their Iowa home and lit a match to them. Every family photograph, every childhood toy and adolescent memento—all were destroyed in the inferno as her mother looked out through the window. She trembled in my arms when she told me the story, and for hours after, I had stroked and held her, having no words that were adequate, but no need for words.

Now though, having finally learned the truth about my family—the reason for Val and George's mysterious remoteness, and Connie's grasping, and the deep, warm sense of safety I'd always felt toward Edwin—I said nothing to Clarice. It seemed to me that to do so would demand more than I wanted to ask of the woman I loved, someone facing her own terrifying series of losses. As much as was possible, who I would be to her now, I decided, was a partner free of her own needs or problems—other than the one great and terrible problem of Clarice's imminent death.

And because I had decided I could not tell Clarice the truth of my discovery, I could not tell Ruth, either. This was not such a difficult decision, actually. Linked as we had been all these years by Connie's birthday sister obsession, I barely knew the woman. All focus and care now went to caring for Clarice, and as much as possible, maintaining the illusion of our old life, which I now understood to have been nothing short of miraculous.

FOR THE FIRST YEAR AFTER we got the news of Clarice's diagnosis, we carried on much as before, though with an acute sense of the preciousness of every day.

At first Clarice's symptoms were minor enough that I allowed myself to believe the doctors might be wrong. Maybe her particular case was different from most, and this was the full extent of the disease. We could live happily with the numbness in her fingers, the way her leg sometimes gave out, and the trouble she had using a fork and knife, particularly at the end of the day when she was tired.

It's a strange thing, how swiftly a person's world reconfigures when illness settles in. One day you're thinking it's a problem that the person you love can't separate one coffee filter from the next one in the box; a month later, all you hope for is that she can hold the mug on her own.

She continued to teach that first year. Apart from one friend in the department, she had told no one about her condition, and neither did I. Even with each other, we spoke of it surprisingly seldom. There had been a time when we made plans—to build a greenhouse someday, to celebrate her fiftieth birthday with a trip (Europe, or perhaps the long-deferred cross-country drive to Yellowstone). Now we avoided all talk of the future, beyond the few days or weeks before us.

A new carefulness overlay what we allowed ourselves to tell each other, or even imagine. A sentence that began "Next year" or even "next summer" now required us to consider other questions. How well could Clarice walk by then? (Could she walk at all was not a question I allowed myself to ask.) Could she get up and down stairs? Would she have trouble with her speech? If the phone rang, could she pick up the receiver?

Five of our goats were due to deliver kids that spring. The first one arrived in the middle of the night, around Valentine's Day, when the temperature was ten below. I had gone out to the barn to check on the animals, and there was the baby. Normally I would have simply left her there to nurse, but cold as it was, I decided to bring them both into the house.

Under normal circumstances, Clarice would have carried one, and I the other, but I brought them both in and laid them on blankets in the kitchen by the woodstove.

Clarice, in her pajamas, knelt beside them. She lay down on the floor by the mother and the baby, her head on the blanket.

"It's good you're strong, Dana," she said. "You'll have to be soon."

By late spring—a few months after Val's death—Clarice was using her cane all the time. By the time I was getting the tomato plants into the ground, she needed a walker, and though she wanted to spend time with me outside, it was hard for her, negotiating the uneven terrain.

"I think we have to sell Jester," she said. "It's not fair leaving him in his stall all the time with no one to ride him."

As she had for several seasons now, on warm days she stretched out in her chaise lounge by the porch while I worked in the strawberry patch. Still developing our perfect strain of plant, I brought her plates of berries to compare for sweetness.

"I think you're getting close to perfection here, honey," she said, when she was finished sampling every one. "They're all wonderful now. Not a single dud in the lot."

"I was thinking the same thing," I said. "This is the summer I'll get the paperwork and testing under way for registering the new variety."

I had always felt the urgency of my timetable lay with Edwin's advancing age—the fact that he was almost seventy-five now. The man I now understood to be my father was no longer farming, and his memory was going. Long before I'd known of our blood connection, I had regarded him as my mentor, and so I felt deep regret that we had missed the chance to pursue the patent on our strawberry plants together, as I had always hoped we would. But there was another force bearing down on me now, more oppressive than the prospect of Edwin's death.

"I wish this could have gone on a lot longer," Clarice said, wiping a drop of strawberry juice from her lip. She had always been the most fastidious person, but lately, it was getting harder for her to take care of herself. "Nothing's over," I said.

"It will be."

———

ONE OF THE THINGS A person learns to live with if she's a farmer, is dying.

We lost goats sometimes—a kid born dead, or too weak to survive. Chickens, if one got out and a fox was in the neighborhood. Katie, our dog, who we buried under Fletcher Simpson's plum tree.

It was not only animals, but crops, too, that reminded you nothing was permanent but the changing of the seasons. For all the years I tended one piece of land or another—flower gardens, strawberry beds—I never got over the sadness that descended every summer, as harvest season approached. The goldenrod and Queen Anne's lace came into bloom, and the days got shorter. The nights were cooler, and I knew that frost would come soon and with it, death.

Somewhere along the line I heard that George had died. That news had come to me in the form of a bill from a funeral home in Austin, Texas, where George had spent his last years. But apart from its inconvenience, that event had seemed to me as distant and removed as George himself had been when he was living.

But picturing Clarice dying was like trying to fathom the ocean drying up, color gone from the world. Nobody I ever knew was more alive to me than Clarice. I could no more imagine her frozen and motionless as the doctor had told us she would be than picture a hummingbird whose wings were stilled. I could no more imagine myself without her than imagine the sky without the sun.

# RUTH

## All This Time

FOR ALL THE years my sisters and I were growing up, my father had prided himself on being debt-free. In the eleven generations that Plank Farm had been in operation there had never been a mortgage on our land. Sometimes, if a winter had been hard, my father would pay a visit to the bank for a five-hundred-dollar loan to help him pay for his seed order and fertilizer, but only until spring, when the money started coming in.

Then came the big rise in fuel prices and proliferating supermarket chains, then the drought, and most crushing of all, the barn fire. Encouraged by Victor, his own right-hand man, my father had taken out a note to build a big new greenhouse for cultivating early-season hothouse tomatoes, but by the time he got it up and running he realized he could not compete with the prices the chains were charging. Then there was the year Esther got a divorce, and my father lent her money to buy out her former husband's share of their house, which had been built on our land.

It was my mother's illness that did him in. Though we knew from the beginning that her cancer was incurable, the bill just for palliative care had gone well over one hundred thousand dollars, and it turned out there was some problem with her insurance.

My husband—whose specialty was life insurance, not health—had been horrified by that one, but by the time he found out, the damage was done. My dad ended up on the hook for more than half of what was owed to the doctors and the hospital.

By 2001 Plank's was in serious trouble. Property taxes were coming due in a few months and we had no idea how we were going to pay them. As usual, the developers were circling, and moving closer all the time.

"Over my dead body," I heard my father say, the last time we'd raised the topic of the Meadow Wood Corporation.

Only the desire to avoid selling out to the developers had brought us around to considering a scenario that would once have seemed inconceivable: Victor Patucci had put together an offer to buy our place—take on the full debt my father owed, if we would offer partial financing ourselves. The farm wouldn't be Plank's anymore, but at least Victor would keep it as a farm. For now anyway.

All four of my sisters were anxious to accept the deal. I, alone, wanted to hold off on the deal while we worked on finding another way to hold on to our property.

"It's the twenty-first century, get used to it," Victor said when I told him how I felt about his plan to open a corn maze and offer a "Build Your Own Scarecrow" activity in the pumpkin field, with pumpkins trucked in at wholesale from other locations to increase our sales potential, and an inflatable bouncy house to lure in kids. "You don't live in Little House on the Prairie with Ma and Pa anymore," Victor pointed out. "Either you step boldly into the future, or you get left behind."

IT WAS NOT ONLY LIFE on the farm that disturbed my sleep at this point, either. Something had changed in my marriage.

In the twenty-four years that Jim and I had been together, I had cared for him deeply—loved him, I thought—but I had never felt for him anything like the hunger or passion I'd known as a young woman, once and once only. I felt childish and immature that even as I passed my fiftieth birthday, I found myself still thinking about Ray Dickerson and still believing—corny as I knew it was—that he had been my one true soul mate, the partner with whom I was destined to spend my life and would have, if my mother had not intervened and convinced him to send me away.

All through my marriage to Jim—from our attempts to conceive a child, to our adoption of Elizabeth, and later the marvelous unexpected gift of Douglas—my husband had remained a loving and loyal mate.

"I still think you're beautiful," he always told me. Whenever we were alone together—our annual Florida trip, or weekends we'd drive to Boston for dinner and a show and a night in a hotel—he'd never ceased his hopeful, almost wistful brand of courtship. He was a man who never let my Fourth of July birthday pass without a glossy card containing a loving message, a man who always thought to have room service deliver champagne and a rose. Though recently he'd given up his old practice of writing me a poem, and simply drew a heart.

"I know you're not in love with me the way I am with you," he told me once. "But I never give up hope that one of these days you'll wake up and you will be. You'll look around at all the other women you know whose husbands don't love them this way, and it'll come to you what a good thing we've had all this time."

"I already know we do," I said.

I just didn't want to sleep with him anymore. I didn't fantasize about being with anyone else. By my fiftieth birthday I just wanted to be left alone to concentrate on my children and work.

I had a few friends—Josh Cohen, oddly enough, among the few with whom I'd stayed in occasional touch from my old Boston days, though he lived in California now. But for me, there was little I liked better than a rare day in which I could go off alone to a museum in the city and wander through the rooms of paintings until closing time.

An exhibition of Bernini sculptures came to the Museum of Fine Arts, from Italy. I'd seen them all, but only in books. So I made the trip down to Boston with my sketch pad, taking a day off work to avoid the weekend crowds.

I loved them all, but there was one, *Apollo and Daphne,* that I could not stop studying. I walked around the sculpture very slowly, taking it in from every angle: the lithe form of Apollo, reaching out toward the woman he loves, and she—her hair flying behind her, a look of desperation on her face—on the verge of capture.

But Daphne had chosen another way of making her escape. She turned herself into a tree. At the moment Bernini chose to freeze her image, she was partially transformed already—her face and arms still those of a beautiful woman, her feet twisting into the gnarled tree roots. Immovable for eternity.

I thought about that sculpture all the long drive home from the museum. It hadn't even struck me until I was on the highway headed home that the name Daphne held another significance for me. The name Ray Dickerson had chosen for the daughter we never had.

It was dark by the time I got home from the museum. Earlier, Jim had fixed dinner for our son and now he was in the living room watching a baseball game.

"Good day?" he asked.

"Great." I asked about Doug's ball game. A meeting I remembered Jim had that day. He turned off the set and walked into the kitchen, where I was pouring a glass of water. He looked, at that moment, like a different person. A man I did not know.

"I have to tell you something, Ruth," he said. "I've fallen in love with another woman. I want to be with her."

# *Dana*

## Specks of Dust

JUST BEFORE LABOR Day, I made the drive to the university, to deliver samples of what I was calling the Plank Strawberry. This was the first step in the long process of pursuing a patent. I'd been told it would take a year or more, during which time my plants would undergo rigorous scrutiny over at least three generations before winning acceptance as an officially registered new breed of strawberry.

That fall, a few weeks before the new academic year, Clarice resigned from the art history department. I had found her at her desk one afternoon, in tears over a slide carousel she'd been trying to load with images for a lecture on the Flemish masters.

"I can't get the slides in the slots," she said.

"I'll do it," I told her. But that was only part of it. She no longer had strength in her leg to work the gas pedal of her car, and steering was now close to impossible. Even if she could get herself to work, walking was getting harder every day, and though I still understood everything she said, her speech had begun to slur. That, for her, was the worst. The worst so far, anyway.

"The good news is, now we can take a trip," I told her.

The next day I went to town in our old Subaru and came home in a brand-new van, outfitted with a gas cookstove and a sink, and a bed in back, a lavatory, a stereo system and air-conditioning. The deluxe model. What were we saving our money for?

"Come with me to Wyoming," I said.

WHEN I HAD FIRST BROUGHT home the van, I'd thought we'd make our trip in the spring, when everything would be green, but in recent weeks the effects of the disease seemed to have accelerated with a terrifying speed. I wanted Clarice to make the trip when she could still get around a little and was no longer sure that would be so six months from now.

So I got the couple down the road to house-sit and cleaned up the strawberry patch in preparation for the winter, laying out the straw mulch to get them through the winter. I hired a helper to tend the goats, which wasn't as big a job in the cold months when their milk dried up and the cheese-making operation ended until spring.

We set out on our great adventure. I drove, naturally, with Clarice perched in the custom-designed copilot's seat beside me, looking out over the road. Our plan was to cover the first eighteen hundred miles as quickly as possible—the stretch from Maine to the Wyoming border—so we could conserve Clarice's energy to spend the most time in the places she wanted most to see: the Bighorn Mountains, the Tetons, Yellowstone.

I had outfitted the van with a good sound system and made tapes of all the music she loved—classical, jazz, show tunes, folk, and though I hated it, country.

There was an album she loved, by an Irish folksinger, with a song that always made her cry, about a woman whose son leaves on a fishing boat and never comes home.

"Does this ever make you think of your brother?" she said. "I wish you two could reconnect."

"He knows where I am," I said, not adding that he wasn't my real brother after all. "Ray's the one who chose to disappear. It would have been so easy to talk to me at Val's service if he'd wanted, but he just left."

"Someday," she said, "maybe you'll make your way back to each other. He may need you. You may need him, too, more than you think. Everyone should have family."

We were on the Ohio turnpike, a long, flat stretch of highway that could have been anywhere, almost.

"You're my family," I said. "All I need."

We found a great piece of pie at a truck stop in Indiana. Clarice was having trouble using a fork now, but I knew she didn't like having me feed her in public.

"Just use your fingers," I said. I did, too, so she wouldn't be the only one.

"Who cares what people think, right?" she said. "That's the least of our problems."

After that we started eating practically all our food with our fingers. Pasta, chicken, salad. She drank soup with a straw now, so I did also.

Nights we'd pull over in some campground. I folded down the bed in the back of the van. First I helped her into the little toilet cubicle and brushed her teeth. Then, with the curtains drawn and a candle lit, I brushed her hair and undressed her.

For a few months after we'd got the diagnosis, we had continued to make love, but it had quickly become harder for Clarice. "Put my arms around you," she said. "Lay me on your chest."

But I knew the truth. She was long past lovemaking now. She was doing this for me. I was happy just holding her.

It was nearing the end of October when we reached the southern part of Wyoming. We had left the interstate now and were on a two-lane highway winding over the Bighorns. Great walls of rock rose up on either side of us, the layers of mineral as clearly delineated as a drawing in a geology textbook. Signs along the way named the particular era in which each rock formation had come into being. 250 billion years ago. 350 billion.

"It's comforting, isn't it?" she said. "Those numbers remind you how small a moment in time this one really is. What specks of dust we all are in the end."

And the stars amazed us. I had thought I knew what the constellations looked like, from nights on our farm we'd lie on our backs in the yard looking up into the darkness, but that was nothing compared with the sky that blanketed us in Wyoming—how brightly stars shone in this place, how clear.

We passed waterfalls and strange, red rock outcroppings that rose alone, like totems, in the middle of a flat expanse of plains. We pulled into a junk shop where Clarice wanted to buy me a pair of spurs, and I bought her an angora skin rug to lie on.

"Do you think I only need invalid-type items now?" she asked, with a sudden sharpness. It was the one moment in ten days that her bitterness had shown itself.

So I bought her a mother-of-pearl penknife for removing the tops of strawberries. I bought her an ivory hair clip, and chaps.

Sitting in her copilot seat, with pillows and a strap under her chin to hold her neck up because she wasn't strong enough to hold her head steady, she sported her chaps over the pajama bottoms that she wore all day now. It was just easier that way, she said. Her pajama bottoms were for comfort. The chaps were for style.

In a town called Buffalo, we found the Hotel Occidental, a place that looked like something straight out of an old western movie.

We pretended she was a rodeo rider, injured in a fall from a horse, and that was why I had to carry her. "You've heard of Calamity Jane?" I stage-whispered to the woman at the registration desk. "This is her great-great-granddaughter. She took a bad fall over in Cody, riding a bull."

They seemed to believe us. We ordered room service and ate medallions of buffalo on the floor by the fireplace and finished off a bottle of wine.

"It doesn't matter if I get drunk now," she said. "I talk like I'm drunk anyway."

"This room looks like a bordello," I said, setting her on a big spool bed with a red velvet spread and slipping her shoes off.

"Let's pretend we're on the run from the sheriff," she said. "We robbed the stagecoach."

My turn again. "We shot a lawman and now the posse's on our tail. We know they're catching up to us. It's our last night of freedom." It was unlike me to make up stories like this—I, the scientist, believer in data. But with Clarice, and only Clarice, I possessed an imagination.

"We can do anything we want," I told her.

Not that we could, really. Our horizons, even in a place as wild and open as this one, were narrowing, and we both knew it.

"I want a whole pint of chocolate ice cream," she said. "I don't care if it's fattening."

For three days, we drove around Yellowstone, pulling over by the side of the road sometimes to watch a moose or a herd of buffalo. We had a picnic on the shores of Yellowstone Lake, huddled under a blanket, watching the pelicans. At the geyser walk was a row of wheelchairs, available for physically challenged visitors.

"I think one of those would be a good idea for me," she said, surprising me. Until now she'd avoided using a wheelchair.

We talked some about the past, and about the wildlife, the rock formations, the way the light fell on the plains, and how much our old dog, Katie, would have loved to run on them back in the old days, or simply be there in the van with us, her head out the window taking it all in.

We did not talk about the future—not her death, or all the stages yet to come between now and then. But one night as we were lying next to each other in our bed at the campground, she turned to me. Her words came out more measured now, and so soft I had to lean close to hear her sometimes, but she was speaking right into my ear.

"I don't think I'll be very good at that eye-blinking system," she said. "I don't have the patience for spelling words out one letter at a time. Going through the whole alphabet to get each letter. By the time I spelled one word I'd probably forget what I wanted to tell you."

There was no point in my saying something cheerful or encouraging, like it wouldn't really happen, or it wouldn't be so bad. It would happen, and when it did, it would be worse than anything we could imagine.

"I need to ask you," she said. "To make sure I don't get to that point. I'll need to end things before I'm so bad I can't tell you anymore. I don't think I can do it by myself. I don't think that I'll be able to do it by myself."

Our campsite was near a deep crevasse. Earlier that day, in the sunlight, we had stood at the edge watching the Yellowstone River raging through and jagged rock rising along the sides, red, rose, orange, yellow. The water smashed down over the rocks with such force that even high above it as we were, we felt the spray on our faces. Now, in the black night, I could hear the roiling current.

*We could hold hands and jump,* I thought. But I could never stand there watching her fall.

"Promise you'll help when I ask you," she said.

I told her yes.

# RUTH

## A Wild and Beautiful Country

I HAD NEVER imagined us getting a divorce, but it happened now with stunning speed. Jim was out of the house by Christmas; papers were signed before the snow melted the next spring. He married again—a small wedding but unlike ours, a real one, with music and guests and the bride in a white gown, I gathered, from our daughter—in late summer.

I had no argument with his actions. Seeing him with his new wife (an insurance client, a widow with whom he had worked, following the death of her longtime husband) I felt no jealousy. I can't go so far as to say I felt free of envy concerning the man with whom I'd spent the last two decades, but the envy I felt was unconnected to any desire to be with him.

I only envied the feeling of being in love. The memory of that was as distant now as what a war veteran amputee might feel remembering a pair of legs blown off in 1967.

By now I had lived half my life without Ray Dickerson, and it was not even Ray I missed. It was the young woman I had been when I loved him. She had disappeared. I missed the way the world had seemed to me then, the richness of the possibilities, the hunger I had felt, the capacity for longing. I had inhabited a wild and beautiful country once, one that I could never find my way back to. I had spoken a language no longer known to me. Somewhere on the planet, music was playing that my ears could not hear.

I thought about Apollo wandering the earth without Daphne, Jackie Kennedy watching the flag-draped coffin of her husband being carried up the steps of the Capitol as Camelot crumbled. I wondered if Neil Armstrong had ever felt this sense of exile: that he had once walked on the face of the moon, and could never return there.

## *Dana*

# The Promise

THE WORLD WAS closing in on Clarice now. The muscles of her body, one by one, were shutting down on her. One day we realized she could no longer walk. Next her right hand went. Then she was down to a couple of functioning fingers on her left, till those two locked. It was the opposite of a growing season, what we were living through now: a slow and relentless catalog of deaths.

She could still speak, though every syllable was labored. With what remained of her ability to communicate, she returned to the subject she had first raised that night in Yellowstone. As much as Clarice loved being alive, once she could not communicate, she would have no more taste for living.

"Not the blinking," she said, again, in her new clipped way of speaking. "Can't do that thing. With the alphabet."

I said there were computer programs that could help her. I was looking into one that picked up the movements of a person's irises to identify commonly used words and phrases on a board. She shook her head when I started to describe it.

"You made a promise," she said.

---

MANY YEARS EARLIER, WHEN I worked at the experimental cattle barns at the university, I learned how to use animal tranquilizers, and in recent years I'd applied my knowledge on occasion, mostly when a need arose to dehorn one of our male goats. There was a chart in my old textbook, identifying the quantities of each tranquilizer necessary to achieve the desired level of inactivity in warm-blooded mammals. There appeared to be no discernible variation in recommended dosages among differing species; the crucial determinants seemed to be simply the weight of the animal undergoing injection and the degree of tranquilization necessary to immobilize an animal without killing him.

An appendix to this text, printed in red, outlined the risks of incorrect dosage, from extended paralysis to coma to death. I learned from my textbook that this was painless.

Because I was a licensed animal breeder, I was able to buy these drugs. Still, I battled with Clarice over her choice, and with myself over my ability to do what she asked of me. For me, it would have been enough to know she was there in the room with me, there on the bed, breathing. But what would have been sufficient for me was for her unbearable.

And even if I wasn't ready yet to act on her request—for what the literature referred to as "a terminal event"—I knew that if the day came when I did, it would be prudent to have an established pattern of making tranquilizer purchases.

So I began buying the drugs and injecting tiny doses of tranquilizer into Clarice's bloodstream at night before she went to sleep.

IT WAS WINTER. FOR WEEKS, I'd barely left the house. Taking Clarice out in the van was too difficult now—not so much because I couldn't carry her as because she could no longer sit up on her own and needed to be strapped in place in her old copilot seat with a breathing tube to do the work her own lungs could no longer manage. She now spent her days on a hospital bed we had set up in the living room after it got too difficult caring for her in our old brass bed upstairs.

I'd put a television and VCR by the bed, with a stack of movies for her. Once a day, I massaged her body with scented oils—a small remaining pleasure.

I brought Clarice a kitten that I laid on her chest so she could feel the purring and the soft fur, and the kitten's small pink tongue licking her skin.

Nights after we finished our third or fourth movie of the day, I'd read out loud to her. She loved Jane Austen novels and the poetry of Yeats, in particular, though one day when I'd made a rare foray to town, I brought home a copy of *Valley of the Dolls* by Jacqueline Susann, and started reading it to her, acting out the dialogue with exaggerated drama. In the old days this would have been the kind of thing Clarice did—never me—but now that she could no longer be that kind of person, I became one, or tried to. Nothing but my love for her could have inspired this.

I was on the chapter where the world-famous fashion model and pill addict breaks off with her millionaire boyfriend because she's really in love with a dashing lawyer who, though he doesn't know it, is the father of her unborn child.

Once this would have made Clarice laugh. Now she just lay there and sighed.

It was getting harder to find anything that provided any form of diversion for Clarice. She was weary of everything now—even the music she'd loved, even the writers, even the pages of her favorite art books. Bonnard's women in their bathtubs, the erotic drawings of Egon Schiele. If it wasn't for Clarice, I never would have known the names of these artists, but because she loved them, so did I.

It was while I held one such book open for her that I had seen her crying. No sounds came out of her, but tears rolled down her cheeks.

"Enough," she said.

"OK," I told her, shutting the book.

"Not what I mean," she told me. "Enough of life. I've had. Enough. Of life."

THAT NIGHT I BATHED HER. I washed her hair with the good shampoo, the stuff she used to ration for herself, it was so expensive. Now I slathered handfuls on her scalp until the suds were piled on her head like a hairdo.

Then conditioner. Then body oil. Bath salts and pumice stone. A loofah on her back.

When every inch of her was scrubbed and patted dry, I carried her to the bed. I rubbed lotion on her. Then I did her nails. I held out six bottles of polish to choose from.

"Curls," she said, after her toes were done.

"I'll do my best," I told her.

I propped her up on the bed. I dug out her round wooden brush and the blow-dryer she'd used to curl her hair with every morning, until she couldn't hold it anymore, and a jar of clips and Velcro rollers.

"This had better be a good hair day," she said with a crooked little smile. It was a long sentence for her now. I knew what that one cost her.

As little as I knew of hair, I knew less of makeup, but I dug out the small velvet bag in which she kept her favored beauty items. Clarice believed in expensive products: swore that a twenty-dollar lipstick possessed properties the drugstore variety did not. Whether or not this was true, the containers her stuff came in were all beautiful little buffed metal compacts with gold-flecked powders, eyeliner wands with long, elegantly tapered brushes, tubes of creamy lipstick that fit in a person's hand like art pastels.

"The trick with makeup," she had once told me, "is to make it look like nothing's there, when plenty really is."

I loved her face best as it was in its most natural state, but because I knew she wanted me to do this, and because I was in no rush—just the opposite; I did not want this night to end, ever—I applied color, then took it off, then put it on again, until it was perfect.

I dabbed perfume on her neck and wrists. Then came jewelry: moonstone earrings and the bracelet I'd given her with charms from all the places we'd visited, the last two depicting a buffalo head and the Old Faithful geyser.

I dressed her in her favorite outfit, an antique lace gown she had found at a vintage clothing store in Portsmouth one time. I put ballet slippers on her feet.

She wanted Joni Mitchell, the *Blue* album.

"I know it's not. An original choice," she said. "But there's a reason. Why everybody. Loves that one."

IT WAS CLOSE TO MIDNIGHT by the time we were finished. I had lit the candles.

"Get it," she said.

The syringe. I thought about my old days at the Ag school barn with the goats. Janis Joplin in the Chelsea Hotel.

"Always remember," she told me. "You made me happy."

"I was the luckiest person on earth," I told her. Only later did I remember who else had said that. Lou Gehrig.

After, I climbed onto the bed and lay down next to her. I put my arms around her, and my face against hers, so I could listen to her breath. Slower, slower, then gone.

I lay there a long time, almost until morning. Then I went outside and buried the syringe. If there was an autopsy, and suspiciously high traces of tranquilizers were found in her blood, I wasn't sure I'd care. As it was, nobody demanded those tests. If whoever it was who examined her body had any questions, they never asked.

# RUTH

## A Different Breed

WE WERE MOVING our father into a nursing home. "Care facility" was what they called the place, but we knew what it was, and as much fog as there was enveloping his brain at this point, my father understood. He was leaving our farm.

"No good will come of this," he said, as my brother-in-law Chip pulled up in front of the building.

"It's going to be fine, Dad," Winnie said.

"What do you know, Ed?" Chip said, as we made our way up the walk to the door—Chip carrying the suitcase, Winnie following behind with a small portable TV. "Looks like they've got a little garden here. Bet you could give these guys a few pointers."

Stooping as if for a low lintel, though none was there, my father said nothing. He was wearing brown corduroys, not his usual Dickies overalls, and the shoes he'd probably last worn for my mother's funeral—or his one brave but abbreviated road trip, that same year, to visit Val Dickerson. Moving along the cinder-block hallway with him now, I observed that all the other residents wore slippers. We had left his work boots back at the house. No use for them here.

His room was the size of a horse stall—single bed, bedside table, chest of drawers. I had brought a few pictures to put up on the walls but when I began to set things out, he shook his head and waved them away. He sat upright and still in the straight chair by the bed—the place for visitors, no doubt—and studied the sliver of sky through the window.

"Looks like rain," he said.

That night, alone at the house, I sat on the porch and looked out over the fields. The cornstalks were down, and the soil turned over for the winter. All evidence of this year's crops gone except the winter squash and pumpkin vines in the far field awaiting the "Make Your Own Scarecrow" weekend that now marked the end of another season at Plank's.

The sun was setting early now. Only the barest slice of light remained, though I could make out the kitchen lamp at my sister Naomi's place down the hill, where she and her husband would probably be fixing dinner now—Lean Cuisine, eaten in front of the television most likely. They didn't eat fresh vegetables even in season, and nobody canned anything anymore.

So here we were—a family scattered to the wind like milkweed once the pod has opened. I was halfway into my fifties, with more gray in my hair now than blond. My daughter was off in Seattle, in her second year of law school and unlikely to live here again. My thirteen-year-old son, though still living under the same roof with me, was counting the days till the Red Sox drafted him starting pitcher, and whether or not he attained that goal, he had his eye on distant horizons.

In the absence of a male heir, management of the farm had fallen to Victor Patucci, though I still oversaw the seasonal farm stand operation.

All of us—the other four girls and the husbands not yet lost to death or divorce—still lived on the property on the one-acre parcels our dad had subdivided for us back in the 1980s. It had only gotten harder to make a go of things on the farm. The only question still before us was which of two courses we'd choose for the dissolution of the property that had been in our family for three hundred and forty years: the Meadow Wood Corporation or good old Victor Patucci. If we went with Victor, we would receive a cash settlement much smaller than that offered by the developers, but at least our family's land would continue to be a farm.

A FEW OF THE GRANDCHILDREN—POSSESSING sufficient sentiment about the property that they still cared to see the land farmed, if not by Planks, then by someone else—were lobbying for the Patucci option. (One, my nephew Ben, labored under the illusion that this was "the green choice." I didn't disabuse him of the notion.)

My sisters themselves seemed ready for the more lucrative buyout. Whichever scenario we chose, it seemed inevitable that the days in which Plank Farm rested in the hands of the Plank family were coming to an end. Everyone but me was long past ready to sell.

My being the lone holdout was odd, actually. If I had a passion in life, it had been art and drawing; but I respected history, too, and it seemed to me that there was a heritage to preserve with this farm of ours, this piece of land of which, like it or not, we had become the stewards.

There were several houses on the property now, of course—mine, and those of my sisters, all of which would be part of the package when the place was sold. Victor Patucci had announced that my house—totally upgraded, of course; his wife favored granite countertops over tile—would work best for his family. Our old farmhouse, where my parents had made their lives for more than fifty years, and my father since birth, was a teardown.

Hearing this, I had considered, briefly, taking the door that bore the marks my father had made through the years chronicling the growth of the Plank sisters. Each pencil mark bore a date:

*November, 1954, Esther.*

*June, 1955, Naomi.*

*October, 1959, Sarah.*

*January, 1960, Edwina.*

*April, 1960, Ruth. Our Beanpole!*

Especially in the later years of childhood, the space between the marks for my sisters and the ones registering my growth stretched wide, whole inches of wood separating us.

I was a different breed from the rest of them. I had always known it. All I was missing was the confirmation.

And then a letter showed up in my mailbox. I didn't at first recognize the name on the return address—Frank Edmunds—but when I opened the envelope I realized who it was who had sent the letter. I had barely known Frank when we were high school classmates long ago, but of course I remembered his mother because she was my mother's friend—her only friend, perhaps, unless you counted Dinah Shore. Nancy Edmunds.

Frank was writing to me now, he said, to tell me that his mother had died recently—in a nursing home in Connecticut where she'd moved some years before, so her son—who worked just outside of Hartford—would be close enough to visit easily.

"Mom didn't say much, those last months," Frank wrote. "But she kept talking about this letter she'd written a long time ago that she'd been holding on to. She made me promise I'd send it to you once she wasn't around anymore. So here it is. I don't even know what it says, but I hope nothing in here stirs up any trouble."

IT HAD BEEN YEARS SINCE I'd seen Frank's mother, Nancy. Back when my mother got sick, people from church had dropped casseroles or cookies by, but it was Nancy, traveling by bus from Windsor Locks, Connecticut, who sat with her and did her hair even, until there wasn't any. She was at the farm the night my mother took her last breath.

Now here came a letter, with my name on the envelope, written in a shaky hand. *For Ruth Plank.*

I didn't open it right away. I sat there for a minute with the pale mauve envelope in my lap, thinking about the woman who had written this, and what might have inspired her to do such a thing. Although I thought of her as having been old forever, I realized now that Nancy Edmunds must have been younger than I was now, when her husband killed himself, younger than I now, on that day my mother and my sisters and I helped out at the yard sale where all the Edmunds family's furniture and most of their personal belongings had been set out on the lawn of the house they had to sell to pay off her creditors—my mother in an apron beside her friend, helping to collect the dollar bills. They had lived through that together, these two women. That and so much else I didn't even know about probably.

I must have known, studying my name on the front of the envelope, that whatever the words were contained inside, they might change my life. Why else would a woman I barely knew have written them, and instructed her son, on her deathbed, to mail this letter to me once its author was in her grave?

And so I registered a measure of dread—mixed with a certain unmistakable excitement—at the prospect of hearing what my mother's friend might have to say to me after all these years. Particularly at this moment. With the full knowledge that of all the relationships of my life, perhaps the least resolved (and least resolvable, now that she was dead) was mine with my mother.

Nancy Edmunds's letter reached me in early summer. For whatever reason—no doubt some would attribute this to some kind of hormonal change but I myself knew it was more than that—a strange melancholy had begun to envelop me sometime earlier that year, for which I could locate no explanation.

My health was fine. My job as an art therapist gave me a certain satisfaction, and—combined with Jim's contributions to our children's support—provided enough money for us to live in relative comfort.

Despite the divorce, our children seemed like happy, well-adjusted people, though I wished Elizabeth called and visited more often than she did. In this respect and few others, I was like my mother—a woman for whom nothing had mattered more than family.

I regretted that my sisters and I weren't closer, though we lived near one another and spent holidays together. Despite our physical proximity, the bond the four of them shared had never seemed to extend to me, for reasons I still tried to comprehend.

We saw the world differently was all I knew. It was nobody's fault, but in a hundred different ways—their quiet, dogged style of living that seemed to leave no room for joyfulness or play; their belief in our parents' brand of self-sacrifice and faith that reward lay in the next life, not this one; even the foods they cooked for family get-togethers—my sisters and I had little in common other than the land we all lived on, those five one-acre tracts along the southern border of our dying family farm. And soon we wouldn't even share that.

FOR SOME TIME NOW I had understood that there was no one in my life—not my sisters, not my father, not my ex-husband or my children, dear though they were to me, not my old friend Josh or the women I worked with now, though I valued their friendship—who fully knew me, not in the way I had briefly believed I had been known only one time in my life. For fifty years I had felt like an outsider in my own family. It was a feeling that began, I knew, with what had taken place between my mother and me. Or what had not taken place, that I had missed so sorely.

A memory came to me then, of Nancy Edmunds and my mother, sewing mother-daughter dresses for Nancy's daughter Cassie and me—dresses with rickrack on the pockets and big wide sashes that tied in back. I had seen a Butterick pattern featuring the dresses at the fabric store and begged my mother to take on the project of making them. Surprisingly, for her, she relented, even going so far as to let me choose the fabric: a girlish print featuring kittens chasing balls of yarn across the yardage. Mint green and pink.

We brought home the fabric shortly before Easter 1960, at the height of the cold war. I was a fourth grader, and the teacher had taught us how to hide under our desks if the Communists came to bomb us. For years afterward, every time I heard a plane overhead I wondered if they were finally on their way to get us.

The picture came to me now of coming home from school on the afternoon of a particularly terrifying air-raid drill and finding my mother and Nancy waiting there, wearing those ridiculous dresses, with their puffed sleeves and sashes tied around the waist, that jaunty row of rickrack trimming the pockets and hem.

Maybe over the course of the years, I reshaped events to come up with the image, but I believe that even my nine-year-old self had registered poignancy in the image of my mother standing in the doorway to greet me that day, wearing the newly finished dress. Young as I was, I recognized this as one of those moments when the dream of how you hope and imagine things will turn out—the picture from the pattern of those two smiling figures in their matching dresses—turns out to bear so little resemblance to how things really go.

I had come racing up the driveway from the bus, carrying my fallout shelter instructions. As always, I longed for my mother's arms around me, at the same time that I understood what I was looking for was not available to me. Only that day, there she was, just outside the house, in the kitten-print dress.

Never anything close to slim, my mother—in her usual clothes—came across as a strong, sturdy, no-nonsense person: not beautiful, not homely, not skinny or fat. Just totally herself.

That day, though—with those puffed sleeves squeezing down on her large arms, and the mint green and pink skirt twirling mercilessly over her thick sausage legs, her feet in their sensible brown oxfords, I remember feeling embarrassed. Not only for myself, but for my mother even more so.

"Let's see you put yours on, Ruth," Mrs. Edmunds called out from her station at the sewing machine in our front room, where she was putting the finishing touches on a dress just like the others, for Cassie's Ginny doll. Mrs. Edmunds's own dress, though not exactly fashionable, hung more successfully on her leaner frame. Cassie—several years younger than I, home from kindergarten hours before—was already dancing around the room in her dress. It was a style, I realized now, best suited to a five-year-old.

My mother was a competent seamstress, but she had cut certain corners, in the interest of saving fabric probably. Instead of a wide sash, and a full, twirly skirt like the ones on the Edmundses' dresses, the sash on mine was narrow, and too short to make a full bow, and because I was not only tall, but long-waisted, it tied somewhere in the midrange between my chest and my belly button.

I had gone upstairs to put on the dress—knowing before I even did so that the whole mother-daughter dress idea had been a terrible mistake. As I came down the stairs, it was clear from the look on my mother's face that she knew this too. But Mrs. Edmunds soldiered on with forced cheer.

"Just look at her, Connie," Mrs. Edmunds said. "She's the spitting image of you. With those dresses on you're two peas in a pod."

MORE THAN FORTY YEARS LATER, I opened her letter to me.

"Dear Ruth," it began. "There is something I need to get off my chest. It seemed about time I told you.

"I know you and your mother had your stormy times, but you should know she tried her hardest to make things work. Right up to the end of her life, she was praying the two of you could get along better."

*That would be my mother all right*, I thought. Saying prayers to some deity to make things better with her grown daughter instead of talking to her about it. Leaving it to God to fix things.

But it was the next words in Nancy Edmunds's letter that stopped me cold.

"She loved you, even though you weren't her real daughter," Nancy had written. "She loved you the best she could."

I read the words over again, to make sure I got them right. Then the air left the room.

NOW CAME THE STORY. NANCY had filled two sides of her lilac-trimmed stationery to explain it:

"Connie knew the day they brought you home from the hospital," she wrote. "She knew you were not the same baby they'd handed her that first day in the recovery room. She just couldn't convince your father to do anything about it."

Facts, then. I could barely breathe, reading them:

The baby they'd brought to my mother that first afternoon had weighed six and a half pounds for one thing. The one she brought home weighed eight.

But more than that, Nancy had written, a mother recognizes things about her child, the same as an animal would. The first baby—the one Val Dickerson brought home and named Dana—had a short, compact body and dark hair. The original baby had short, thick fingers like my mother's own, and—unlike any baby she'd ever seen—brown eyes with green in them. But the one they said was hers (we were speaking of me here) had fine blond hair, blue eyes, long legs, and long thin fingers. Her real baby (this would be Dana) had such a good appetite they couldn't get the bottle in her mouth fast enough.

My parents' real daughter slept easily and often; I was always fussy, not much interested in the bottle, and colicky.

"She said you smelled different from her child," the letter continued. "Mothers recognize these things."

I, mother of two myself, knew this was so.

The part of the letter that was hardest to read—and harder still to comprehend—was Nancy's account of what happened after Connie and Edwin Plank brought me home from the hospital, when my mother—Connie, the woman who would go on to raise me, though I was not the child who had come out of her body—explained to her husband, the man I called my father, that there had been a mistake.

"Edwin told Connie what's done was done," Nancy had written. "He said making a fuss about it would embarrass the doctor, and he was a friend from church. You were such a pretty baby, he said. More so, truthfully, than your sisters had been.

" 'Leave well enough alone,' he said. He decided this was God's will, evidently.

"You wouldn't understand how it was for us wives back in those days," Nancy went on. "You obeyed your husband if you knew what was good for you."

There I had it, finally—the truth: I was not the baby they'd put in Connie Plank's arms that first morning in the summer of 1950, though I was the one she brought home with her two days later.

Sometime in between—a bath, maybe?—the birthday sisters were switched. Maybe it occurred in the middle of the night, when both of us—Dana and I—had wakened at the same moment, crying, and the nurse on duty had been only half awake. However it took place, the result was clear: I was a Dickerson who became a Plank. Dana was a Plank who became a Dickerson. We had lived over fifty years, and neither of us had ever known who we really were.

I told no one about Nancy Edmunds's letter, or what her words had revealed to me. I wanted some time to think about this and consider what it meant. You spend more than half a century thinking you're one person and then it turns out you're not. Or maybe it is that the person you always were is suddenly revealed to you and all kinds of things make sense that didn't before, and all kinds of other things that used to make sense no longer do.

Of course I wondered about Val, the woman I was now recasting in my mind as my real mother. She'd been dead more than a dozen years, and I didn't even know if she had come to understand the truth about my parentage, though remembering that day at the Isabella Stewart Gardner Museum, when she had studied my face with tears in her eyes, I have to guess that at some point along the line—later than Connie, but sooner than I—she realized what had happened, and—not out of character for a woman who seemed most herself away from her family, alone in her studio—chose to do nothing about it.

The only two people with whom I might have discussed this were the Dickerson children—their one real child, at least, and the one they had raised as theirs: Ray and Dana. Ray—the thought of whom, even after all these years, caused a wave of sadness to wash over me.

Ray, who was—it had taken me a while after hearing the news to realize this—my brother.

It would have been easy finding Dana, who lived less than a half hour's drive away, but I hadn't called her. What would I say?

"I got your life. You got mine. What do you want to do about this now?"

As for Ray, he had not been the kind of person for whom any Google entries were likely to exist. And even if I could have tracked him down, I was not sure that I'd want to, although at one time it was my most fervent wish. The last time I'd seen Ray I had been looking out the window of the taxi taking me away from our little cabin on the island in Canada, as the taxi pulled away down the road, with the woman I now thought of as Connie Plank, who had come to take me away from him. On what I had considered, until now, the worst day of my life, or close enough.

Now I knew why she'd done it, and though it was no less terrible, and she was wrong not to tell me—and the cost was incalculable—I forgave her at last.

## *Dana*

# That Would Have Been Better

TIME PASSED. PLANTING seasons. Baseball seasons. Baby goats. Strawberries. Cheese. Winter. Seven of them, without Clarice.

It was early spring—I got the phone call from my brother. He was at the South Station in Boston, waiting to board a bus to Concord, New Hampshire, having spent the last ten days on a Greyhound making his way east from Oregon. He wondered if I could pick him up.

I was fifty-six years old now, which meant my brother, Ray, was sixty. The last time I had seen him had been at Valerie's memorial service a dozen years before—but the picture of him I still carried in my head was that of the young boy with the harmonica and the unicycle, with that restless, haunted look in his amazingly blue eyes.

I was not ready for the man who stepped off the bus that day. All his life, my brother had been such a lean person, with that basketball player's easy speed and grace, that heartbreakingly handsome face. Sometime since I had last seen him his body had taken on a certain heft, but he carried himself very straight, though with a certain appearance that doing this took effort. He still had all his hair—longer than it was the last time, and mostly gray now.

"Long ride," he said, easing slowly into the front passenger seat, like a person suffering from that disease in which every bone is brittle and subject to breakage at any given moment.

"I bet you're hungry," I said.

He shook his head.

I had thought, briefly, that it might be a good thing for Ray to work on the farm, tending the goats or the strawberries, but he was restless, unable to focus. I'd come home and find him sitting on the front porch holding a rake, or lying on the chaise that had been Clarice's spot, those last few hard years. He took a lot of naps. Nights, I fixed us dinner and he usually ate in silence. Afterward, he watched television sometimes, though he liked playing solitaire. Sometimes I'd get the feeling there was something he wanted to say, but he hardly ever spoke.

"Remember all those magic tricks you used to do for us?" I asked him one time, when he had the cards out. "Do you remember that one you did, where the queen of hearts ends up on top of a person's head?"

"That was somebody else," he told me.

One night, when we were sitting at the table finishing our pie, I told him about Clarice. I wanted my brother to know me. And maybe, too, I just wanted to talk about her to someone. Little as he said, telling him was better than talking to the goats.

"We loved each other so much," I said. "Until then, I didn't know it was possible to feel that way about someone. But I would have died for her. Even now, I think about her a hundred times a day."

"I used to know a person like that," he said.

A FEW WEEKS AFTER HE came to stay with me, Ray said he couldn't remain on the farm anymore. He didn't like being around all the animals, he said. And though I knew he had lived in the woods for a number of years, back on that island in Canada, being out in the country made him uneasy now. Many nights he would knock at my door to say he'd heard a noise, or he thought there was an animal on the roof, or a person trying to get in.

"It's nothing," I told him. "Sometimes there are raccoons. They won't do anything bad."

But he couldn't sleep at the farm. Too many stars, he said.

The goats made him nervous. The refrigerator gave off a humming noise that left him wondering if maybe it was radioactive. One time I came in from the barn and found my brother sitting at the kitchen table totally naked, looking out the window. His clothes hurt, he said.

I had come to understand, by now, all the things there were in the world that made it almost physically painful for my brother to get through the day. Even when he was young, I could remember times when Ray found it hard to get out of bed, and other times he'd feel a need to jump on that unicycle of his and disappear without telling anyone where he was off to. But back then those times when clouds seemed to envelop him were rare.

When I thought of Ray, as he was growing up, I saw this wildly funny, joyful person whose appetite for the world was so great he'd run outside in the middle of a rainstorm without caring that he got soaked—the boy who came to get me out of school with a note forged to look as if it had been written by our parents, so we could be at the record store for the release of a Fats Domino album.

One spring when we were living in Vermont, Ray had made the discovery that a surprising number of tiny and very beautiful lizards known as efts had emerged—seemingly all at once and all together—from wherever it was they'd spent the winter, and were now, on that one moonlit night, making their way like a parade of refugees across the dirt road in front of our rented house to the creek on the other side. He had awakened me in the middle of the night so I could see the red eft exodus take place, and another time—in the dead of winter—bundled me up in blankets before lifting me onto his shoulders to bring me out in the yard so I wouldn't miss a lunar eclipse.

He'd told me very little—nothing, really—about how he'd spent those years in Canada, but it would not have surprised me to learn he'd been homeless for at least a portion of that time. Now I called a social services agency in Concord and scheduled an appointment for Ray and me, and then more visits, and testing. He accepted these visits and tests without argument.

The term they applied to my brother was schizophrenic, and because of this, he qualified for a group home, where a half dozen or so people with a similar diagnosis—some much younger, one in his late seventies, all on some form of psychological disability—lived together under the part-time supervision of a counselor who oversaw things like grocery shopping and bills. Surprisingly, for a person who seemed so totally without interest in social interaction up to that point, Ray liked the place when we paid a visit there, and we filled out the paperwork. A few weeks later a space became available and he moved in.

One of Ray's new housemates—Natalie, who suffered from some form of OCD, but managed to hold down a part-time job at a dry cleaner's—told Ray about a weekly workshop she attended: art classes for adults with emotional disabilities, or "special sensitivities" as she described it.

"My mother was an artist," Ray said.

So Natalie took him to the class.

That night I was surprised to get a call from my brother. Even before he told me what had happened I could feel the agitation in his voice.

"It was her," he said. "She has a different name now," he said. "But it's the same person. Only not really."

The woman running the art workshop was Ruth Plank.

I HAD NEVER KNOWN THE full story of what happened between the two of them, all those years ago when he was living in British Columbia. But I knew enough to understand that something terrible had taken place.

"Were you happy to see her?" I said. I had learned, by now, that it was a good idea to ask Ray questions that allowed for yes or no answers.

There was a long silence on the other end of the line—the way there would be sometimes, in the last stages of Clarice's illness, when if I needed to be away for a few hours, I'd call her from a pay phone even though I knew talking was barely possible for her. Just so she could hear my voice, and I her breathing, as now I heard his, as if the air he was letting out of his lungs had been there a long time.

More silence. I thought he was finished. Then came his voice—quiet and low and filled with sorrow.

"I never told anyone this," he said. "But we were going to get married. We were going to have a baby. Then it turned out she was my sister."

I wondered how he'd learned the truth, but there was not much point in asking. He had been carrying this around with him a long time. That was enough.

"I actually figured most of that out, too. A while back," I told him. "They should have told us before."

"That would have been better," he said. And then he was gone. All I heard was a soft *click* as he put down his phone.

# RUTH

## A Long Way from Boston

EVEN AFTER SO much time, I still recognized him. The old Ray didn't enter a room so much as he took it over—bursting through the door, generally, with some amazing thing to show you, a trick or a joke or a song, maybe. One time, I remember, he had actually cartwheeled into the Dickersons' kitchen.

Now the man I had come to understand was my brother moved slowly, as if on ice. He seemed to be studying the floor when he entered the room, in fact. So it took him a moment to catch sight of me. When he did, it was as if a curtain was slowly lifted, and the years fell away. There were those long dark lashes I remembered so well, and under them those blue eyes that used to study me for hours. In spite of all life had handed him, he was still a handsome man.

I had thought about this moment—dreamed about it—for so long that it took a few moments to realize, with a slight, sharp stab of regret, that the feelings he had inspired in me once were gone. There had been a time when the sight of him caused me to draw in my breath. My body had been so tuned to his, one touch of his hand and I melted.

What I felt now was a sadness no different from what I felt for any of the people I worked with in those classes. Sorrow that the world had become, for them, a place so painful to inhabit that they had simply had to leave it the only way they knew.

He spent the afternoon working with clay. What he formed that day was a perfectly shaped egg.

Before he left, he shook my hand and said, "You still look good."

"I have thought of you often," I told him. "I hope you're doing OK."

"Do you have any children?" he said.

"A girl and a boy."

He nodded and left. He never returned to the workshop, and truthfully, I was relieved.

NOW THAT JIM WAS GONE and my father was in the nursing home, I quit my part-time job at the elementary school and cut back on my hours with my adult art therapy students. I was running the farm stand that summer, and as much work as that required of me, it was where I wanted to be. I knew this would be my final season at Plank's. Every time one crop matured and another passed by (peas, spinach, strawberries, broccoli, tomatoes, peppers) I marked it as my last on the farm. We were at corn now. Next would be winter squash and pumpkins. Then it would be over.

Douglas was quite independent now, and able to get himself to school and ball games—which I took in when I could. I even sat with his father on the bench sometimes.

The family had voted to sell the farm to Victor Patucci—mine the lone dissenting vote. We were due to sign the papers as soon as the Patuccis' loan came through that fall. One afternoon, a BMW convertible pulled up at the stand. The top was down and an old 1970s R & B song was blasting from the stereo.

Though I knew he was well over fifty now, Josh jumped over the side of the car, the way one of the characters used to in *The Dukes of Hazzard,* an old TV show that we used to joke about.

"I've been visiting a woman on the Cape," he said. "I thought I'd drive up and surprise you."

He did that all right, I told him.

"You're a long way from Boston," he said, looking around. "Times sure have changed." For him, too. He was living in Santa Monica. Making adult films. *Tasteful ones,* he said.

"I have something for you," he said, holding out an envelope. "We brought the book back out last year. Would you believe, it's been selling like crazy?"

Inside was a check made out to me for seventy-three thousand dollars.

## *Dana*

# Matchless Sweetness

A FULL FIVE years after I'd submitted my registration application, a letter arrived from the horticulture department at the university.

After all the years of work it was almost anticlimactic to finally get the news that our new strawberry variety had been approved and now qualified for a patent. The board would be happy to refer me to an expert in the field of horticultural law (who would have known such a field existed?) for the purpose of "pursuing a possible sale of rights to propagate and sell the breed." For the moment, my strawberry was known as *Fragaria* S–4762, but I was free to provide a name of my choice for future identification of my strawberry variety.

Not right away, but some time after this—when the contract had been signed and the paperwork and testing completed, the Ernie's A-1 Seed Company purchased exclusive rights to feature an exciting new variety of strawberry plant in its next season's catalog. Boasting a rating of four stars, with a particular recommendation for growers in the northeastern part of the country, the berry was described as not overly large in size, but possessing a matchless sweetness. I named the strain Clarice.

———

AN ODD THING HAPPENED WHEN I was driving my truck to Burlington, Vermont—the headquarters of Ernie's Seeds—to sign the final paperwork. I had the radio tuned to a country station that morning. I was thinking about Clarice, of course, who had a weakness for that brand of music. I dismissed most of it as incredibly sappy.

A song came on that I recognized, or half recognized. It was a duet between a couple of female singers whose intermingled voices had the effect of sounding like a couple of angels. Suddenly I found myself singing along with this song. Not only that, but I was weirdly able to anticipate the next line before it was sung.

At first I thought it must have been one of Clarice's favorites, something I'd heard time and again and never really gave much thought to. Then with a shock I realized: it was *George's* song. Who knew by what odd route it had made its way into the hands of this duo, whose names I didn't even know, though evidently many others did. The station was playing "the country countdown." The song was a hit.

I suppose I could have pursued this. Maybe I could have sued someone and made a bundle. But I chose to let it go. I was picking up a big check that day for work of my own creation—mine, and that of the man I now knew to be my true father. This was enough.

# RUTH

## What Happened

AFTER I LEARNED from Nancy Edmunds's letter about the secret that had transformed and haunted my family, it had proved surprisingly easy to see myself as the daughter of Valerie Dickerson. No doubt this was made easier by the fact that Connie had never acted like my mother anyway. There was some comfort, actually, in finally understanding why.

The harder part was viewing George Dickerson as my true father. Not only because George had been such a cipher. More so, though, because I adored the man who raised me, Edwin Plank. And so, whatever the DNA might tell me, I knew that for me, Edwin would always be the person I thought of as my father.

Most days when I visited him at the nursing home, he would say almost nothing, and what he did say to me seldom made any sense. If the weather was nice, we might walk around the grounds of the nursing home, not that there was much to see. A few straggling geraniums. A little patchy grass.

Who knows why it was different that day, but I recognized this the moment I walked in the door—a kind of alertness in his expression I had not seen in years. His eyes, which for some time now had looked at me with nothing but blankness, were focused and clear, and a little moist, as if he'd been crying.

Things were different for me, too. A week earlier, I had opened Nancy Edmunds's letter and learned the news that Dana Dickerson and I had been sent home from the hospital with the wrong families. And that my father had known all along. For seven days now, I had been trying to make sense of what this meant for my life. Who might I have been if not for my family's unlikely and disastrous intersection with the Dickersons?

I had been thinking about writing a letter to Dana. I knew she had a goat farm in Maine. It would be easy enough to get her address. I just wasn't ready yet to talk about what happened.

Meanwhile, here I was at my usual Wednesday afternoon visit with my father. I don't know what it was about that day that made my father view me as he did then. My hair was loose rather than pinned up as I normally wore it, and I was wearing a dress. Or maybe it was just that I happened to catch him in a rare moment of reflection.

Seeing me as I walked into his room that day, my father looked up from his chair and for the first time within recent memory, smiled.

"It's about time you came," he said. "I kept wondering where you'd got to."

"I was here last week, Dad," I said, but he didn't seem to be listening.

"You were right about that music," he said. "That Peggy Lee knows how to sing them."

"I brought you a tomato," I told him. "I've had my eye on this one for a couple of weeks now, with you in mind."

"You don't have to bring me a thing, sweetheart," he said. "Just yourself."

I was sitting on the edge of the bed now. He was propped up with a pillow, his hair white as the fluff on a baby chick. With surprising force and energy he pulled himself up and reached out so his hand brushed my cheek in a way he'd never done before. The way a man does with a woman, not his daughter. It came to me then: he thought I was someone else.

"You're still a beauty," he said. "That never changes. You're wearing your hair the way I like it."

I sat there. I had no words for him. I wanted to hear this and I didn't.

"What happened, Edwin?" I asked him. "How did Ruth end up coming home with you and Connie? And Dana went to—" For a moment I could not finish the sentence, knowing who my father believed me to be. "To Val," I said.

We sat in silence for a long time then, me facing my father, him gazing out the window, his thoughts seemingly off in some other place I could only guess at. Studying his face, that I loved so well in spite of everything, it was almost as if I were watching a hint of changing weather roll in over the horizon—clouds gathering, and the sun disappearing behind them, the first signs of rain.

"What happened. What happened," he said, shaking his head. The way he said the words, they were less a question than a statement. Watching him, I was reminded of all the times he'd pushed on our heavy barn door to open it.

I waited.

One part of the answer I would never know, of course, and it was likely my father didn't know it either. The name of the nurse who put one baby in the bassinet with the other one's name on it. The precise event—diaper change? feeding time? bath?—that was both so small and so large as to change all our lives forever. It didn't even matter anymore, when you got down to it.

The part I wanted to understand came after, when my father—my father alone, among the four people named on our birth certificates as parents—had chosen to keep me on that farm, and to leave his real daughter, Dana, with the Dickersons. I sensed the moment had come when he might finally be able to tell me. It was unlikely there'd be another.

"What about the babies, Edwin?" I asked him. "The girls."

"Oh, darling, our girls," he said. He let out the longest sigh. "Please forgive me." His hands, that had laid the seeds in miles of rows all those years and tended the plants those seeds became, were trembling.

"I'm trying to understand," I told him. "When you found out what had happened, why didn't you do something about it?"

"It was an accident, the two of them getting switched like that," he said. "I never expected such a thing. But when Connie realized and told me we had to call the hospital and fix things, I just thought, maybe it's supposed to be this way. I knew I'd love the girl we brought home, because she was yours."

"What are you talking about, Edwin?" I told him. I understood now, I was Valerie. At least, it was Valerie to whom my father spoke. But I didn't understand why he was so sure he'd love her baby.

He didn't answer my question. He continued as if I hadn't said anything.

"It wasn't fair to you or Connie," he said. "Or the girls, of course. Or any of us, probably. I just let my heart get the best of me."

"You mean taking Ruth?" I said to him then. "Instead of Dana?"

"They were both my girls, was the thing," he said. "Either way you sliced it, I was going to be one daughter short. I just wanted that little reminder of you. I wanted my little Beanpole."

My father was crying now. This was the kind of moment they told you at the nursing home you were supposed to call an aide to come and give your loved one a sedative. I could push the button and in five minutes, he'd be snoring. Then I'd never know.

"I don't understand what you're talking about," I said, holding his hand. "Start from the beginning, Edwin."

Then finally, it was as if the door swung open at last, and we stepped into our old barn.

He sat up. His eyes seemed to focus then, though not on anything in the room. It was as if he was watching a scene in a movie, only a movie that was playing inside his head. I wasn't Ruth anymore, or Valerie either. To my father, I doubt anybody was even there. But he must have needed to tell the story, finally, if only to the four walls of his room. And so—for the first time, and the last—he did.

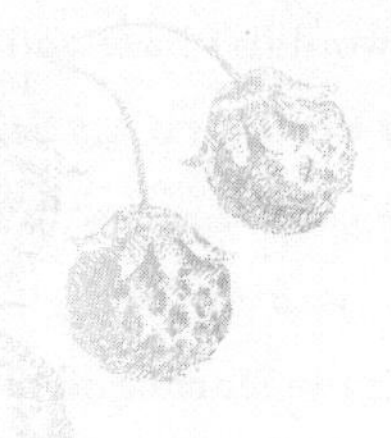

# Edwin

## Lucky You Came Along

It was only the second hurricane of the season, and you could tell from the way it came on—fast and dark—this one was going to be a doozy. It was October, so we didn't have to worry much about the crops—just the pumpkins in the field, but back in those days we weren't doing a big business in pumpkins yet. If I had a worry, it was the barn roof, and a certain stand of hickory up along the far edge of the property, where the strawberries were planted.

We were young then, Connie no more than twenty-six, me just past thirty, but I had the weight of the world on my shoulders: two hundred acres to tend and four girls to keep fed—whippersnappers, the oldest of them not even six years old, the youngest on the bottle. And a good wife, though not the kind to keep the bed warm, summer nights or winter.

It was supposed to be the first game of the Series that night, but I knew the power would likely go out before the game got started. The Yanks versus the Dodgers. The Sox had folded as usual in September. Some things you can count on, regular as rain, and that was one of them.

Connie was bringing in the laundry when the call came. It was the dispatcher on the line—ten more minutes and she wouldn't have gotten through. There was a tree down on the old County Road, and me being head of the volunteer firemen, it was my job to take care of it. I threw on my slicker and hopped in the truck, told Connie not to wait up, though I had been thinking before the call came that maybe with the storm and all, I'd get lucky with my wife that night. It had been months since she'd let me give her more than a peck on the cheek, and I was craving her affection sorely.

So now I'm out on the road, headed toward the spot where the dispatcher told me the downed tree was blocking the bridge. No other vehicle in sight, of course. It's crazy to be out there. Even my old half-ton feels unsteady in the wind. I can imagine one good gust pushing me over.

Suddenly, up ahead, I can make out a figure in the road—yellow slicker in my headlights. I see a person's arms waving as the water blows across the road, not even coming down anymore so much as going sideways.

When I get closer, I cut the engine and climb out. Once I get close I can make out that it's a woman with a child, a boy around the age of one of my girls—four maybe, or five.

"I need help," she says. "My car went off the road. We can't see to get home."

I help them into the truck, the mother and her son. With her hood off now, I recognize her from the times she stopped in at the farm stand that past summer, once for strawberries, another time for corn. I had noticed her all right, with her long blond hair—a tall woman, close to six feet, and beautiful. Her son looks like her. He's shivering in the seat between us.

"We're lucky you came along when you did," she says. "I didn't know what we were going to do."

We make it to her house, just barely—though I stop on the way, to take out my chain saw and move the fallen tree. I'm soaked through, of course. Water in my boots even. My hands so numb I can barely work the saw, but I manage.

No lights on inside her house. The power's out.

"Your husband will be worried," I say.

"Not likely. He's on a trip," she says. "He never worries like that, anyway."

She invites me in then. "You should dry off," she says. "I'll give you a shot of whiskey. George keeps a bottle on hand."

I don't drink as a rule, or rather, Connie doesn't like me to, but I follow the woman in. I think back on the time I saw her at our farm stand and how, after she bought her corn, Connie had watched her go, then commented how odd it was that a woman her age would still wear a ponytail. And I remember thinking to myself that I liked it.

We're standing in the kitchen now. The boy has run upstairs with a flashlight in search of dry clothes, but me and the woman are still standing there in our wet clothes, the water forming pools around our feet on the linoleum.

Then comes a cracking sound, louder even than anything the storm has produced so far. It's a crash like the end of the world, or close, and when I open the door I can just make out a tree broken in two—the big old elm in the front yard that had been swaying as we pulled up.

Now there's branches covering the house. The trunk is severed—not clean, of course, like if I'd done it with my chain saw, but all jagged. And the top of the tree is lying horizontal over my truck. I'm thinking maybe the vehicle is salvageable but for the moment, there's no telling. The only thing I know for sure: I'm not going anyplace tonight.

There's no food in her house. Here's one more way—one of a million—this gal standing in her kitchen now, soaked to the bone, bears about as much resemblance to my wife as an artichoke to a potato. Connie's the kind of woman that could feed her family for three months off the contents of her larder, where all this blond stringbean could offer us was a few crackers and a bowl of something I never tasted before: yogurt. And the thing was, I didn't care. It was nourishment enough, her being there.

She offers me more whiskey. She sets the bottle on the table, next to the candles. We drink from the same glass.

At some point, the son goes up to bed, looking at me sideways as he heads up the stairs. "Who are you, anyway?" he says.

"I'm a fireman," I tell him, but I can't blame the boy for wondering. Where's the uniform, the hose, the truck?

After the boy's gone, the woman brings out dry clothes for me. A shirt and pants belonging to her husband. No need to go someplace else to change, it's that dark. The clothes are on the small side, since evidently this husband of hers is considerably shorter than me and less well fed, no doubt. The woman goes upstairs herself for a bit, and when she gets back she has also put on dry clothes—a bathrobe; I can make out there are flowers on it and lace—nothing Connie would wear, and if she did, I have to say, the outfit wouldn't have the same effect or anything close.

She laughs at the sight of the pants on me, which leave a full six inches of shin and ankle uncovered. "Planks tend to come tall," I tell her, "although all four of my girls take after their mother in the height department." After I say this, I'm wishing I hadn't mentioned my wife, but the woman seems not to notice.

"I think I'll put on some music," she says.

"The power's out, remember?" I tell her. Thinking of how it is at our house, Connie's and mine, with the radio permanently tuned to Bishop Fulton J. Sheen.

"We have a Victrola," she says. "I like the sound of 78s so much better."

She puts on Peggy Lee. "Bali Ha'i." That one.

She stands there in the dark room, in the flickering light of a couple of candles burning down to the stubs, with the wind moaning. The rain pounds on the roof. From upstairs, I hear her son calling, "I'm scared."

"He's always been afraid of storms," she says, turning to make her way up the stairs in the darkness.

I tell her I love the rain. "That's a farmer for you. Always thinking about the crops."

When she comes down again, to say the boy's calmed down now, that's when we dance.

*Dana*

# Life on Earth

I DROVE OVER to Plank Farm. Though no contract had ever existed for our strawberry propagation project, I had never questioned that half of the money for the licensing of our new strain belonged to Edwin Plank, but I had other reasons for going to see Ruth. It seemed about time the two of us talked about what had happened all those years back, when for no fault of ours, we got each other's families instead of our own.

It was October, hurricane season, and as I pulled up the drive I saw her sitting on the old front porch, looking out over the fields. She poured me a glass of wine, as if she'd been expecting me. Less explanation was necessary than I'd anticipated. I'd figured it all out by now.

When she told me that despite her resistance, the remaining Planks had decided to sell the farm, it seemed like a particularly good moment to let her know I had a check for a hundred thousand dollars in my pocket. It turned out Ruth had recently come into some cash unexpectedly, too. That, combined with the money from Clarice's life insurance policy, allowed us to counter Victor Patucci's offer with a better one of our own. The family accepted.

We ended up renting out our sisters' houses, after they got their cash and moved away. (For St. Pete, Florida. Las Vegas, Nevada. And in Winnie's case, for a succession of RV campgrounds and Walmart parking lots across North America.)

Not without sadness, I sold Fletcher Simpson's place and moved with my goats to Plank Farm. It turned out that years before, when Edwin had carved out those one-acre plots on his land, he had designated a sixth for me. That's where I built the cabin where I make my home now, just up the hill from Ruth.

I run the farm now. Victor has moved on. Our brother, Ray, lives in the group home, where one small good sign of a little progress is his having recently started playing the harmonica again.

Ruth and he did eventually get a chance to talk about what happened so long before. He had always remembered the fireman who rescued him and his mother the night of the storm but it wasn't until years later, when Connie came to Quadra Island, that Connie had revealed to him the part of the story that broke his heart. He'd always been different and mercurial. I suppose the loss of Ruth, in many ways his touchstone to reality, did him in.

Sometimes, now, when I go to visit Ray, I'll hear the strains of some old tune coming from the back step and there he is, oblivious to whatever weather the state of New Hampshire may be offering us that day—including snow. Often the song is "Shenandoah."

Ruth makes her paintings, and does her art therapy, and sometimes her kids and grandchildren come to visit and during busy times like strawberry season and pumpkin time they all pitch in at the farm stand. Ruth's the one in charge of that operation, of course, same as always. There is a good man with whom she keeps company now, though she has no need to move in with him, she tells me.

Our father lives out his life at the Birch Glen Home, where we visit him—sometimes alone, sometimes together—a few times a week, and sometimes we sneak him away for the afternoon or the weekend, and bring him to the farm again to walk the rows with us. Summer evenings, in corn season, we boil a big pot on the stove and drop a baker's dozen of ears in the water, and afterward, when we eat them, we roll the cob on the stick of butter. It was the Plank family custom to butter corn this way, Ruth tells me, and now it's my custom too.

It was on one of our father's visits home to the farm—a night the Silver Queen had just come in—that an extraordinary thing happened.

He had been sitting in his old place as he always did evidently, at the head of the table, with a steaming cob of corn in front of him. He didn't pick it up, just looked at the plate. He started to shake his head, and I realized there were tears in his eyes.

"It's OK, Dad," Ruth told him.

"You were a good father," I said. "You were the one person who saw us both the way we really were. Not how everyone else wanted us to be."

"Daughters," he said. "What can a man have, better than good daughters?" Then he picked up his corn.

LATER WE DROVE HIM BACK to Birch Glen. Then the two of us, Ruth and I, sat on the porch, looking out over the farm. Neither of us said anything or needed to. Nights like these, I know I am part of a family, though not the one I started out with, precisely, or the one I'd expected. I love this piece of land and the people with whom I share it, though in general I prefer plants and goats, dogs and chickens, to people.

Concerning the rest: the Clarice strawberry has gone on to become one of the most popular varieties ever sold at Ernie's A-1 Seeds, a perpetual favorite. Not long ago, I was interviewed by a graduate student from the university where Clarice once taught. This woman was working on a thesis with some catchy title along the lines of "Effective Use of Daughter Plants in the Evolution of Superior Hybrid Strawberry Species."

It was her hope, the young botanist admitted, that this particular work of scholarly research would support her upcoming application for a teaching position at the university. I might have said some things to her then about faculty politics and factors other than those of an academic nature which could have bearing on her professional future. But I hope that times have changed, that things are better now.

Regarding her field of specialty, I told this young woman how, like my father, I had always loved the study of plant propagation. There is a perfect symmetry to nature and natural selection, I said, brutal though it may be. Survival of the fittest. Some very beautiful examples of life on earth—my brother comes to mind here, as does Clarice—do not endure, for reasons that may be utterly beyond their control. Others—and I am one, and so is the woman I now name as my sister, who is as dear to me as any living being—survive against all odds. Sturdier stock perhaps, or simply luckier, if you can call us that.

# Acknowledgments

MUCH OF THIS NOVEL WAS WRITTEN in a log cabin on a ranch in the state of Wyoming, with the support of the UCross Foundation and its staff, to whom I owe enormous gratitude. Though my story is set in the granite state of New Hampshire, I was filled with newfound love of Wyoming as I wrote, which is why I decided to send Dana and Clarice on a road trip through the Bighorn Mountains to Yellowstone—a trip I made and loved during my time at UCross.

My thanks to my early readers—Andrea Askowitz and Gail Venable. Wonderful friends, wonderful editors.

Though my story is an invention, inspired only very loosely by a couple of news stories from recent years, the farm and farm stand operation that I used as my model for Plank's does in fact exist. It is Tuttle's Red Barn in Dover Point, New Hampshire—America's oldest family farm, and a favorite destination of my own childhood on the New Hampshire seacoast, in the days when homegrown organic produce was not yet in fashion and there was no other place like Tuttle's.

Throughout the writing of this book, I drew on the knowledge and experience of Rebecca Tuttle Schultze—an eleventh-generation Tuttle. My friend

Becky—who used to drive the tractor for her father, Hugh, and count out the bakers' dozens of corn, and haul irrigation pipe, and renovate strawberry beds, and set out the bouquets of zinnias, when she and I were girls in neighboring towns—oversaw every page of this manuscript to make sure I got the farming part right, along with the history of her beloved Red Sox. I have yet to ask Becky a question about growing vegetables or doing farm chores that she was unable to answer, though I treasure her friendship most of all for what she knows about the human species.

I am indebted to my agent, David Kuhn, for wise and farsighted representation and guidance, assisted by Jessi Cimafonte and Billy Kingsland at Kuhn Projects. Likewise, my thanks to Judi Farkas, who weighs in with rare insight from the other coast. Warm appreciation as well to Emily Krump, Tavia Kowalchuk, and the wonderfully supportive team at William Morrow.

My editor, Jennifer Brehl, did something with this manuscript that went beyond anything I had known before in the editing of a work of fiction. There is evidence of her red pen on every page here—occasionally more red ink than black—and always her work makes me a better writer. To Jennifer goes deepest gratitude, deepest respect, as well as deep affection.

Finally, for four years now, a quiet voice of loving support has remained a constant in my ear, even when I failed to hear or listen well. To David Schiff, my love always.